Guns in Sage Valley

Center Point
Large Print

Also by Wayne D. Overholser and available from Center Point Large Print:

The Durango Stage
Proud Journey
Pass Creek Valley
Summer Warpath
Fighting Man
Ten Mile Valley
High Desert
The Waiting Gun

This Large Print Book carries the Seal of Approval of N.A.V.H.

GUNS *in* SAGE VALLEY

A Western Duo

Wayne D. Overholser

CENTER POINT LARGE PRINT
THORNDIKE, MAINE

ISBN: 978-1-68324-932-0 (hardcover)
ISBN: 978-1-68324-936-8 (paperback)

Library of Congress Cataloging-in-Publication Data

Names: Overholser, Wayne D., 1906-1996, author.
Title: Guns in Sage Valley : a western duo / Wayne D. Overholser.
Description: Center Point Large Print edition. | Thorndike, Maine :
    Center Point Large Print, 2018.
Identifiers: LCCN 2018024547| ISBN 9781683249320
    (hardcover : alk. paper) | ISBN 9781683249368 (paperback : alk. paper)
Subjects: LCSH: Large type books. | BISAC: FICTION / Westerns. |
    GSAFD: Western stories.
Classification: LCC PS3529.V33 G86 2018 | DDC 813/.52—dc23
LC record available at https://lccn.loc.gov/2018024547

Land Rush

I

For months Colorado had rung with the cry that the Utes must go. Now they had gone from the Uncompahgre, filing pathetically westward to new, unwanted homes in Utah, a defeated people who had taken their last look at the San Juan Mountains they loved. Along the reservation boundary, the white men waited for the Army's signal to move in on the vacated land, many of them greedy and triumphant now that another victory had been won over the Indians. But there was no feeling of victory in Steve Regan.

Steve was camped next to the river. From this position he could see the long line of wagons, the smoke of the fires that drifted upvalley with the wind. He could see men and women moving about, friends today, but tomorrow they would be bitter rivals as they raced for the valley land.

Steve did not see the Madden girls until they came around his wagon, Ila calling: "How long now, Steve?"

He had been hunkered beside his fire, the day being unseasonably cold for early September. He jumped and whirled, hand dropping automatically to his gun. Then he laughed, embarrassed at this show of nerves. "Say, you'd better give a holler

7

when you sneak up. I thought the Utes were back."

"I don't think I like that." Ila cocked her head, pouting. "Are you comparing me to a squaw?"

"That's sure what I'm doing." He winked at Ruth. "Now I suppose she'll want my scalp."

"She's wanted it all the time," Ruth said. "Didn't you know?"

"Why, I didn't have the slightest notion," Steve answered.

It was idle talk, yet Steve sensed that there was more meaning to it than was apparent. The Maddens had camped beside him for two weeks, and although he had become well acquainted with the womenfolk, he had only just met Joe Madden. Those few moments convinced him that the man was stronger on talk than action. Madden had had the bad luck to get caught on the wrong side of the line. Now he was locked up in the Army post's guardhouse along with fifty other boomers who had been a little too eager. The Maddens struck Steve as being like many of the settler families, rainbow chasers with big hopes. With the exception of Ruth, they seemed too weak for the hardships that went with the taming of a new land.

Ila tossed her head, still pouting. "I'm insulted. I came over to invite you to supper, but now I'm not going to. You can eat your own grub."

"Well, if there's a meal at stake, I'll apologize." Steve winked at Ruth again. "I didn't mean you look like a squaw. It's the way you move, quiet-like and graceful."

"Oh, that's different." Ila's pout changed to a smile.

"She isn't fooling you, is she, Steve?" Ruth asked. "I mean, you knew all the time she was going to ask you, didn't you?"

Ila held her smile with an effort. Steve looked from one to the other, sensing that there was little sisterly love between them. Ila was twenty, a startlingly pretty girl with auburn hair, dark eyes that at times seemed nearly purple, and an awareness of her beauty. Talk came easily to her, but her mood changed as quickly as the wind. She had been invitingly friendly to Steve, but she was the same with most men. Ruth was the quiet one, about eighteen, Steve judged, and with no family resemblance to Ila at all. She was small and slender, but roundly shaped with early maturity. Her hair, pulled back and tied with a bit of red ribbon, was smooth ebony, and her eyes were as black as her hair. There was a gentleness about her that he liked, a depth of character that was genuine, and more than once when he was alone during these idle two weeks, he found himself dreaming of her like a schoolboy, remembering the dulcet melody of her voice, the sweet set of her lips. He had not told her he loved her. He had nothing to offer a wife. Besides, he had his brother Al to think of.

Ila glanced at him. "You think they'll let Pa out in time?"

"Don't know about that. I'll help you harness up in the morning."

"That will be wonderful. Well, we've got to get back and help. Oh, bring Al over for supper, if he's here."

"Sure," Steve said. "If he's here."

He watched them walk away, Ruth straight-backed and proud, Ila's hips swaying, knowing his eyes would be on her. He rose, sudden dissatisfaction in him. Mounting, Steve reined away from the line, making a wide swing through the scanty sagebrush before he turned north again. He knew where he would be likely to find Al.

With the late afternoon sunlight glinting upon the spiny ramparts of the San Juan range to the south, Steve thought about Al, and bitterness was like a corrosive acid in his blood stream. Work was not to Al's liking. He had resented the labor of filling a woodcutting contract that Steve had made with the Army post. They had started in early spring and kept at it until two weeks ago, Steve doing the hard work of sawing and splitting, Al the hauling. Even though Al had the easier job, he had continually grumbled about it.

Al was twenty-one now, and they had come to the fork in the road. It would be settled tomorrow. Steve had been on the reservation; he knew what the valley land was and he was convinced that the mesa soil was better than that along the river. Because he had been there longer than anyone else in the line, the boomers had asked him about the choice locations. He had told them, but no one had believed—not even the Maddens. They could irrigate valley land from the Uncompahgre, they said, and in a very dry country like this, water was life.

Steve swung to his left and came to Bronc Vedder's camp. He did not understand Vedder, or his two men, Todd Brashada and Sandy Smith. They would have seemed more at home with the Wild Bunch, or on a cattle ranch in Texas, than in line with these boomers along the edge of an Indian reservation. But Al, not sharing Steve's distrust, had taken to them from the first.

The four were squatted around the fire playing poker, when Steve rode up. Al looked at him, lips tightly pressed. He was taller than Steve, blue-eyed, with tawny hair and handsome features that brought girls' eyes to him as naturally as a magnet pulls steel. But Al Regan had no time for women. They tied a man down, he said, and cut out his fun. They wanted kids and a home, and to hell with all of it.

Steve reined up, greeting the men. Vedder rose and nodded, remaining silent while he waited for Steve to make his errand known. He was a rail of a man, with the bowed legs of a rider, and gray eyes that held the shine of freshly honed steel. Steve had a feeling that Bronc Vedder could not be trusted.

Todd Brashada said: "Well, if it ain't Mesa Steve Regan. Staked that claim out yet?"

"I will, come morning," Steve said.

Al said nothing, but Steve felt the antagonism that was a wall between him and his brother. He had felt it before, but when a showdown had come, Al had always followed Steve's lead, though reluctantly, as when Steve had taken the wood job. Now, his brown eyes locking briefly with Al's, Steve sensed that the break had finally come.

Sandy Smith laughed easily. "Well, Mesa, you come to run herd on your kid brother?"

"No," Steve said. "I quit running herd the day he was twenty-one."

"Well now, I'm sure glad to hear that," Al jeered. "Why didn't you tell me?"

"I reckoned you knew," Steve answered evenly.

"What's on your mind, grandma?" Brashada asked.

Anger burned in Steve. He had pegged Brashada as a bully from the first. Now he saw his judgment had been right. He bent forward in the saddle, his lean face expressionless. "That's tough talk, Brashada. You aim to make it stick?"

Brashada grinned in anticipation. "You're damned right."

12

Steve would have swung down if Al had not laid a hand on Brashada's thick arm. He said: "Behave, Todd." He looked at Steve, his pearl-gray Stetson tilted at a rakish angle. "Let's get this straight. I'm throwing in with Bronc. We're taking our four claims together about ten miles down the river. If anybody beats us to 'em, they'll get hell kicked out of 'em."

"Five can work together as well as four," Vedder said. "We figure to build a ditch that'll put water on all our places, which same will be a damned sight cheaper than digging five ditches."

Steve shook his head. "I'll take the mesa."

"There's a big opportunity here," Vedder pressed. "The mining camps need hay. I know for a fact they've paid as high as a hundred dollars a ton." He swung a hand out toward the other wagon men. "They're rabbits. We won't have no trouble with 'em. We'll sell hay to the camps, Regan. All the hay. I tell you it's a gold mine."

Sandy Smith laughed. "We'll let the miners dig the gold, and we'll swap hay for it. Easy *dinero*, Steve."

They were watching Steve, all four of them, and suddenly it struck him that this didn't add up. Brashada was pushing for a fight, but Vedder and Smith were holding out an invitation to throw in with them. Al was keyed up, blue eyes on Steve's face as if a great deal depended on what he said now. Steve shook his head again. "Thanks, but I reckon I'll go it alone."

"You chuckle-headed fool!" Al shouted. "I told Bronc you couldn't see no farther'n the end of your nose."

No matter how Al had grumbled about the moves they'd made and the jobs Steve had taken on, he had never talked this way before. Steve felt color deepen in his face, felt an aching emptiness creep into his middle. "All right, Al," Steve said. "Come over and get your stuff."

He would have reined away if Al had not cried out: "I didn't mean that, Steve, but damn it, you've always done our thinking for us! Now we've got something good right in our hands, and you're too stubborn to change your mind."

"It ain't that I'm stubborn. It's just that I know what I want. If you're sure you want this, go ahead and take it."

Brashada shoved his thick thumbs into his belt, his great head cocked. "Looks like Al got off your apron strings, Mesa."

Al whirled on him. "Keep your mouth shut."

Vedder said: "That's right, Todd." He nodded amiably at Steve. "Think it over, Regan. If you change your mind, let me know."

"I forgot to tell you what I came for, Al," Steve said. "Ila asked you over for supper."

"Naw," Al mumbled. "Ain't no woman gonna get her hooks on me."

14

"Keep your eyes open for them female traps." Smith sighed loudly. "But that Ila is a mighty pretty gal."

Steve turned his horse, knowing there was nothing more he could say or do at this moment.

II

Mrs. Madden probably had a good supper. Steve ate, but there was little taste to the food. Mrs. Madden's chatter was a meaningless flow of sound. He gave monosyllabic answers to Ila's questions, but he was finally jarred back to consciousness when Ruth asked pointedly: "What's the matter with you, Steve? Friends aren't worth much if they can't share your troubles."

"That's right," Mrs. Madden said as if only then she became aware that something was wrong. "Goodness knows what would have happened to us if you hadn't been so kind. Why, after they locked up Joe in that awful place, I felt like going back to Kansas."

She was a plump woman with traces of gray showing in her chestnut hair. There might have been a time when she was as attractive as Ila, but the hard years in Kansas coupled with the daily problem of living with a husband who talked success but never achieved it had taken the flair for living from her. Now she seemed able to do nothing but worry.

Ruth laid a hand on Steve's arm, a spontaneous gesture that held none of the subtle meanings that would have accompanied it if it had come from Ila. Ruth said: "Tell us, Steve."

"Just thinking about tomorrow, I guess," he said.

"Scares me." Ila dropped to the ground on the other side of him and pressed a soft shoulder against his. "Steve, won't you drive our wagon tomorrow?"

"Don't ask him to do that," Ruth said sharply. "Hasn't he done enough for us?"

"He's done a great deal," Mrs. Madden said, "but I would feel better if he held the lines. I just don't know how we'll manage if they don't give Joe back to us."

Steve held no sympathy for Joe Madden. The man had known the rule, but like fifty others who were locked up in the post guardhouse, he had sneaked onto the reservation to pick out the location he wanted. Steve said: "Sorry, ma'am, but I've got a claim to stake out for myself."

"I'll drive," Ruth said. "All you and Ila have to do is to hang on, Mamma."

"Joe picked a nice place," Mrs. Madden said. "Right along the river where there are some cottonwoods for shade. If he isn't with us, we may not be able to find it."

Steve knew the place, adobe soil that would mire a feather after a rain. It was like Joe Madden to pick such a spot. Steve said: "I could find a better farm for you, ma'am, but I've quit arguing with folks about it."

The sun was down now and dusk was deepening about them. To the north the long flat line of Grand Mesa was lost against the dark sky. Steve stood by the fire, packing his pipe, not wanting to go, for he had a feeling of companionship with Ruth that Ila's flirting had not destroyed. For a moment he thought of asking Ruth to go walking with him, of saying he loved her. He was alone now, for he felt no responsibility to Al. Still he hesitated. It would be a hard life on the mesa with no close neighbors, and he would have very little money after his cabin was built and a small herd of cattle bought.

"Someone's coming from the fort!" Ila cried suddenly.

"Joe!" Mrs. Madden shouted, and would have run toward the rider if Steve had not caught her arm.

"Hold on, ma'am. I don't know when they'll let your husband out, but it won't be before sunup. I'm sure of that."

Mrs. Madden stopped, taking a long sighing breath.

A lieutenant from the fort rode into the firelight. He said: "The bugle will blow at five in the morning. You're free to go in after that. Anyone caught disobeying will be locked up."

"You've got my husband locked up now," Mrs. Madden said. "When are you going to let him out?"

"I don't know," the lieutenant answered, "but if he had obeyed the law, he wouldn't be there."

The lieutenant rode toward the next fire. Mrs. Madden, staring after him, began to cry. Ila said harshly: "Now you hush that up. Pa will be all right. Steve's promised to help us in the morning."

There was a moment of awkward silence. Mrs. Madden stopped sniffling. Then Ruth burst out: "I think we'll have time to get back to Kansas before winter sets in. I told you we weren't the kind who could make a living out here."

"If you're so smart . . . ," Ila began.

"Now, now," Mrs. Madden said. "We'll just have to pray and hope the Lord will bless us."

A rider drifted up, calling: "Meeting at Tobert's wagon. Right away!"

It was Sandy Smith. Ila, recognizing him, called: "Get down, Mister Smith. I'll get you some coffee."

He had stopped in the fringe of firelight, leaning forward in the saddle, bold eyes on Ila. "Now I'd sure like to, miss, but I've got to get back. You coming, Steve?"

"Sure," Steve said, wondering why the meeting

would hold interest for a man like Sandy Smith.

Smith rode off.

"We'll go along, Steve," Ila said. "At least I will, and I suppose Tagalong won't miss a chance like this."

"Of course not," Ruth said.

"Well, I'm going to bed." Mrs. Madden put a hand to her throat as if finding it hard to breathe. "I don't suppose I'll live through tomorrow, but maybe I'll get one night's sleep before I'm scalped."

Steve said: "Thanks for the supper, Missus Madden."

He walked away, Ila on one side of him, Ruth on the other.

III

They passed the Bain outfit, the Ashtons', and then Pete Delaney's big wagon and trailer outfit. Delaney had said he wasn't going to be in the race. He'd mosey in on the tail end of things. He aimed to start a store and he had agreed with John Tobert on the best site for a town about twelve miles downstream. "I'm having a load of lumber hauled in the first day the reservation's open," he had said. "Before the week's out, I'll have a building up and goods on the shelf."

Now Delaney stepped in beside Ila, saying: "I

don't see no sense to this meeting. Folks ought to get all the sleep they can, having to get up in the middle of the night."

Delaney was a middle-aged bachelor who had spent a good many hours courting Ila. She had taken his gifts, smiled her encouragement, and confided in Steve that she couldn't stand the man. Now, assuming a proprietary air, she took Steve's arm.

A crowd had already gathered at Tobert's wagon. He had built up a big fire, the flames throwing their flickering light upon the weather-beaten faces of the settlers and their wives. Tobert was in the center, talking loud and beating a fist against the palm of his other hand to emphasize his words. He was a newspaperman who had promised he'd have the first issue of the Uncompahgre *News* off the press within the week. He had political ambitions, for he'd made himself known to every boomer in the line.

For a time Steve remained in the fringe of the crowd, Ila still gripping his arm, Ruth standing stiffly on the other side of him. Delaney muttered—"Can't hear him out here."—and finally drifted away.

But Delaney should have had no trouble hearing Tobert, for the newspaperman had a clarion voice that must have carried halfway to the fort. "Tomorrow is the biggest day any of us will ever see," Tobert was shouting. "By the next sunset the valley will be settled, this beautiful and fertile land that has lain idle for so many years. Sagebrush and greasewood will be grubbed out, the soil will be turned, homes will be built, towns will spring up. Ladies and gentlemen, our hour of destiny is at hand."

Bronc Vedder was standing in the front line on the far side of the circle, half a head taller than anyone around him. A smile was set on his lips, but his eyes were sharp and cold. He broke in: "Fine words, Mister Editor, but we've got business. Let's get to it."

Tobert's thin face darkened with resentment. He was a lanky man of perhaps fifty, with heavy irregular features and faded blue eyes. Like Delaney, he was no farmer, but they had one thing in common with the others. They were shutting their eyes on the failures that lay behind, hoping fortune waited for them in this new country.

"I'm getting to it, Mister Vedder," Tobert said. "Despite our bright future, we must be honest with ourselves. The valley has not been surveyed. We are to fix our corners as best we can. That may mean trouble. We have no law, no officials. True, we have the Army, the same Army that has thrown fifty of our members into the guardhouse, the same Army that holds us on this line, dangling us like hooked fish until it pleases the commanding officer to have a trumpet blown. Ladies and gentlemen, we must organize tonight, and through our own efforts set up a government that will keep law and order."

Vedder stepped toward the fire, making an impatient gesture with his right hand. "Tobert, I can say it in a lot less words, even if they ain't as pretty as yours. Boys, we need a vigilance committee. If there's any claim jumping, we've got to be in shape to set things square."

Delaney pushed through the crowd to occupy the spot Vedder had vacated. He shouted: "Sounds good to me! Right here and now I nominate Bronc Vedder to head the committee. He looks to me like a right solid gent. All of you who agree say so."

They agreed with considerable gusto, cheering and whistling as if it were entirely spontaneous. Steve, because he doubted Bronc Vedder's integrity, distrusted the whole proceedings.

Ruth whispered: "What does it mean, Steve?"

"I don't know, but it looks like a rigged play to me."

Vedder was grinning broadly. "Thanks, boys. I'll do my best. Now I say we need a committee. Not a big one. Just a couple of the boys to work with me in case we hit something that needs more'n one head to figure the answer. How about Delaney and Tobert?"

They cheered again, not as wildly as before, but it seemed to be enough noise to elect Vedder's candidates.

"Hold on, Vedder," Steve broke in. "This bunch is about ninety-nine percent farmers, but you've named a committee that ain't got a farmer on it. Looks to me like you'd better throw Tobert or Delaney out so you'll have room for a farmer."

"Maybe you want to be on it, Mesa," Brashada said.

Brashada stood on the wagon side of the circle, thick legs spread, big head jutting forward on his massive shoulders. Sandy Smith and Al were directly behind him, the tough reckless grin on Smith's face, cold fear on Al's. In that moment Steve had his first premonition of trouble.

"No I don't," Steve said sharply. "I'm just saying that what's being done tonight may have a lot to do with how we get along tomorrow. I claim we need a farmer on that committee."

Several settlers yelled: "That's right!" Another man called: "You've been here a while, Regan. How about you being on the committee?"

"Not if I'm going to be chairman of it," Vedder said curtly.

"What's the matter with Regan?" someone demanded.

"I'll tell you," Brashada said. "There's something mighty wrong, or he wouldn't have been whooping it up for the mesa like he has. What's your game, Regan?"

"I don't have any game," Steve answered

angrily, "but I was in the valley last spring. I saw the river go on a rampage and I know what the adobe land's like when it's wet. It don't make me no never mind where you boys settle. Far as I'm concerned I'm heading for the mesa in the morning."

"You'll go alone!" a settler yelled.

"He ain't going, alone or otherwise," Brashada boomed. "You boys do a little figgering on what it means if half our bunch follows Regan. I look for the Utes to sneak back. They'll do just like they done to Meeker and everybody else at the agency. If we're strung out over a million acres, they'll lift every scalp we've got before we can get together or the Army can show up."

Vedder nodded agreement. "Todd's talking sense."

"You boys that have got women and children better think about them," Delaney threw in. "If we don't settle within shouting distance of each other, our blood will make the Uncompahgre run red from here to the Gunnison."

For a moment there was silence, as tension built. Now the full impact of this thing hit Steve. *They aimed to make him settle in the valley!* And Vedder and his bunch were calling the right tune to do the job. Fear of the Utes had been a dark shadow upon Colorado's western slope from the day of the Meeker massacre.

"For our own protection," Brashada burst out,

"we've got to keep everybody together. Regan, you're settling in the valley."

"A man's got the right to settle where he wants to," someone called. "If this committee figures on telling us what to do, I don't want any part of it."

"Hold on, now," another said. "This talk Regan's been putting out looks fishy to me. That there mesa is as dry as hell's back yard."

"A creek comes through there," Steve said. "It'll do for me. If others come, we'll build a dam and hold the spring runoff."

"That'll take money," Delaney said.

"Yeah, and it gives the answer to why Regan has been trying to get folks to settle up there," Brashada broke in. "He's hooked up with some moneybags from Denver to organize a ditch company. You know what you'll pay for water then."

"Water is the life of the country," Delaney said sagely.

John Tobert could stand it no longer. He cried: "This is all wrong, gentlemen. When I proposed the organization, I did not anticipate anything like this. If Regan wants to settle on the mesa, it's his business, no concern of the committee."

"We'll stick together!" Brashada shouted.

He took two quick steps toward Tobert and struck him on the side of the head, the blow sending the newspaperman reeling into the packed

25

circle of men. "Now you'd better think twice before you bust things up, mister." He wheeled away from the stunned Tobert, adding piously: "I'm thinking about the women and children, folks. I've seen what the sneaking redskins do, and I'm remembering Father Meeker."

Then Steve understood the fear that had been in Al. This had been planned. Brashada wanted a fight. Steve had no choice. He grabbed Brashada's beefy shoulder, turned him, and drove a hammering right to his jaw. Brashada bawled like a great bull, shook his head, and charged at Steve.

Someone yelled: "Give it to him, Todd!"

But there were other cries of: "Knock hell out of him, Regan!" After that Steve heard only a blended roar of voices, for he found himself fighting for his life. Brashada was big, heavy, and strong, and an expert at barroom fighting, but the advantage of reach and speed was with Steve. He ducked, swiveled, side-stepped, keeping away from Brashada's big fists, and all the time his right was flicking out to the man's wide jaw or red-veined cheeks. He backed around the fire slowly, watching closely, while his lightning right slashed Brashada's face like the cutting tip of a rapier in a skilled hand.

Steve had no time to look at the crowd or to see where he was, for his attention was focused on the panting, bloody man who kept rushing him, only to find that his clubbing fists never quite connected. Then Sandy Smith stuck out his foot and Steve sprawled over it, landing on his back. He heard Ruth scream, heard Al yell: "Damn you, Sandy, he gets a fair fight!" Others, crazed by blood lust, bawled: "Boot him, Todd." Or: "Cave in his ribs. You've got him now!"

Brashada jumped at Steve, intending to grind him under his heavy boots. Steve rolled, Brashada landed heavily beside him, and Steve grabbed his legs and dumped him to the ground in a jarring fall. He came to his feet, as thoroughly angry as he had ever been in his life. He had time to say: "I'll see you later, Smith." He glimpsed the flushed, reckless face of the gunman, heard his cursing angry voice, and saw that Al had rammed his gun against the man's back.

Steve whirled on Brashada as the big fellow struggled to his feet, his breathing labored. Steve had fought a careful fight, vaguely realizing that there was more back of this than his own defeat. Now he drove in, taking chances he would not have taken a moment before. Brashada gave way under his attack, backing toward the wagon as he hammered Steve with defensive fists.

Men broke away, and now Steve had Brashada pinned against the side of Tobert's wagon. He rolled his head with a punch, took another on his shoulder, then he was in close and had his opening. For the first time in the fight he threw his left into the man's muscle-ridged stomach. Brashada's breath was knocked out of him a second time. He bent forward, fighting to suck air back into paralyzed lungs. Steve's right came through to his nose, flattening it and bringing a spurt of blood. For a moment Brashada was stunned. He stood motionlessly, fists half lifted. Steve grabbed him around the middle and, lifting his great weight, spun him and dumped him hard against the back wheel of Tobert's wagon. He fell on his back and lay there, a bloody mass of bone and flesh.

Steve turned away, knowing that he had taken more punishment than he had realized. He wiped a sleeve across his bruised, sweaty face. For a moment everything was blurred, and he swayed uncertainly until his vision cleared and he found strength to say: "You boys go where you want to in the morning. Me, I'm staking a claim on the mesa." He turned to his brother, who still held his gun against Sandy Smith's back. He said: "Thanks, Al."

"I like to see a fair fight," Al said tonelessly.

"No more trouble now," Vedder called, hiding what must have been both surprise and disappointment.

"Sure," Smith said, "no more trouble." But his face held the promise of it.

Steve moved through the crowd, men falling

away before him. Al dropped into step with him, and for the first time that Steve could remember, Al's voice held frank admiration when he said: "That was a hell of a good fight, Steve. A hell of a good fight."

IV

Ruth and Ila were still standing at the fringe of the crowd where Steve had left them. Now they walked back along the line with the Regans, neither saying anything until they had reached the Madden wagon. Then Ruth said: "I'll heat a pan of water, Steve. You've got some cuts on your face."

"He didn't lay a hand on you till Sandy tripped you," Al said. "Guess that made you mad."

"Yeah, guess it did," Steve admitted.

Ruth built up the fire, poured water into a pan, and set it on the grate. Ila stood motionlessly, flustered and useless. She said in a small voice: "Steve, you aren't really hurt, are you?"

"No."

"I was worried," she whispered. "It was so unexpected and useless. John Tobert's an old man. Why did Brashada hit him?"

"Maybe you can answer that, Al," Steve said.

Al stared at the fire. He said sullenly: "No, I can't. Todd just likes to fight, I reckon."

"There was more to it than that," Steve pressed. "They don't come any slicker than Vedder. He's working on something."

"I don't know what it is," Al said, still sullen.

Ruth brought cloth and turpentine from the wagon, and lifted the pan of water from the fire. She motioned for Steve to sit down, tore the cloth in two, and washed the blood and dirt from Steve's face. "This will sting," she said, and, soaking the other piece of cloth with turpentine, swabbed the bruises and cuts. It did sting, but he said nothing, and when she rose, she said: "You're a tough man, Mister Regan."

"And an awfully brave one," Ila added.

Ruth was looking at Al, her dark eyes thoughtful. "Al, I don't pretend to understand what's going on, but I think Brashada aimed to kill Steve."

"You don't kill a man with your fists," Al muttered.

"You do with your boots," she flung at him. "If he'd jumped on Steve like he aimed to, he'd have broken half of Steve's ribs."

Al stared resentfully at her. "Steve's looked out for himself for a long time." Then he turned his eyes to Ila and he said, with more bitterness than Steve had ever heard in his voice: "You're to blame for this as much as anyone. You've been seeing Sandy Smith, and you've got Delaney out of his head. That's why he wanted Steve banged up. He'd be out to get Sandy, too, if he knew all I do."

Al turned toward Steve's wagon, leaving Ila staring after him, white-faced and angry. Steve said: "A woman can sure raise hell, can't she?"

Steve had supposed Al had come back to join him. Now he saw he was wrong, for his brother got his bedroll out of the wagon, saying: "Keep your eyes peeled tomorrow. Todd won't forget the licking you gave him."

"You going back to 'em?" Steve asked incredulously.

Al stood motionlessly for a moment. Steve's fire had died, and there was no moon in the sky. The star shine was too thin to see the boy's face, but Steve could hear the hard pull of his breathing. He said finally: "I've got to."

"No, you don't. Damn it, Smith'll shoot you in the back for what you done. It ain't fair, anyhow. We've planned on this all summer. We need each other. Maybe I've treated you like a kid, but from now on it's a straight partnership."

"I've got to go back," Al muttered. "I ain't cut out to be a farmer."

"But it won't just be farming. There's the making of the best cattle outfit in Colorado on the mesa. All we need is a half section to raise hay. I'll do the farming and you can do the riding."

Al shook his head. "It won't work. You'll be

31

getting married, and I've got a notion I want to see some country."

Al walked away, and the pain that was in Steve Regan did not come from the hammering of Todd Brashada's big fists. For those few minutes he had thought everything was all right between him and Al, that Al had seen through Vedder and his men. But nothing was right. When Al had shoved his gun into Sandy Smith's back, he had only done what he would have for any man who deserved a fair fight.

It must have been close to midnight when Steve dropped off to sleep. He was awakened almost immediately by a sound he could not identify. He stiffened, reaching for his gun, then he glimpsed a vague shape in the darkness. Throwing the blanket back, he pulled his gun free of leather.

"Steve, are you awake?"

It was Ila's voice. He shoved his Colt back into leather, weak with relief. He said: "Someday you're gonna get yourself shot doing that. Don't you know nothing?"

She dropped to her knees beside him. "No, Steve, I don't know anything. I've always thought I was smart, but I'm not. I'm just the biggest fool that ever walked."

"Now what . . . ?"

But he didn't finish. She buried her face in the blanket that still half covered him and began to cry. He sat there, stiffly, not knowing what to say or what to do, and resentment washed through him. He had enough to worry about without having a crying woman wake him in the middle of the night.

She lifted her head and wiped her eyes, her face so close to his that strands of hair touched his cheek. "Steve, you have every right to be angry with me. I shouldn't be here, but I couldn't stand it. I tried to sleep, but I can't. Not till I've talked to you."

"Tomorrow . . ."

"I know. I'm scared. That's part of it, and seeing you fight Brashada is some of it, too. But mostly it's what Al said. I don't love Sandy. It was just kind of exciting, meeting him at night as I've been doing, listening to him, hearing about the places he's been and the things he's done. But I didn't mean any harm. Steve, I'm trying to tell you something."

"If you want to see Sandy Smith, it's your business."

"But it's yours, too. And if I've made any of this trouble by smiling at Delaney, I can't do anything but promise it won't happen again."

"It's all right. Go back to bed."

Her hands came up to his shoulders. "Not till you kiss me, Steve."

Angry now, he said: "No. I don't want to kiss you. I love Ruth."

"But you need me. I know what Vedder's up to. Sandy told me. He's got cattle . . ." She stopped and sat back. "What did you say about Ruth?"

"I love her. I ain't got anything to offer, but I'm going to ask her to marry me."

"Steve, doesn't it make any difference to you that I'm here?"

Her face was a faint outline in the star shine, but he felt the sudden fury that seized her. He said: "No, it don't mean a damned thing."

She said: "All right, Steve, but I'll promise you one thing. You'll never marry Ruth."

She jumped up and ran away. He lay back, pulling the blanket over him again, and tried to sleep. He had never been one to worry, and now he told himself that there was nothing Ila could do to hurt him. Still, he could not get her out of his mind, could not forget what she had said. She was, he thought, capable of putting a knife into a man's back while she kissed him, if it would be to her advantage.

There were these long moments while the boomers slept, moments of silence except for an occasional coyote call from some cedar-covered ridge that flanked the valley. At such a time a man's thoughts ran wild and free. Perhaps every boomer in the line was awake, dreaming and hoping and planning, forgetting yesterday and thinking of tomorrow when failures would be erased and opportunity would gleam like a bright sun tipping upward into a clear sky. Then, as if by signal, the line came to life.

Someone lit a lantern. Another man began chopping wood. A querulous woman's voice asked if it was time to get up. A sleepy child started to cry. A dog barked. Horses whinnied, metal clinked on metal, the sounds running sharply through the thin chill air. The day of destiny had come.

Steve watered and fed his team and his sorrel saddler. He tossed his bedding and a few odds and ends that were on the ground into the wagon, threw gear on the sorrel, and tied a sack of food behind the saddle. It had been his plan to ride out the instant the bugle sounded and stake his claim on the mesa. Then he would wait for Al to bring the wagon. Now it would not be that way. He would have to return for the wagon. If no one settled on the mesa, it would make little real difference, for there would be no one to jump his claim. Still, he could not lose the sense of uneasiness that plagued him. It would be with him until he knew what Bronc Vedder planned.

The Maddens were up. He smelled coffee and frying bacon, and felt the stirring of hunger. Then Ila was there, a lighted lantern in her hand, her face holding none of the fury that had been in her a few hours before. She said, as if nothing had happened: "Come over for breakfast, Steve. It

35

will be ready by the time you harness our horses."

"I'll water them," he said.

Ruth was fixing breakfast when he came to the Madden wagon. She glanced up, tight-featured, and her voice was very low when she said: "Good morning, Steve."

He said—"Howdy."—a little awkwardly, wanting to be alone with her and seeing there was no chance for that.

He took their horses to the river and watered them, brought them back and fed them. He ate quickly, for time was crowding now, harnessed the team, and drove them to the front of the wagon. He asked: "Got everything buttoned down?"

"Almost," Ruth said, her tone sharp.

Old man Bain next to the Madden wagon called: "What time is it?"

John Tobert bawled back: "Five minutes to go, yet."

Hoofs thudded as a detail from the fort moved up the river. The moment was almost here. Ruth bent over beside the lighted lantern as Steve pulled the team to a stop. It was not the time to ask her, but he could not wait.

She straightened when he said her name, gripping the lantern in one hand, a sack in the other. The murky lantern light showed the frozen set of her features, and he saw that she had been crying. She asked stonily: "What?"

He had never seen her this way before, the gentleness gone, no hint of a smile on the thin line of her mouth. They were storm signals he should have observed, but he hurried on: "I should have said this yesterday, but I didn't, so I've got to now. I love you, Ruth." He swallowed, seeking encouragement and finding none. "I'm asking you to marry me after I get some kind of a cabin up."

"I didn't think I'd hear anything like that from you after what happened last night." She blew out the lantern and handed it to Mrs. Madden in the wagon, giving Steve her back.

Ila came up then, asking briskly: "All ready, Steve?"

"No."

Swinging the team into position, he hooked up, puzzled and hurt, fingers numb as he worked. He had never met a woman before who meant anything to him. Now it seemed that anything he did today held no real importance, for he had not realized until this moment how fully his plans and hopes had included Ruth.

"Good luck, Steve," Ila said, her tone honey-sweet. "I'll see you soon."

He looked up at Ruth on the seat, the lines in her hand. She had kicked off the brake and was leaning forward, her body tense. She was wearing a heavy sweater, the collar turned up around her neck, and her face seemed frozen by the cold. He turned away. That was not the kind of look he wanted from her.

The soldiers were drawn up along the river, waiting, the lieutenant holding a watch, his eyes fixed on it. Steve mounted his sorrel, glancing along the line at the wagons and buggies and carts, and at this moment there was silence while each second dragged out through an eternity of waiting.

Then Steve was aware of the pounding beat of a running horse. He turned in his saddle, wondering. Al swung around the back of the Madden wagon. He called: "Stake your claim and hang onto it, Steve! I'll have the wagon up there before sundown."

"What happened?"

"Haven't got time to tell you now, but watch out for Brashada and Sandy."

A lot of things were right with Steve Regan then. This was half of what he had hoped for. Now, with the last blue chip down, Al was with him again. He leaned forward, peering at Al in the deepening light, and he knew he might be imagining it, but it seemed to him that the antagonism he had seen so many times in his brother's face was gone. "Good boy," Steve said.

Al waved his hand toward the soldiers. "It's time, Steve. Keep moving."

Steve glanced at Ruth, still hunched forward on the wagon seat, waiting. She did not look at him.

She might have been a million miles away for any awareness she had of his presence. Then the lieutenant said something, and the bugle sounded clear and sharp, the call racing out across the valley. Before the echoes died, the line surged forward, the earth trembled with the thunder of a thousand hoofs and rolling wheels. It was the moment of destiny on the Uncompahgre; it was flood tide again for the surging whites, and far to the west the sullen Utes must have heard it.

Steve swept out ahead of the wagons, passed the detail of soldiers who seemed dourly unaware of the history that was being made. He followed the river for a mile, the onsweeping racket of the wagons fading behind him. He forded the Uncompahgre, low now at this season, as it ran gray with tailings from the mines cradled among the high peaks of the San Juan range. The sorrel plunged up the bank, and Steve pulled him to a brief stop and looked back.

White alkali dust banked high above the wagons. One overturned, spilling man and wife and children into the sagebrush with their goods. Half a dozen buggies and carts were out ahead. Then Steve saw three horsemen far in the lead, streaking across the valley and angling toward the river.

Steve went on, holding his sorrel to a ground-eating pace. He passed the fort, a huddle of buildings out here in the flat, drab and uninviting.

He held steadily toward the steep hill that marked the mesa, reached it, and pulled up again to rest his horse. He hipped around in the saddle, eyes scanning the valley, but he could see no trace of Vedder and his men.

He angled up the hill, stopped again for his horse to blow, and then saw the three riders. The sun was up now, bright and glaring above the granite peaks. Distance had silenced the roar of the wagons. He could see some of them, made small by the miles, and brought his eyes to Vedder and his men again. They had crossed the river and were heading directly toward the mesa. He puzzled over that for a time. It didn't seem smart, for they had taken the long way, and they seemed to be moving without haste. He shrugged, and went on, certain that he would beat them.

V

The sun rolled up into a cloudless sky. It was warm now, contrasting to the chill weather that had held on through most of the time they had waited in line. A few clouds gathered above the long crest of the Uncompahgre Plateau to the west. Across the valley the barren adobe hills lifted their eroded summits skyward, looking like the great hands of an aged giant, splayed fingers tipped downward toward the valley.

Near noon Steve reached the spot he had wanted from the first day he had taken the wood contract and had ridden out across the mesa. A sizeable stream curled down out of the spruce and aspens of the Plateau to the west. Here it would take only a small dam to lift the water above its banks and spread it out upon the mesa. He had planned it many times, where the main ditch would go, the laterals, the place for his house and corrals and barn.

Dismounting, he drove a stake for one corner, rode east for what he judged would be the proper distance, and drove a second stake. He drove a third and fourth, and returned to his first, still having seen nothing of Vedder and his men. Loosening the cinches, he let his horse drink, then picketed him in the tall grass beside the creek, and built a fire.

He cooked and ate a meal, and then, suddenly and without warning, a rifle shot splintered the silence. He rose and looked around, but it had been some distance to the southeast. No one was in sight. He pondered the matter for a moment, thinking he should investigate, then he decided against it. He had the choice claim on the mesa, and at such a time possession was nine-tenths of the law. The shot might have been fired to lure him away from his claim.

Time was a drag. It seemed to Steve he had spent a lifetime waiting with the others along the line. Now he was waiting again. He smoked innumerable cigarettes; he got up and walked around, eyes searching the mesa for Al and the wagon. It had been easy, too easy, and Steve was always suspicious of anything that came easy.

The sun was well down toward the crest of the Plateau now, and Steve could wait no longer. He saddled his horse, knowing he had to find out what had happened to Al. A nagging suspicion that his brother had stolen the wagon began to plague him. Maybe Al had intended to stick with Vedder all the time. Steve was ashamed of the thought, but he could not dislodge it from his mind.

Steve mounted, but he did not ride away from the creek, for Todd Brashada's voice boomed at him from the willows upstream: "Stand pat, Regan, or you'll get what your kid brother got!"

He sat frozen in the saddle, seeing the glint of the dying sun on the rifle barrel thrust through the willows. Then Sandy Smith came out of the thicket, a gun in his hand, the cocky grin on his lips.

"Get down," Smith said. "You know, Regan, you're going to look real good swinging from a rope. It's my guess that's what the vigilance committee will do to claim-jumpers."

Brashada stepped out of the willows, Winchester held ready, bruised face filled with gloating triumph. He said: "You were lucky last night, Regan, but your luck's run out. Unbuckle your gun belt."

Steve hesitated. He would die now if he made a try for his gun. If he didn't, he'd have a few hours of life. They were holding a pat hand, and he had no illusions about what would happen at the end of those hours. Still, it was natural to play it out, for there was a chance something might turn up. He stepped out of the saddle, unbuckled his gun belt, and let it drop.

Brashada laid his rifle down and moved toward Steve. "Now I'm gonna beat hell out of you."

"No," Smith said sharply. "Bronc said . . ."

"I've got a damned poor memory," Brashada said.

"No," Smith repeated. "You had your chance, and you weren't man enough to do the job. You bust him up now, and you'll start the boomers to thinking."

Brashada stood glowering at Smith. He said reluctantly: "All right, all right. Tie him up."

Smith did not holster his gun until Brashada had bound Steve's hands and feet so tightly that the rawhide thongs cut into his skin. Then Smith said: "Build up the fire, Todd. I'll get some grub to cooking."

"What about Al?" Steve asked.

Brashada's puffy lips fashioned a grin. "He won't bother us none. Didn't you hear that shot this afternoon?"

Steve lay motionlessly, watching them cook a meal. He was sick with a sense of failure, for letting himself be caught, for his doubts of Al, and most of all for failing Al. He tugged at the thongs, but he succeeded only in wearing the skin off his wrists. Smith, hunkered by the fire with a cup of coffee, gave him a mocking grin.

"Take it easy," Smith said. "When Todd ties a man, he stays tied. You know, Regan, you ain't real smart. Not as smart as your kid brother. He hung around till he got onto Bronc's scheme. But he wasn't so smart, either, come to think of it. He'd be alive now if he hadn't got the notion he wanted to throw in with you again." Smith drank his coffee and put the tin cup down. "Bronc's the smart one. He didn't want you up here on the mesa. Me and Todd had looked it over this summer when we was cutting hay. It looked good to us, so we wrote to Bronc, telling him we could have a mighty pretty spread here if we could keep the boomers in the valley. That's why we fixed it so they wouldn't listen to you."

"You're talking too much," Brashada grunted.

"I like to see him squirm," Smith said. "It's a real kindness to let a man know he ain't smart like he thinks he is. You see, Regan, Bronc had it figured two ways. If Brashada busted you up so you couldn't stake out this claim, we'd nab it without trouble. Or if you sucked in and went down the river like he asked you to, you'd

44

be out of the way. We told Bronc there was just one place where we could take water out of the creek without much work, so he says we'll grab it. In a couple of days he'll have his herd up here, and we can stop worrying about boomers."

Steve should have guessed what Vedder was aiming at. Once a herd had been thrown on the mesa, Bronc Vedder could hold it for years, or until the pressure of population was so great that he was forced back into the dry hills to the west. "You're holding the high cards," Steve said.

"We've raked in every pot," Smith said complacently. "Even got Ila where I want her. I had her make a play for you last night, figuring she could make it plumb inviting for you to settle in the valley. A woman can't do no more than that for a man, can she?"

It was dusk now, the last brilliant color of the sunset flaming above the crest of the Plateau. Brashada pulled gear from the horses and staked them out, then returned to the fire.

A moment later Vedder rode in from the east and reined up in the fringe of firelight. He looked down at Steve, laughing silently. Then he said: "So they nailed you, did they, Regan?"

"Didn't you figure we would?" Smith asked.

"I wasn't worried. Too bad you weren't willing to stay on the river with the rest of 'em, Regan. I told you Al would wind up with a rope on his neck, but I was wrong. He's got a bullet in his head. You're the one who'll have a rope on your neck. I just had a palaver with Tobert and Delaney. We fixed up some rules and regulations. Like hanging a man who jumps a claim."

"Then you'll hang Smith and Brashada," Steve burst out.

"Why, I guess you'll have a hard time proving that, seeing as Sandy and Todd will swear they were here first and you tried to run 'em off with a gun."

"How are you going to satisfy folks about coming up here after that talk about sticking together in the valley?" Steve demanded.

Vedder shrugged. "I don't give a damn what the boomers think. They're in the valley where I wanted 'em, and I'll have my cows on the mesa." He gave his silent laugh again. "Ain't real talkative, are you, Regan? Well, you got the short end of the stick and that's a fact." He nodded at Smith. "Fetch him in, come morning. We'll make an example out of him."

"I ain't sure about Tobert," Smith said. "You'd better put a little starch down his backbone."

"He's all right," Vedder said impatiently. "That crack Todd gave him last night taught him a hell of a lot."

Vedder rode away. Complete darkness was all around them now, except for the light from the fire. Brashada kicked it up, and for a time played cards with Smith. Then he yawned and said he'd get some sleep.

"I'll stand guard," Smith said.

"No sense in that," Brashada grunted.

"How about tying me a little looser?" Steve said.

"Just the way I want it," Brashada said. "You won't be going nowhere when you're tied that-a-way."

A glow of hope warmed Steve. If they both went to sleep, he had a chance, for he lay within ten feet of the creek and the thongs that bound him were rawhide. But Smith didn't seem to be satisfied. He argued with Brashada, but the big man was stubborn.

"What the hell you worried about?" Brashada demanded. "He can't get loose, and Al ain't coming to help him."

"It's Vedder I'm worried about if this yahoo gets away," Smith said. "I'll sleep close to him. If he makes a wrong move, he won't live for his own hanging."

For a long time Steve lay motionlessly. Brashada's snores left little doubt about him, but Smith made no sound. It would be like the gunman, Steve thought, to wait until he made a move and then shoot him. He was the kind who needed an excuse, but a slight one would do.

Two hours passed, and Steve was not yet sure of Smith. It was quiet except for the hooting of an owl, the barking of a coyote, the rustling in the sagebrush of some furtive night prowler. Steve had no judgment of passing time, but he knew he could stand it no longer. Slowly he edged through the grass toward the creek, moving his legs a few inches, and then working his shoulders a little closer. There was no sound but the sibilance of body movement on the grass. It was loud to him, his ears straining to catch any sound of wakefulness on Smith's or Brashada's part.

It seemed a long time, although it must have been only a few minutes. Then his hands were in the water. It was very cold, but except for that sharp, needle-like sensation, there was little feeling in his hands. He twisted them, putting all his strength against the rawhide, and presently it stretched. He rolled back so that his hands were out of the water and continued to tug. His right slipped out of the loop. He flung the thong off his left, and sat up, rubbing one wrist and then the other.

He was free. It was all he could have hoped for. He thought his gun was still on the ground, for he had not seen either man pick it up. During the waiting hours he had gone over this in his mind many times. Brashada and Smith had murdered Al, and he would kill them with as little feeling as he would kill a pair of rattlesnakes. He pulled a knife from his pocket and slashed the thongs that bound his ankles. He lay back quickly, for Brashada stirred and rolled over.

Again the minutes plodded by. Then Brashada was sleeping soundly again. Cautiously Steve came to his hands and knees. Both men were motionless, vague mounds in the darkness. Steve crawled around the edge of the remains of the fire toward the spot where he had dropped his gun. He heard a sound behind him.

Steve grabbed the end of a stick that had not burned and lunged to his feet, but he had no chance to use the club in his hand. Smith caught him across the head with a vicious blow of his gun barrel, and Steve sprawled on his face, the blackness complete.

Smith laughed softly. He said: "Good thing I'm a light sleeper, bucko."

VI

Daylight was creeping across a dark sky when Steve came to. He was conscious first of a throbbing headache, then of his tied hands and feet, and the last hope faded from his mind. He had come close to escaping, but not close enough.

Presently Brashada woke, knuckled his eyes and yawned loudly, and built a fire. Smith sat up, rubbed his face, and then began to taunt Brashada over his failure in tying Steve. At first Brashada didn't believe it until he looked at Steve. Then he cursed Smith and told him to shut up. Smith obeyed, sensing the big man's ugly mood.

They ate, offering nothing to Steve. They saddled horses, and Smith cut Steve free. He said: "Mount up, mister. You're taking your last ride, so enjoy it."

Steve rose stiffly, reeling as a wave of nausea struck him. He grabbed the saddle horn, held himself there for a time until the earth quit rolling under his feet, and then pulled himself into leather.

"You ride with Todd," Smith ordered. "I'll be right behind you."

They struck off across the mesa, angling to the north, and within half an hour reached the hill that broke off sharply to the river bottom. Countless pillars of smoke stood motionlessly in the still morning air beside the scattered covered wagons. Steve thought of the Maddens and wondered if Ruth had brought the wagon through to the spot her father had selected. It was not in the cards that all the boomers would win the claims they coveted.

They slanted down the mesa hill, the sun well up now above the San Juan peaks, and rode across the river bottom through a jungle of *chico* brush. Reaching the Uncompahgre, they forded it and came to the site of Tobert and Delaney's town. It was on a slight bench above the river, and they had already cut a path through the sagebrush and had put up a sign that bragged: Main Street. Both Tobert's and Delaney's wagons were here, and there were two more a short distance to the south.

Vedder rose from the fire, where he had been hunkered, eating breakfast with Delaney and Tobert. He asked: "Who you got there, Todd?"

"A claim-jumper," Brashada said.

Tobert and Delaney got up, looking uneasily at each other. Steve said nothing, but he had recognized the other wagons. One was his own, the other the Maddens'. As he reined up, Joe Madden came around the rear of his wagon and moved toward them in his lumbering walk.

"We're pulling out for Kansas this morning, Steve," Madden called, "but I sure want to thank you for looking out for my womenfolks. This country is tough."

"We've got some dirty business to attend to," Vedder said curtly. "Unless you want to side a claim-jumper, you'd better get back to your outfit."

Steve swung to the ground. "I need a lawyer, don't I, Vedder? Maybe Joe'll do."

Madden stopped, his lips working nervously as understanding struck him. "I ain't in this," he muttered, and shuffled back toward his wagon.

Smith and Brashada dismounted, and Brashada led the horses away. Tobert shifted uneasily, his gaze touching Steve's face briefly. He asked: "Did you jump a claim like they say?"

"No." Steve motioned to Smith. "I beat these *hombres* to the mesa and staked out my claim. They got the drop on me, and they've been holding me prisoner ever since."

"That's a damned lie," Smith said as if indignant at Steve's accusation. "He threw a gun on me and told me to get off his claim. That was after I'd staked it, mind you. He'd have pulled his steal off, too, if Todd hadn't showed up."

Brashada returned in time to hear what Smith said. He nodded agreement. "That's right, Tobert. Get out your Bible and I'll swear on it. If you're going to get this country started off right, you've got to make an example of one claim-jumper. Then you won't have no more trouble."

"That's right," Vedder said. "That's why we were put on this committee. What do you have to say to that, Delaney?"

The storekeeper licked his lips, glancing at the Madden wagon. Then he blurted: "I say to hang Regan. We've got to have law and order."

Tobert threw up his hands. "This isn't the way. We'll hold him and call in a jury. He has a right to a regular trial."

"The hell he has!" Vedder shouted. "I've been through these things before, Tobert. String up one man, let folks see him, and the job's done. Dilly-dally around, and the toughs get the jump on you."

"I'll get a rope," Delaney said.

"Got it all cut and dried, ain't you?" Steve asked bitterly. "Can't you see you're playing into Vedder's hands, Delaney? What kind of a country do you figure you'll have, letting Vedder run things the second day the valley's settled?"

Brashada struck Steve on the side of the head, knocking him down into the dust.

Steve got to his hands and knees. A red haze danced before his eyes. He shook his head and came upright. His destiny had been decided when the crowd had elected this committee. It was partly that Vedder wanted him out of the way because he would always be dangerous to the cowman's ambition, and it was partly that Vedder understood the boomers. One hanging, and Vedder, by a show of force, could bull through to anything he wanted.

Then Steve thought he must be dreaming, for he was seeing something he had never thought he'd see. Ruth was coming toward them from Steve's wagon, Al beside her, one hand holding to her arm as if uncertain of each step. His tawny hair was disheveled, and a bloody bandage was tied around his head.

Brashada swore as if he refused to believe what his eyes saw. Smith cried out, his tone shrill: "You're dead, Al! Get back into hell where you belong."

"Shut up!" Vedder shouted. "He ain't dead.

Either way, it's got nothing to do with Steve jumping your claim."

"Yes it has!" Ruth cried. "If hanging is your punishment for a claim-jumper, what do you do to a murderer?" She pointed a finger at Smith. "He is a murderer, or he tried to be. His own words condemned him. Bring out your Bible, Delaney. I'll swear to what I know."

They came on, Ruth straight-backed and defiant, Al so weak he could hardly remain on his feet but doggedly holding himself upright. Then Vedder recovered his self-possession. He said coolly: "Take Al back to bed, Miss Madden, and stay out of sight. This is not something you will want to see."

Still they came on, Ruth's head high. "Delaney, you want Steve hanged, don't you? You think Ila will marry you if he's out of the way. Well, you're wrong." She pointed her finger at Smith again. "He's the one who'll marry Ila, but you'll let them use you to kill Steve and you're so blind you won't see what they're doing until it's too late."

"It's Steve, Ila . . . ," Delaney began.

"I'm marrying Steve," Ruth cut in. "Not Ila. Al knows the story about how Vedder wants the mesa for his cattle range, so he has to prove that Steve jumped Smith's claim. If he lets one man stay up there, he'll lose the mesa eventually."

There was no better time than this. They were

watching Ruth and Al, not knowing quite what to do, for it was something Vedder had not foreseen. His tactics with men would not work with a woman like Ruth. Tobert was nodding his head and saying: "I can believe it." Brashada stood one step away from Steve, holstered gun on his left side, within Steve's reach. Steve took the one step, pulled the gun, and jumped back as Brashada whirled, a big fist lashing out and missing by inches.

Vedder bawled an oath and grabbed for his gun, but he was slow. Sandy Smith was the dangerous one of the three. He wheeled, his gun sweeping up from leather as if it had been released by a spring. Steve fired only an instant before Smith's gun thundered.

Both shots rolled out as if one were an echo of the first. Smith's bullet breathed past Steve's head, but he had no strength to fire again. He broke at knee and hip and spilled forward into the dust.

Steve's action had been a desperate one born of necessity. There had been little real hope of survival in him, for no man, not even an expert like Sandy Smith, would have been fast enough to take three men, and Al was in no shape to help. But now another gun came into the fight, and Bronc Vedder, gun half lifted, stumbled and fell.

There was no time for Steve to see who was siding him. Brashada, cursing like a maniac, jerked his second gun from leather and threw a shot at Steve. It slammed through his left shoulder, the bullet shocking and numbing him, but he kept his feet. He fired twice, fast, and Brashada's second bullet went wide.

The big man teetered there for a moment, pale eyes filled with the knowledge of death. Blood was on his lips as he struggled to bring his gun into line again, but strength had fled from him. He fell forward, strangely awkward, his dogged will unable to hold his bullet-riddled body upright. His right hand, empty now, was flung out, and he lay like that, very still.

Al fumbled for his gun, but the fight was finished before he could lift it. Turning, Steve saw that it was John Tobert who had shot Vedder. Steve said—"Thanks, John."—and Tobert, sick with the knowledge that he had taken a human life, brought his gaze to Steve.

"I've never been a brave man," Tobert said, "but I made a fool of myself that night at my wagon. I didn't know till then what Vedder was doing." He swallowed. "I'm glad I killed him. We've got a new country to build, and we can't do it on lies and greed."

"How about you, Delaney?" Steve asked, still holding the gun.

The storekeeper's face was shiny with sweat. He wiped it now and, stepping back to the wagon, gripped a wheel to steady himself. Ila was running toward them, crying: "Sandy, Sandy!"

Then she saw his body, and, falling on her knees, she cradled his head in her lap and rocked back and forth.

Delaney said—"I'm here, Ila."—but she gave no indication that she heard him. He turned his head to look at Steve. "I'll be moving on, Regan," he said. "No place for me here."

Ruth was beside Steve, holding his right arm. "Can you walk to the wagon?" she asked.

"Sure. You help Al."

They moved toward the wagon, Al muttering: "I'm no damned good, Steve. Seemed like my gun weighed a ton."

"You're mighty damned good," Steve said warmly. "Took a lot of guts for you to be there. Smith told me you'd stuck with them till you found out what Vedder was up to. Why didn't you tell me?"

"I had to find out first," Al said. "I've always been a kid to you. I wanted to show you I'd grown up."

"You showed me," Steve said.

They reached the wagon, and Al dropped wearily to the ground. "They ambushed me yesterday. Ruth came along and took care of me. Brought the wagon in. She was going up on the mesa this morning to see about you. Vedder didn't know I was alive."

Ruth started to help Steve take off his shirt. "Looks like it's just a flesh wound."

"It'll wait. I've got to know if you meant it about marrying me."

She looked up at him, her face very grave. "If you want me. I should have known Ila was lying, but I guess I wasn't thinking very straight. You see, I knew she had gone to your wagon. When she came back, she told me you loved her and had asked her to marry you. She's always had a way with men, and you hadn't told me how you felt. Then after I had time to think about it, I . . . well, I'm sorry about the way I acted yesterday morning."

"She'll do," Al said, with more feeling than Steve had ever heard him have when he spoke about a woman. "That fool dad of hers got out of the guardhouse in time to catch the wagon. He made her stop and got up and took the lines. He told her to walk so the wagon would be lighter. Just a damned fool. If he'd let her drive, they'd have got the claim he wanted, but it was lucky for me. If she hadn't been walking, she wouldn't have heard the shot that got me."

"Anyhow, they're going back," Ruth said.

"You're not," Steve told her. "This is your country, yours and Al's and mine." He kissed her, thinking John Tobert had been right in saying that a country could not be built on lies and greed, but it could be built with the right tools—work, faith, and love. Those were the tools they would use, the three of them.

Guns in Sage Valley

I

At twenty Dave Logan held the promise of a strong man in his bony frame; his heart held the unfulfilled dream of a new raw land, waiting to be owned and tamed and made to produce, a dream that would grow with the years. Now it was enough to feel the wonder of each day, the challenge and beauty of the valley, the vague uneasiness that stifled him when he was near Nan Romney. It was enough to feel the wind strike his face when he put his buckskin into a run and the sage was a blur streaming by.

The crop was in and at the moment work was slack. He saddled up, telling his mother he was going rabbit hunting, and rode out of Logan Pocket toward Bill Hanna's place. Then, reaching the rim, he swung north toward West Lake. There was nothing for him at Hanna's shack, only dirt and the splashing of dishwater and the smell of unclean living, but to the north was Mary Romney's house. Her daughter Nan would be there.

Dave pulled his buckskin up atop the rim, eyes moving from the gray alkali water of West Lake to the unstained blue of neighboring Sage Lake. He could see the Romney house between them, set there beside the toll bridge that spanned the

Channel, a swift stream carrying the overflow from Sage into West Lake that was locked within rocky walls. Below him Logan Creek, born in a spring above his home, cut a turbulent escape from the pocket, its route marked by the green of willows. Beyond the lakes Sage Valley stretched away toward the broken rims on the east and the west and the piney Blue Mountains on the north, its bottom made gray and green by sagebrush and grass and greasewood.

The minutes piled behind him, unnoted and unmarked. Here was a wilderness, primitive, overlooked by man except for a few patches of turned grass and the Romney house and the town of Sage, but it would not remain this way. Lacey Markham, the schoolteacher, had talked to Dave about it.

"It's land for the plow," Markham had said earnestly. "Idle now because it's off the beaten path and because the Paiutes held the settlers out of valley, but it won't be idle long. They'll come like miners attracted to the mother lode. Plows and teams and cabins. Towns and railroads. A living for settlers driven by drought and grasshoppers from Kansas. We'll see them come, Dave, spiritual descendants of those who followed the Oregon Trail."

But Dave had not been convinced. There were other rumors that ran like wind across the valley. Perhaps the stories were true, perhaps nothing more than idle gossip, for the few who were in the valley lived with a dozen tales that did not agree and grew with the telling. These few were the hearty ones, strong enough to have survived the Paiute-Bannock War, strong enough to live by themselves despite the rumors that breathed across the valley. Of the stories one seemed, by virtue of repetition, to be true. A California cattleman was coming north with his herd and *vaqueros*. No one knew his name or how many cows he was bringing, but the story was that he had bought the valley as swamp land, bought it for a song from a swamp angel who had finagled thousands of acres from the state of Oregon for less than a song. If the story was true, Lacey Markham was wrong, for Sage Valley was not big enough to give both homes to Kansas farmers and range for a rancher's stock.

Dave put the thought from him. Tomorrow was another day. Today was Dave Logan's day unstained by threats that might be no more than false whispers. He looked down at the valley, silver where the sun was bright upon the sage, purple below the eastern rim where morning shadows clung with stubborn persistence. He looked beyond to the black barrier of the mountains and shook his head, gaze dropping again to the valley. He hated mountains. They closed about him and imprisoned his mind within the confines of cañons and forest. This was Dave

Logan's valley; he looked at it and loved it. Here were broad horizons where his thoughts could range from a boy's fantastic dreams to the hard realities of a man's future. There was both boy and man in Dave. He was man when he thought of Nan Romney, picturing himself married to her. In that picture was a house and ranch, horses and cows. He did not place it exactly, but it must be in the valley where the wind breathed unchallenged across the gray-green flat. Then the dreams would fall apart, for he was a boy again. A man would talk to Nan, tell her of his plans, tell her he loved her, but the words would not slip off his tongue when he was with her. He put his buckskin down the twisting trail to the valley, suddenly ashamed. He could talk to her mother, but when he was alone with Nan, his thoughts became fuzzy, his tongue anchored, and embarrassment touched its torch to his cheeks.

He reached the Romney house with the sun high in the midmorning, gave his buckskin a drink at the trough, and loosened its cinches. He felt the touch of a damp wind from West Lake; the lake smells came to him. He heard the steady wash of the Channel, the rustle of the tules. A mallard shot by to skid into the water below the bridge. Then Mary Romney called: "Come in, Dave! It's been a long time."

Dave led his horse to the rack. "Been busy," he

said. "Got the corn in, but reckon I wasted my time. Corn won't do nothing here."

Dave tied his horse and walked up the path to the house. Mary Romney held the door open for him, a smiling beautiful woman. There was much Dave did not understand about her, why she was never referred to as Mrs. Romney, why his mother hated her and called her "a bad woman," why the saloon man in Sage winked when her name was mentioned, but to Dave Logan she was the finest woman in the world. Involuntarily he compared his mother to her, her round-bosomed attractiveness making his mother seem as barren of life as a stick figure.

"People have to learn by doing in a new country, Dave." She closed the door behind him. "Cookie day. I'll bet you smelled them baking clear down in Logan Pocket."

She stood close to him, looking at him as if she considered him a man, woman smell a strong fragrance about her. He stepped away, feeling his face go hot. At that moment he was a boy with a man's body, and shame clutched his middle.

"No, ma'am. I just thought maybe you needed some wood cut."

Sobering, Mary looked down at her hands. They were calloused and hard, her fingernails split. She had kept her face as pretty as when she had come to the valley. Her expensive clothes were in good repair. She spent hours brushing her long yellow hair until it held the gloss of silky gold, but her hands were a farmer's hands.

"It would be nice, Dave," she said quietly. "All the cookies you can eat. Is that a fair bargain?"

"Fair enough," he said, and went on through the front room into the kitchen, walking on tiptoes because he always felt uneasy in Mary's front room with her fine furniture around him and her thick rug under his feet.

Nan was shutting the oven door when she heard him. Straightening, she turned and smiled. Again, as always when he saw her, he felt his heart race, his tongue glue to the top of his mouth. He muttered—"Howdy, Nan."—and struggled for breath.

"Good morning, Dave." She brushed a strand of hair away from her forehead, leaving flour streaked above her eyes. "I thought you were mad at us."

Mary Romney remained in the doorway, very still, good humor gone from her face. Dave wondered if she knew what his mother said about her, or how the saloon man in Sage winked when her name was mentioned. Anger stirred in him. There was nothing right about it. Mary Romney had never hurt anybody. She lived by the toll from her bridge over the Channel. Sometimes she kept travelers. Her meals were good, her beds clean, and she never overcharged. Still she had no friends in the valley except Dave, and perhaps Bill Hanna.

"I'm not mad," he said with more violence than he intended. "I've just been busy."

"He's been planting corn, Nan," her mother said. "How's your father, Dave?"

"He ain't well. I reckon he won't live the summer out."

"I'm sorry," Nan said. "We hadn't heard."

Dave stood awkwardly, shifting his weight from one foot to the other, looking at Nan and wondering why she wasn't as pretty as her mother. She was boy-bodied with too many freckles across her nose. Her hair was braided in pigtails down her back instead of fluffed up like her mother's, and her dress was of faded calico, plain with none of the doodads that her mother's had.

Then Dave was aware of the pressure of the silence, of Nan turning from him and scurrying into the pantry, of her mother's short laugh as she said: "Don't forget your cookies in the oven, Nan."

"I'll get at the wood," Dave said, and walked on through the kitchen.

The wood was juniper brought from the rim beyond Bill Hanna's place. Once Dave's mother had scolded Hanna for chopping and hauling it to Mary Romney, but the scolding had only angered him.

"She's got good money, Mary has," Hanna had snapped, "which same is more than most settlers around here have, including you." Then he'd stomped out of the Logan cabin and he'd never come back.

It was slow work, sawing and splitting the scraggly juniper. Dave stacked the straight pieces for the cook stove and tossed the rest into a pile beside the back door. Nan brought him a plate of cookies and a glass of milk, and he leaned the axe against the woodpile and sat down on the chopping block.

"Must be kind of hard living without a man," Dave said.

Nan watched him eat for a moment. Then she said stiffly: "We get along."

"Yeah, sure."

He emptied the glass with a long drink, covertly watching her, afraid he had made her angry. He never had understood why it was hard to talk to Nan. He could talk to Dixie Joslyn. Dixie was the storekeeper's daughter and a sight prettier girl than Nan, but he didn't like her as well.

"What makes you think it's hard to get along without a man?" she asked.

Dave shoved another cookie into his mouth. Nan had a pitcher of milk in her hand, but she didn't notice his glass was empty. There were spots of red in her cheeks; her lips were straight and sourly sober.

"Well?" Nan asked.

He swallowed, knowing he shouldn't ask for the milk, but he shoved his glass at her anyway. The cookie was swelling like a mouthful of cotton. Nan giggled, the barrier breaking between them.

"I'm sorry, Dave. I should have noticed."

She filled his glass. He drank it dry again and wiped a sleeve across his mouth. "I didn't mean nothing by saying it's hard to get along without a man. I just meant there was things to do like chopping wood that's man's work."

"There's nothing a man can do we can't," she said, her face turned sober again. "Don't you ever forget that, Dave Logan."

She sure was touchy, Dave thought. Might be better if he rode off before she lost her temper. He said: "Sure. I just thought chopping wood was man's work. Same as cooking and washing dishes and tending garden is woman's work."

There was a moment of silence, Nan staring at him. He squirmed, wanting another cookie, but she didn't offer him one.

"Why did you look at me that way in the house?" Nan asked.

"I don't know."

He swallowed. He knew, but he couldn't tell her. His thoughts were fuzzy again, his tongue sucked against the roof of his mouth.

"There's nothing wrong with us," she flung at

him. "You don't need to come in and stare at me like maybe I was something terrible."

"I didn't. I mean, I didn't think of that." He kicked a stray piece of juniper toward the pile. "You going to school next winter?"

"You know I'm not," she blazed. "I never have and I never will. Someday I'm going to get out of here. There must be a place where people are decent and friendly." She stopped, lips tightly pressed. Then she said, deliberately and slowly, each word spaced so that it was a slap: "Some place there must be people who aren't like your mother."

He got up, sick. "Thanks for the cookies," he said, and walked around the house to his horse. He didn't look back, didn't see the tears on Nan's face, didn't see her run into the house and slam the door.

He was in the saddle when Mary Romney called: "Thank you for cutting our wood, Dave! Come back again."

"Yes, ma'am," he said, and turned his buckskin up the trail toward Logan Pocket, puzzled and hurt and feeling the prick of conscience because he had not defended his mother.

II

Dave did not go home until the necessity of time drove him back. The chores must be done and it had been three months since his father had been able to do anything. He had shot and cleaned three jack rabbits, the first fresh meat they'd had for more than a week. He took them into the house, nodding at his father who sat in a rocking chair in front of the cabin, a skeleton of a man who knew he would die soon and did not care.

Mrs. Logan was darning a pair of Dave's socks when he came in, holding them close to the window so that she could use the last of the afternoon sunlight. The kerosene lamp on the shelf had been empty for a month. Mary Romney always had money to keep her lamp filled. Dave wondered if that was the reason his mother didn't like her.

Dave laid the rabbits on the table. He paused there in the middle of the room, looking at his mother, thin and flat-bosomed and always tired. He had been thinking all afternoon about what Nan had said: *Some place there must be people who aren't like your mother.* A new thought shocked him. All the women of the valley were like his mother except Mary Romney. Some were fatter or shorter or taller. Perhaps their hair was not white like hers. Some had good dresses and shoes that hid their wearer's toes. But those were not the important things. Dave searched his mind, unable to identify the likeness he sensed in the valley women. Then he had the word. Starved! That was it. The squeezing poverty of their meager existence had killed their capacity for living. Work was the only thing left for them, work so they could prove up on the land they claimed.

"I was over to Mary Romney's this morning," Dave blurted. "I like her and Nan. Why don't you go to see them?"

He didn't know why he said it. It was a mistake, but he couldn't have held the words back.

She raised her head and stared at him, her eyes angry sparks in a flat-lined angular face. She said shrilly: "I'll never step into Mary Romney's house, and I want you to stay away from there."

"I like Nan," he said doggedly.

"Like mother like daughter. There are decent girls in the valley. Like Dixie Joslyn. Go take her to the dance if you want to go, but don't go back to the Romneys. You hear?"

He stared at his mother, sullen, resentful, and he would have said more if his father had not croaked: "Dave! Ma! They're coming into the Pocket. Cows. Millions of 'em."

Dave ran out of the cabin ahead of his mother. He heard the yip of the riders, the bawling of cows, and smelled the dust that was drifting toward them. They had come from the south, dropping down the trail into Logan Pocket, a long line of swaying red backs, their horns bright as freshly honed swords, their tips catching the last of the slanting sunlight.

Mrs. Logan swore. It was the first time in his life Dave had heard her use those words. She whirled into the house, grabbed a shotgun from the corner, and rushed back into the yard.

"Get your rifle, Dave. They can't come in here. They'll mud up the spring and break our fences. They'll take our home away from us." She ran toward them, a gaunt figure, the hammer of her shotgun back. "Get out!" she screamed. "Drive 'em back up on the rim!"

Dave didn't get his rifle. He saw the big man riding toward them, a stud horse of a man, deep-chested and great-muscled, a granite block of a man who sat his saddle as if lightning could not take him out of it.

"I'm Matt Strang, ma'am!" he called. "I'll pay you for any damage . . . !"

Mrs. Logan raised her shotgun and fired. Dave, beside her, batted the barrel down and twisted the gun out of her hands. The buckshot rapped into the ground, dust and smoke boiling up around them, the big man's booming laugh rolling into the thunder of the blast.

"I've got a tough hide, ma'am, but it ain't tough

enough to bounce buckshot off it. You better thank your boy you didn't murder me."

Trembling, Mrs. Logan tried to jerk the shotgun out of Dave's grip. She screamed: "Why shouldn't I murder you? What have you done for the country, stealing land under the robbers' act, bringing your cows in here to shove us off our homes. Look at 'em! Breaking down our fences just like I knew they would. Get 'em out. You hear? Get 'em out!"

"Sorry, ma'am," Strang said. "They need water. We'll hold 'em here tonight, and tomorrow we'll push 'em into the valley." He turned to one of his men. "Clab, hold 'em against yonder wall. Keep 'em out of the grain." He tossed a gold coin at Mrs. Logan's feet. "Here. That'll more'n pay you for the damage they've done."

"You can't buy me!" she screamed. "Keep your dirty gold. Take 'em back to California."

She whirled and ran toward the cabin, crying, one hand clutching her apron against her face. The shotgun was still in Dave's grip. The yip of the riders and the bawling of cattle seemed far away to him. He looked up at Matt Strang, thinking how wrong Lacey Markham had been when he'd talked about the spiritual descendants of those who followed the Oregon Trail. There would be no room here for the Kansas settlers. Cows had beaten them to the valley.

"I'm right sorry your ma took it that way,"

Strang said. "You keep that gold piece. She'll change her mind after a while."

He rubbed his wide face, dark with stubble. Then he cuffed back his hat, and Dave saw that his hands were big, his fingers square-tipped, his wrists heavy-boned. Strength was in Matt Strang, great unyielding strength. Dave, staring at him, read the future. His folks and Bill Hanna and Mary Romney would lose or keep their homes according to the humor of this man.

Dave picked up the gold piece and dropped it into his pocket. "Ma was right," he said stiffly. "What have you done for the country?"

"Nothing yet, sonny, but I will, and I aim to do something for Matt Strang." He lifted a cigar from his coat pocket, amusement touching his dark face. "I ain't never real sure about this business of being right. I reckon there's something to say on your ma's side. Likewise on mine. I bought this land. Your place belongs to me. Savvy?"

"I savvy you've got guns and money and the law on your side, but all of them don't make it right."

"We'll auger this some other day," Strang said amiably. "Right now maybe you'd like to show me the trail that'll get me up to yonder rim." He motioned to the north wall of the Pocket. "I want to take a look."

Dave hesitated, thinking of his mother. He kept

his eyes on Strang's face, friendly and amused. He had seen cowmen in the valley before, but none had stayed and none had looked like Strang. He had the appearance of a California cattleman, his horse a big blaze-faced black, his saddle and bridle bright with silver trimmings. A *vaquero* wearing a *rosadero* rode up in answer to Strang's motion.

"See they don't tromp that spring up." Strang hipped around in the saddle, watching the twisting line come down the trail. He turned back to Dave. "How about it, lad?"

"I'll show you," Dave said, and, walking back to the house, mounted his buckskin.

As he rode up the trail, a haunting Spanish tune from a *vaquero*'s throat came to him. Change, he thought, had come to the valley. Nothing would be the same again, but he was thinking of Mary Romney and not his folks. They had little to lose, a cabin and a few acres of plowed ground, but Mary had a fine house and a toll bridge that paid her a good living.

They reached the rim and only then did Dave look again at Matt Strang. The valley lay below them, purple-hued, the sun lost for the day with only a transient scarlet glory a fading reminder of its passage. Strang was a man hypnotized. Dave had heard the stories of gold discoveries on the John Day River to the north. Now, watching the cattleman, Dave thought the gold-seekers must have had the same enraptured look on their faces that Matt Strang's had now.

Strang lifted his great body in the stirrups, a hand sweeping out before him. He said hoarsely: "Mine. All mine. I own it, every acre."

"What about us folks that live here?" Dave demanded.

Apparently Strang did not hear. He said, as if totally unaware of Dave's presence: "Fifty thousand acres. I bought it, sight unseen. Crazy, they said I was, but I wasn't crazy. An empire. Matt Strang's empire. Sweet water and grass. Cool days and no anthrax. I'll have bigger cattle than California ever saw."

"What about us?" Dave demanded. "My folks and Bill Hanna and Mary Romney? We came here before you bought any swamp land."

Strang turned to him, his face a wide blob in the dusk. "It's my land, lad. What would you do if you was in my boots?"

"I'd keep folks out who wasn't here, but I wouldn't bother them that was."

Strang folded his hands around the saddle horn. "Why would you leave the folks alone who was already here?"

"There's just three of us this side of Sage. Bill Hanna, he don't hurt anybody. Hunts and cuts wood for Mary Romney. And Mary, she don't hurt nothing. Mary and her girl Nan have got a nice house on the Channel. They live off their

77

toll bridge that saves folks going around one of the lakes. And my pa's got consumption. He'll die this summer. Me and Ma wouldn't do you no hurt."

"You say this Mary Romney's got a nice home?"

"Best in the valley. I guess she's got money. Cost her a pile to build that house and put up lacy curtains and bring in them fancy carpets and furniture. Awful pretty, Mary is, but folks don't like her."

"Why?"

Dave shifted in the saddle. "I don't rightly know."

"What's your name, lad?"

"Dave Logan. We was here in the valley before the Paiute trouble. We got out in time and made it to Fort Pacific over on the other side of the valley. Mary and Nan got there, too, but Bill Hanna and his brother didn't make it. The Injuns got Bill's brother."

"You're trying to say I'm a little late. That it?"

"That's right," Dave said defiantly. "I don't know much about what folks call the robbers' act that let you grab the valley, but we was here first and we fought Injuns. We got a right to our homes."

Strang turned his horse back toward Logan Pocket. "How'd you like a job, Dave? You don't know anything about cattle, but you'll learn, and I need somebody who knows the valley."

Dave took a long breath. "I'd like that." This, he knew, was how his dream would become reality. It had been his destiny from the first.

III

Dave was up with dawn holding a gray promise of day. He paused beside his parents' bed. His father's face seemed dead, the yellow skin pulled tightly across his cheek bones. He stood there, listening to the old man's feverish breathing. His mother's hair made a white spill across the pillow. The light was too thin to see her face clearly, but he pictured it, narrow and unforgiving and bitter. He wished he had known her when she was younger. There had been money. A good farm in Ohio. He had seen the tintypes. She had been good-looking and life had held some sweetness. There was none for her now.

He tiptoed out of the room, fearing the violence of her temper when she read his note. He remembered Matt Strang saying: *I ain't never real sure about this business of being right.* Dave was not sure himself.

Dave went out into the air still sharp with the night chill. He saddled his buckskin, telling himself there was nothing that had to be done on the place now except the milking and his mother could do that. He had left Strang's gold piece on the table. The money he earned would buy flour and sugar and kerosene, luxuries they had not been able to afford. Maybe she would forgive him when he brought his first month's pay home. He swung into the saddle, uncertainty bringing a biting worry into his thoughts.

Strang's men were sitting, cross-legged, around the fire eating breakfast when Dave rode up. Strang nodded, and said: "Git down, Dave, and pitch in." He motioned toward a stringy man at the fire. "Clab Holland, Dave. He's the foreman, so you'll be working for him when I ain't around. Clab, you'll make a buckaroo out of the boy."

Holland grunted, his sharp calculating eyes coldly studying Dave. Dave said—"Howdy."— and met the foreman's stare. Holland was about Strang's age, Dave thought, thirty-five or so, a leggy man with a long head and a knife-thin nose. Grinning, he wheeled to face Strang. "Matt, looks to me like we've got enough trouble without playing nursemaid to a granger brat."

Dave's fists knotted. Holland had a missing tooth in the front of his mouth. He spat through the opening, the stream plopping into the ashes of the fire and sizzling, a contemptuous gesture that Dave did not miss. He felt their eyes upon him, Strang's and the *vaqueros'* and the fat cook's, and he knew what he had to do. Dave's action was quick and accurate. One long step brought him within reach of Holland. His right fist lashed out, caught Holland on the jaw, and flattened him, the foreman's head banging against a Dutch oven.

"Nobody plays nursemaid to me," Dave said hotly.

They were surprised, Holland and Strang and the rest. Dave supposed that finished it, but Strang did not move to stop the fight. Holland bounced up and came at Dave, wasting no breath in talk.

Dave had been in plenty of fights mostly during the school term when the boys were penned up inside and needed violence as an avenue of escape for their dammed-up energy, but they were nothing like this. It seemed to Dave that Holland had ten fists. He felt their sting and tasted his own blood. He swung and missed, or hit nothing more vital than a shoulder or elbow. Holland would land half a dozen jarring blows before Dave could cover up. The foreman was like a turning, twisting dust devil that stayed out of Dave's reach, bobbing and ducking and slashing with cutting knuckles.

"That's enough, Clab!" Strang called.

The words came as a distant sound to Dave. He dropped his fists, reeled a little, sweat and blood rolling down his face. Then Holland stepped in close and sledged him on the chin with a wickedly turning fist. Dave dropped and blackness was all around him.

"He hits hard." Holland rubbed the side of his face, grinning at Strang. "I should have seen that coming, but I didn't think a granger kid would stand up and fight."

"He'll do," Strang said, motioning to a rider to throw a bucketful of water on Dave.

Dave sat up, wheezing and choking and swinging wildly with his fists.

"All right, Dave," Strang said. "The fun's over."

Dave rubbed his face, his vision clearing. Holland was back on the other side of the fire, finishing his breakfast as if nothing had happened. The riders were spilled out on both sides of him and the cook was walking back to the chuck wagon. Dave looked at Strang, suddenly angry. "I didn't have much fun. I reckon we'll try it again."

Strang shook his head. "No. Fun's over. Clab won't have a man on the payroll he can't lick. Likewise he won't have a man who won't fight. He was just washing out a pan to see what your color was. Pitch in now and eat."

Dave ate, but his jaws didn't work right. One eye was closed and blood dripped from a cut on his right cheek. He finished his coffee, watching Holland, but the man ignored him.

"Fetch 'em into the valley, Clab, and let 'em spread out," Strang ordered. "There's grass for ten thousand head instead of two." He stepped into the saddle. "We'll ride, Dave. I want to see this fine Romney house. While we're at it, we'll go on into town."

They rode out of the Pocket, the sun a widening arc above the eastern rim. Strang said nothing until they were in the valley and Mary Romney's house stood before them and the rush of the Channel was a steady sound in their ears.

Strang pulled up and hipped around in his saddle, eyes on the trail behind him. He said: "I'll build my house on that rise just below the rim. The creek flow all year?"

"I've never seen it dry," Dave answered.

"Good water?"

"Best in the valley. Comes out of that spring just above our house."

"Then that's the place. I've got ten men now, but I'll have a hundred." He turned back in his saddle, eyes raised to the distant wall of the mountains. "Pine?"

Dave nodded. "Lots of it."

"Is there a sawmill?"

"A little one above the fort."

Strang looked at Mary Romney's house, two-story and painted white with a picket fence in front and a patch of grass. "I'd never expect to see that out here. Might be cheaper to take her house except I don't like it down here by the lakes."

"You drive her out of her home and I'll kill you."

Strang's black brows lifted. He pinned his eyes on Dave, searching the boy's face. He murmured: "I thought you said this woman wasn't liked?"

"I like her," Dave said hotly.

"I don't want trouble with any of the settlers," Strang said. "I came here to raise cows, but if I've got to fight, I'll do it."

"You won't have to do no fighting on account of her. She ain't got no friends who'd help her out if you took her house." Dave's good eye was fixed on Strang's face, his tone level. "Just me."

"Mostly I don't have much curiosity," Strang said, "but I have after hearing you talk. Reckon we'd better visit Mary Romney."

Strang stepped down and racked his horse. Dave hesitated, not liking it and afraid of what Strang would do. He reached down for his Winchester, and then decided against it. Dismounting, he left his buckskin beside Strang's black and followed him.

Strang's big fist beat a series of racketing blows on the door. It swung open and Mary Romney stood there, her hair combed, her face composed. She was wearing a long form-fitting robe tied by a silk cord above her round hips. Dave took a deep breath. He had never seen so much lace before.

"If you're crossing the bridge," Mary said

evenly, "you can pay your toll without knocking my door down."

Strang's hat came off his head in a quick, involuntary motion. His lips were parted; his shirt was stirred by the depth of his breathing. Dave said: "This is Matt Strang, Mary. He brought in a herd. He owns the valley."

"I see. Won't you come in?"

She stepped back, and Strang followed her into the house. He said: "I usually can talk when I can't do anything else, ma'am, but looking at you makes me tongue-tied. It ain't believable, finding you in a wilderness like this."

She smiled, pleased. "Have you had breakfast?"

"Yes, ma'am. Dave was telling me about you. I just stopped to get acquainted." He looked around the room at the starched lace curtains, the high-piled rug, the red so dark it was nearly black, the melodeon set against the front wall, the oak center table with the tall lamp, the Bible, and the bouquet of lilacs in a blue vase. "To a man who's seen nothing but cows and dust all the way up from Nevada, this is like stepping into heaven."

Some of the composure passed from her face; her lips were stirred by interest. "Come on back to the kitchen, Mister Strang. You'll have coffee at least."

Strang followed her, Dave, hat in hand, walking behind him. Nan was sitting at the table. She rose, uncertain. Her mother said: "This is my daughter, Mister Strang."

"How do you do?" Strang said it quickly as if the girl held no interest for him, his eyes swinging to her and back to Mary Romney. "My friends call me Matt. I'm hoping you'll do the same."

She held a chair at the table for him. "Dave said you owned the valley. That makes us trespassers."

"You don't need to worry." Strang dropped into the chair, his flesh flowing over the sides. "I've got to get acquainted with the valley folks, and then I'll know what to do to protect myself. I'm glad I started here."

Nan moved back to stand unobtrusively by the stove. Dave had stopped in the doorway, feeling awkward and unwanted. Mary Romney had brought a filled coffee cup from the stove and placed it before Strang. Dave, watching, thought that he and Nan might as well have been a thousand miles away. There were just the two in the room, Matt Strang and Mary Romney.

Something had happened that Dave did not understand and did not like. He looked at Nan once and brought his gaze away. She was staring at her mother, stiff-bodied with apprehension.

Mary moved back around the table, hips swinging. She said: "Thank you, Matt. I'm glad you started here, too."

He picked up his cup and drank, eyes black living stars in a muscle-ridged face. He put it down, gaze clinging to her as if held there by some power greater than his will. He said: "I won't bother you, ma'am. I'll give you a patent for this quarter-section and it won't cost you nothing."

She lowered her head, fingers tapping lightly on the table. "Nothing is free, Matt. I'm not sure I'll pay your price."

"This is free." He clutched the side of the table, great body hunched forward. "I tell you it's free. Soon as I can get the papers fixed up, you'll have a patent on this quarter-section."

"Perhaps I have my price, Matt." She looked at him now, boldly, invitingly. "There are other folks here. Bill Hanna, Dave's people."

"All right. I'll let them alone."

"And the folks in town. The storekeeper, Bob Joslyn. Lacey Markham, the schoolteacher. Tildie Fields who runs the hotel. A few others. You could take their homes away from them, but I know how they feel."

Strang looked questioningly at Dave as if to say: *You told me this woman had no friends in the valley.*

Dave was staring at Mary Romney, his mind gripping this thing he had heard her say and making no sense of it. He blurted: "You don't owe them nothing, Mary."

"We all owe everybody something, Dave." She stood with her head high, her cheeks pale. "Matt, I'd like for them to know why you're letting them stay."

Strang rose. "I'll tell 'em. You're damned right I'll tell 'em." He picked up his hat. "Lot to do today. A lot to do for the next ten years." He stood there, hands fisted, a hungry man not wanting to leave. "I'll stop in later."

He said it hesitantly as if it depended on how she felt about him. Her smile came quickly, brightening her face. She said: "I hope you will, Matt."

Still he did not stir for a moment. Again Dave felt that something had happened between them, changing everything in the valley. He looked at Mary Romney, her face alive and vibrant in a way he had not seen it before. Then he brought his gaze to Matt Strang, and he saw the same thing in the big man's face, the hunger and the reaching.

Without a word, Strang wheeled into the living room and walked out of the house, spurs jingling. He mounted and reined toward the tollgate. Nan was there ahead of him, opening it, and when he asked—"How much is the toll?"—she answered stiffly: "Nothing to you."

Dave followed him across the bridge, looking at Nan and hoping she would lift her eyes to him, but she did not. There was misery on her face, and that was not like her. Dave caught up with Strang and swung his buckskin in beside the big black. He thought about Nan, not sure but believing he understood. There had been just her and her mother. Now there was Strang.

"Dave," Strang said, "from now on she's got two friends in the valley, and heaven help anybody who don't treat her right."

Strang rode in silence then, looking like a man who has waked from a pleasant dream and was fondling the memory of it, but Dave's thoughts turned to Nan and they were troubled.

IV

It was a complimentary extension of the truth to call Sage a town. There was one weed-grown street that was a series of ruts in dry weather and a sea of clutching mud in wet. A few of the buildings were false-fronted frame structures built of lumber hauled to the valley from the little sawmill in the Blue Mountains, but all the dwellings except Bob Joslyn's were one-room log cabins, most of them poorly made and inadequate except when the weather was warm. Joslyn's house, next to his store, was a four-room cottage, painted white, with a picket fence in front.

Strang reined up in front of the Gold Bar

saloon, eyes raking the town. Joslyn's Mercantile was across the street, Tildie Fields's hotel beside it. The blacksmith shop flanked the saloon. A schoolhouse was beyond the Mercantile at the other end of town.

"How many in the valley, Dave?" Strang asked.

" 'Bout fifteen families."

"Farmers?"

"All but four or five that live in town."

"Might as well talk to them that's here. Round 'em up, Dave. They'll tell the farmers." Strang stepped down and dropped the reins over the hitch pole. "Better have 'em come to the store, seeing as a woman runs the hotel. Otherwise, I'd say the saloon."

Dave dismounted and racked his buckskin, apprehension filling him with uncertainty. There had been a good deal of wild talk about what would happen if a cowman invaded the valley. Lacey Markham had said repeatedly: "This is farm country and our only chance of survival is to hold it for the farmers." Strang did not carry a gun. It would have been safer, Dave thought as he turned into the Gold Bar, if Strang had brought half a dozen armed men with him.

"A cowman named Strang has bought the valley!" Dave called to the saloon man. "He wants to see all of you in the store."

The saloon owner was a fat man who went only by the name of Hambone. He had driven a team and wagon into the valley the year before and set up the saloon, but where he had come from and why he had stopped in an isolated place like Sage were questions that had gone unanswered. "The hell," he said angrily. "He can come here if he wants to talk."

"Was I you, I'd go," Dave said, and left the saloon.

He told the blacksmith, George McNair, crossed the street to the hotel and gave the same invitation to Tildie Fields. He walked past the store toward Lacey Markham's cabin, seeing that Strang had gone inside and was talking to Bob Joslyn, the storekeeper.

"Dave. Come here."

Dixie Joslyn was in the doorway of the Joslyn house, motioning for him to come to her. Dave stopped, irritated, not wanting to talk to her but lacking the decision to go on.

"Come here," Dixie repeated, and, when Dave stood rooted at the corner of the store, she left the house and walked quickly toward him.

"I've got to get Markham," Dave said.

Dixie was beside him then, her hand on his arm. She was a small dark girl who had a way of pressing close to him, the nearness of her body never failing to send an undefined disturbance through him. Her lips were parted now, her black eyes searching his. "Dave, who is the man you rode into town with?"

"Matt Strang. He owns the valley."

"What are you running around town for?"

"He wants to talk to everybody."

Dixie was not the mystery to Dave that Nan was. He had never been sure Nan liked him, but Dixie made no secret of her feelings. She was pretty with the perfect features of a doll, and she had a talent for making Dave feel her helplessness as if he were the only person in the world who could do anything for her. "Does he want to talk to me?" she asked. "Is he going to drive us out of the valley?"

"I don't think so."

"Dave." She pulled him off the path and around the corner of the store building. "You're on our side, aren't you? We've got to fight him together, haven't we?"

Her lips were parted, expectant. He had kissed her before when she had looked at him this way. She would welcome it now. Then he wondered if she invited his kisses because he was the only man in the valley who was her age and was single, or whether she really liked him as much as she pretended.

"I've got to get Markham," Dave muttered.

"Dave, you haven't been to see me for a long time." She was facing him, her hands on his arms, her lips softly pressed. "Dave, you know what this means, don't you? Dad says it's bound to come, and he's going to fight."

"Maybe there won't be any fighting," he said, and, jerking away from her, went on to Markham's cabin in a fast pace that was close to a run.

"I'll be along," the teacher said when Dave told him about Strang.

When Dave walked back, Dixie was not in sight. He tried to whistle, tried to focus his thoughts on Nan, to tell himself it wasn't right to love her and kiss Dixie every time she held her lips up to him. Still, the lost opportunity brought a vague regret to him.

All of them but Markham were in the back of the store, sitting around the potbellied stove when Dave came in. Hambone, his oiled hair carefully combed with a drooping curl pasted against his forehead. McNair, the blacksmith, a bearded man with thick hairy arms. Middle-aged Tildie Fields, tiny and prim, who held herself proudly from the rest as if she felt she was the only aristocrat in the valley. Bob Joslyn, almost as small as Tildie, a white-haired man who, like Lacey Markham, believed that this was agricultural land. All the townspeople but Tildie were armed. That was the first thing Dave noticed. The second was the sullenness that gripped them. They were silent and tight-lipped, eyes on the floor, but if Matt Strang sensed the feeling, he gave no indication of it.

"Any more, Dave?" Strang asked.

"Just the schoolteacher," Dave said.

"What happened to you?" Tildie Fields demanded.

Dave hesitated, gaze swinging to Strang's smiling face. He couldn't tell the truth. Suddenly it seemed to him a foolish thing to take a beating the way he had from Clab Holland and keep on working for Matt Strang. No one would understand if he told them. He was not sure he understood himself, but it was the thing he must do. If there had been any doubt, Strang's feeling about Mary Romney had settled it. Dixie had said—"We've got to stand together."—but the only thing the settlers could agree on was their feeling about Mary. "Met up with a wildcat," Dave said.

"I never saw a wildcat . . . ," Tildie began.

"Several kinds of wildcats," Strang cut in blandly. He turned to the counter, eyes scanning the shelves. "Joslyn, I want you to outfit Dave. Give him the best boots in the store. That black Stetson yonder will do. Shirt and pants." He scratched his cheek, fingernail grating against the stubble. "Better give him a gun and holster."

"I can't afford it," Dave burst out. "I've got to take my wages home."

"Well, I should think so," Tildie Fields said. "I never dreamed you'd work for a man like this Strang. Your folks were among the first in the valley."

That was what they were all thinking. Dave knew his cheeks were red the way they always were when he was embarrassed. He turned toward the door, giving them his back. Why couldn't he keep his mouth shut? He had taken his direction and he would keep it. From this day on there would be two sides in the valley without room for the neutral. Dave swung back, suddenly angry, feeling the need of justifying himself. "Sure, they were the first in the valley. Right after Bob started this store, but I don't know yet why we came. I don't know why Bob came. I don't know why any of you came. Look at you, rotting out here in the sagebrush while you talk about how good it's going to be."

He paused for breath, but before he could plunge on, Lacey Markham called from the doorway: "It will be good, Dave, but not if we sell out to a land pirate."

Dave had always liked Markham. He was not yet forty, a tall gaunt man who looked older than he was. His eyes were a mild blue with red rims from too much reading, a visionary, Dave's mother had said, so lazy he wouldn't file on a quarter-section because he'd have to farm it. If it had been anyone else in the room, Dave would have had an angry response, but Lacey Markham was a gentle man who talked of fine ideals and lived by them. So Dave said mildly: "Even a land pirate might improve the valley, Lacey."

"No." Markham gave Strang a searching look, then brushed past him to sit down beside Joslyn. "Progress has flowed to the north of us, leaving our valley on the fringe of the frontier, but it won't always be that way. Real progress comes with the plow. You've read some history, Dave. Have you ever known of nomads making a real contribution to civilization?"

Strang had been listening, an amused smile lingering in the corners of his mouth. Now, ignoring Markham, he said: "Joslyn, we'll fit Dave out after our palaver. Don't worry none about paying for this, Dave. We'll settle that next year if you need your money now."

"Dave, are you working for this man?" Markham demanded.

"That's right," Dave said defiantly. "Who else is there to work for?"

"Nobody now, but there will be. Wait a year. Perhaps two." Markham licked dry lips, his face lighting up as it always did when he talked about the valley's future. "Wagon trains and settlers. Cabins and farms. Railroads. There'll be a million opportunities for you then. Now your job is to prove up on the land your folks . . ."

"That's the damnedest hogwash I ever heard," Strang cut in, the smile wiped from his face. "You know this valley has been declared swamp land and has been turned back to the state for sale. I bought it. I'm promising you one thing, mister. Starting today, this valley is cattle range, and I can promise you it'll be a hell of a long time before you see a railroad in these parts."

"It was designated as swamp land," Markham said coldly, "and we know how. You bought this valley from a weasel named James Harl, a swamp angel if you prefer that term, but I say weasel is the fitting one."

"Call him what you want, I bought the land." Strang waved the thought aside. "Whether you stay here or not is up to me."

"We'll lick no boots!" Bob Joslyn cried. "This is my town site. I staked it out. I've sold lots to these people. There'll come a day when Sage is the biggest city in southeastern Oregon."

"You've delivered damned poor titles to any lots you've sold," Strang said. "Go ahead and stake out your town site. My cows will be grazing in these streets fifty years after you're gone."

"I think not," Markham breathed. "Only a small part of this valley is actually swamp land. You saw that when you rode across it this morning. I told you we knew James Harl and we know how it comes to be designated as swamp land. We'll get the robbers' act repealed if it takes a lifetime, and this valley will be thrown open to settlement."

"I ain't here to auger," Strang said. "The land's mine. I can show you on a map. The land that was returned by the government survey as swamp land is marked with a red S. The whole valley is marked except the part around the fort."

"Damn it," Markham flung back, "a red S on a map don't make swamp land. Look at it! Do you call sagebrush swamp vegetation? The biggest land steal in the history of the country was right here in this valley. The state sells it for a dollar an acre, but a paltry twenty cents an acre secures possession. Then if you cut three crops of hay within ten years, you've reclaimed the land, and for eighty cents more per acre you get full title as far as the state can give it. I say that's robbery even if this valley was all swamp land."

For a moment Strang struggled with his temper. Then he laughed, and, lifting a cigar from his pocket, bit off the end, and spit it on the floor. "You've got a smart man's gab, Markham, but I think you're a fool. I know what this valley looks like, but when the survey was made, the agent swore he rowed over the valley in a boat."

"That, my friend," Markham said bitterly, "is a question of spelling. The agent r-o-d-e in a boat, but the boat was in a wagon. Perhaps a matter of conscience, but conscience or not, bad spelling and law and governments cannot change Nature."

Strang stared at the teacher. Then he burst into a laugh, winking at Dave. "I hadn't heard about his boat being in a wagon. Sharp, wasn't he?"

"Too sharp," Markham insisted, "but we'll beat

him and you, too. The land sale will be revoked and the valley will be settled."

Strang picked up his Stetson and jammed it on his head. "There's one thing I always say. I ain't never sure about this business of being right, but I know the facts, and the facts are that this valley is mine. I was thinking I'd run the lot of you out of here, but Mary Romney asked me to let you stay. Don't ever forget you owe your homes to her."

They stared at him, no sound in the store but the whisper of their breathing. Even Lacey Markham had nothing to say. It was the blacksmith, George McNair, a pious man whose plain-faced wife dictated his thinking, who rose and pinned resentful eyes on Strang. "I don't want a home if I owe it to a woman like that . . ."

He didn't finish. Strang, moving fast for so big a man, reached him and, gripping his left arm, began to twist. There were men besides McNair with guns on their hips, men who were McNair's friends, but none of them moved and none of them said anything. The blacksmith was slammed against the wall and held in that position, right arm pinned by the weight of his body against the wall, His face went white, his eyes bulged as pain increased, and sweat burst through his skin to make a shiny film across his forehead. He tried to lunge free and failed, tried to smash a knee into Strang's crotch, but Strang smothered the blow, his face entirely expressionless as if this was nothing more than another incident in the day's work.

It was Matt Strang's will that held McNair's friends in their seats as his strength held the blacksmith against the wall. In that moment Dave understood more about Strang than he had understood in all the hours he had been with him before, and he understood Markham and Joslyn and Hambone. He thought: *They're just talk.*

Then McNair cried out in a wild voice made shrill by the pain; he lunged and twisted and aimed a knee upward again, but he gained nothing. It was like trying to turn the flow of destiny. The break of the bone was an audible snap. Strang stepped back, his face wiped clear of expression. McNair's left arm hung awkwardly at his side, a sickness crawling into his face. There was a sickness showing in the faces of the others, too, but it was a sickness that came from shame, not from physical pain.

"I said I was leaving you your homes because Mary Romney asked it," Strang said evenly. "Everybody who's in the valley will get patents to the land they're squatting on, but if I hear of any of you speaking of Mary like this man did, either to me or anyone else, I'll break your neck." He wheeled to the door. "Let's ride, lad. I've got duds in camp that you can wear."

Dave followed Strang out of the room, feeling

the sting of their hatred and refusing to meet Lacey Markham's eyes. He thought: *He's got no right to look at me that way, not after his sitting there with a gun on him and doing nothing.* Then Dave was outside and in the saddle and the wind was in his face, the sage clumps running beside him as the town dropped behind. He glanced at Strang. The big man was looking ahead at the rim beyond Mary Romney's house, his face showing no concern. He had already forgotten what had happened in Joslyn's store. Dave thought: *It didn't mean any more to him than if he'd broken a kindling stick.*

V

Strang made no mention of what he had done to the blacksmith. Now, watching Strang as they rode, Dave thought again that the destiny of every settler in the valley was in this man's hands. If it had not been for Mary Romney, Strang would have cleared the valley. He was power; he was fate. Lacey Markham, rich in book learning, could discuss questions of right and wrong with profundity, but in the end Markham, for all of his knowledge, would be destroyed, snapped like a slender reed before a glacier's slow and pitiless power. When that end came, Matt Strang would still be here.

It was afternoon when they clattered across Mary Romney's bridge. The tollgate was open. Strang waved to Mary who stood on the porch, but kept on. Dave, eyes searching the yard and windows, could not see Nan. Later, with the house behind them, Dave looked back. Mary was still on the porch, her gaze following Matt Strang.

Already the cattle were fanning out across the valley. The chuck and bed wagons stood beside the creek below the rim, smoke from a small fire curling away from them. Reining up, Strang swung down. He asked: "What do you think of it, Clab?"

"Hell, you don't need no buckaroos. All you've got to do is to let 'em eat and get fat."

"Looks good, don't it?" Strang filled a plate with steak, beans, and bread. "What about the winters, Dave?"

"Sometimes they're cold." Dave followed Strang, and turned from the fire with a heaped-up plate and a cup of coffee. He sat down, feeling Strang's and Holland's eyes on him. He added: "Last winter we had four feet of snow on the level."

"Four feet," Holland breathed. "That change your mind about sending for the rest of the beef?"

Strang shook his head. "No. We moved from California to Nevada. Now we're moving to Oregon, and this is where we stay." He jerked a

102

hand toward the rim. "There'll come a day when you'll bury me up there where a man can see the valley." He turned to Dave. "We may need some hay come spring. Has Joslyn got any mowers and rakes?"

"A few."

"I reckon the grangers ain't against working, are they?"

"They need money," Dave said.

Strang grunted. "I never seen grangers who didn't need money." He nodded at a *vaquero*. "Juan, light out for Winnemucca and get them wagons moving north. Tell Sandow that Clab will be down for the rest of the cattle and tell Hayes at the bank I'll take his offer for the spread. Everything stays but the stock and the furniture in the house." Strang filled his coffee cup again, and drained it. He said: "Mike, there's a sawmill yonder . . ." He stopped and turned to Dave. "Hell, Mike would be a month finding it. Come sunup, you hike out for that sawmill. I want a house. Savvy? A good one. Cost ain't no matter. Get some lumber heading this way. Who built Mary's house?"

"Some carpenters at the fort."

"Get 'em. Promise 'em heaven and hell both if they want it. Just get 'em here." He wiped the bottom of his cup against his leg and dipped it into the coffee pot again. "What's this Hanna *hombre* like?"

"Easy-going. Hunts when he ain't cutting wood for himself or Mary."

"One thing we'll have in this valley is law," Strang said. "The county seat's to hell-and-gone on the other side of the mountains, ain't it?"

"That's right. They don't even know we're in the county. The sheriff ain't never been here that I've heard of."

"Go get Hanna. I want to see him."

Holland reached for tobacco and paper, eyes on Dave's buckskin. "You're riding the tail off that horse, Dave. Better give him a rest if you've got to head out in the morning. Take that paint yonder."

Strang gave his foreman a sharp look. "That buckskin's his long horse, Clab."

"It's my only horse," Dave said.

"The paint'll get you there and back," Holland said casually. "He don't look like much, but he's got four legs that git out and move."

Dave rose and carried his plate and cup to the shelf at the back of the chuck wagon. The paint didn't look like much for a fact. He was standing outside the rope corral, saddled, his head down, but Dave was remembering his fight with Holland that morning and how the foreman had hit him after Strang had called: "That's enough, Clab."

"Hey, you damned fool," the cook bawled. "Get them dirty dishes into the wreck pan. What'n hell do you think . . . ?"

104

"Under the wagon," Strang said.

Dave grabbed up his plate and cup, swinging to face the cook. "Don't get in a lather," he said defiantly.

The cook grabbed up a butcher knife. "You figger I don't need to get into no lather, do you?"

Dave saw the big dishpan under the wagon and dropped his plate and cup into it. Turning his back to the cook, he walked toward the horse. Holland's lips held a small grin. *Vaqueros* began drifting toward the paint. Strang rose and opened his mouth to say something, but no words came. He shook his head at Holland, plainly irritated.

Dave missed none of it. He'd need glue on his pants to ride the paint, but he'd had a turn at breaking horses at the fort. Unless the animal was an outlaw, Dave could ride him, and he didn't think the horse was an outlaw, for it wasn't likely Strang would bring a worthless horse as far as he'd brought his outfit.

Dave got his leg over and his toe in the stirrup when the paint cut loose. He went up headed north, but he was pointing west when he came down. It was an old story to the men on the ground, for only Clab Holland rode the horse. It was Holland's way of deflating a man his first day with the outfit. The horse exploded again, cat-backed, all four hoofs two feet off the ground. He came down, stiff-legged, reared, and threatened to fall backward, but Dave was still

105

in leather. Front hoofs down, the paint swapped ends. He started to run, stopped, and kicked at the sky. He ran some more, stopped, and bucked for another twenty seconds, but his heart wasn't in it. His rider should have been off before now. Then he started to run again, and this time he kept going until he was out of sight, headed for Bill Hanna's place.

"Reckon he'll run his mainspring down," Strang said with satisfaction. "Disappointed, Clab?"

"You know damned well I'd have given odds he'd pile the kid," Holland said as if he still didn't believe what he'd seen. "I figgered your boy would get thrown so far he wouldn't get back for breakfast. Been good for the size of his head."

"He ain't hurt from swelling of the noggin."

Holland rolled a smoke, still staring at the dust the paint had raised. "He's no granger kid. Where'n hell did you find him, Matt?"

"Granger, all right." Strang walked back to the fire and dipped another cup of coffee. "Folks are like cows, Clab. Get 'em trained and they'll stay in line. This kid's gonna help us get 'em trained. Don't forget that, Clab."

Holland shrugged. "You're the boss, Matt. I reckon we can make a buckaroo out of him."

"He's more buckaroo now than half the crew." He turned his gaze to Mary Romney's house.

"If his judgment's as good on cows as it is on women, he'll be the best man I've got."

Dave was back with Hanna by late afternoon. He swung down and dropped his reins, the paint standing docilely enough. Dave said: "He's got four legs all right, Clab, and he gits out and travels. That's a fact."

"I didn't figger you'd stick," Holland said a little grudgingly.

"That's what I thought you figgered." Dave turned to Strang. "Here's your man, Matt."

"Next time you want to see me, you can do the riding," Hanna said in an aggrieved tone.

Strang gave Hanna a cool study. "There's no law in this end of the county, Hanna."

"Why," the settler said with some sourness, "that comes as no surprise to me." He stepped out of the saddle, a fat man who buckled his belt below the roundness of his belly. He rolled a cigarette, stubby hands awkward with the paper, pale eyes returning Strang's cool stare. "You mean to tell me I rode to hell-and-gone just to hear you say something I've known for years?"

"No, I ain't telling you that, but I'll tell you something you don't know. I'm aiming to give you a patent to your land as soon as I can get the papers fixed up."

Hanna licked his cigarette into shape, his gaze swinging to Holland and on to the chuck and bed wagons, the fire, and the *vaqueros* lounging around it. Then he looked out across the valley to the cattle. He said, puzzled: "You know, if somebody had pointed to you when I came up, and said . . . 'There stands Santa Claus' . . . I'd have said he was a damned liar."

Holland laughed. "You would have been right, mister. Matt's gonna have to change some to pass for Santa Claus."

Strang nodded, unruffled. "I'm playing my own string, Hanna. Dave gave me a notion that struck me as being a good one. I ain't bothering the settlers that's already here. There might come a day when I'll need friends who ain't on my payroll. I figger a few nesters don't hurt a range, but if any more come along, I'll build a fire under the seat of their pants."

Hanna rubbed a fat cheek, still not understanding. "I'll do my thanking when I get that patent."

"There's one more thing," Strang said as if it were a minor matter. "I aim to have a deputy appointed to look after things in this end of the county. I'm gonna make sure that law in this valley is more than a pretty theory."

"Quit beating around the bush," Hanna said testily.

"I ain't beating around the bush. I'm just getting around to telling you that you're gonna be that deputy. If the county won't pay you, I will.

Fifty dollars a month, and I'll back you if you ever get caught between a rock and a hard place."

"Mighty sure I'll take the job, ain't you?"

"It's a good job, Hanna, and I'm on your side. I don't want nobody to get the idea I'm playing Santa Claus. I aim to look out for Matt Strang. To do that, I've got to have law that'll protect a man's property."

Hanna lowered his head, smoke a shifting shadow before his fat face. He said: "All right, Strang. I'm your man."

Strang dug a star from his pocket and handed it to the settler. "You're deputy, starting now. I'll see it's fixed in Cañon City."

Hanna pinned the star on his shirt and polished it with his sleeve. Dave, watching him, knew that he was pleased.

"We ought to have a jail," Hanna said.

"We'll have one," Strang said. "If you've got any extra time, and want to cut wood, I'll buy all you can spare."

Hanna grimaced. "If I ain't careful, I'll turn into a respectable working man. Might even have some of that property you were talking about, and I wouldn't want to lose that." Grunting, he lifted himself ponderously into the saddle, and rode away.

VI

At sundown the wind raised a stirring in the grass, and the killdeers, flying low, made the air plaintive with their cries. Dave, sitting alone on the talus slope, looked at Mary Romney's house and saw it in a different way than he had from the rim. From here it seemed a square strong structure, boldly rising above the flat, symbolic of Mary's strength in facing the valley. Again Dave gave thought, as he had since early that morning, to Mary's reason in asking Strang to leave the settlers in their homes. It was something Lacey Markham, wise in his knowledge of human motives, might understand, but it was inexplicable to Dave.

Strang stood beside the fire, thick legs spread, eyes on the flames. Dave, looking at him, was reminded once more of a granite block. Like a huge boulder solidly lodged in a streambed, he would be unmoving regardless of the pressure that the torrent of human opposition laid against him. He stood in that position a long time, his great body motionless. Suddenly he turned and called: "Dave!"

Dave toed out his cigarette and moved toward the fire, sensing what was in the big man's mind.

"We'll take a ride," Strang said, and gave no explanation.

Mounting, Strang turned toward the Romney house, Dave following. Dusk had thickened before they reached the Channel. The air, richly spiced with sage smell, still held a remnant of the day's heat. Westward, the sky was touched by a dying sun, and for a moment cottony clouds above the horizon were gold and scarlet. Along the edges of the valley the rim threw purple shadows across the flat. A blue heron, standing stilt-legged along the bank of the Channel, now took flight.

Without preface, Strang said: "You like the girl, don't you?"

"Yeah, but I ain't sure it goes double."

Reaching the house, they dismounted and racked their horses. Strang said: "This is the night you find out. Keep her outside till we go."

That, then, was the reason Strang had brought him. Strang had shaved and put on a clean shirt, the only concession he had made for the occasion. Resentment touched Dave. There was no fairness about it. Mary wouldn't stand for it. Nan had a right to sit in her own house no matter who was calling on her mother. Then the resentment passed and anticipation made a pleasant warmth in him. This had been a red-letter day, a day that had changed him even more than it had changed Mary and Lacey Markham and McNair and the rest. Tonight he would be able to talk to Nan.

For a moment Dave stared at the wide blob of Strang's face, uncertainty touching him, for he had never been sure of Nan or what she would say or do. He said: "I don't know she'll stay outside."

"Keep her interested," Strang said, and turned toward the house.

Mary stood in the doorway, waiting for Strang, her round graceful body silhouetted against the light. She wore a blue silk dress that rustled as she moved; her hair was piled high on her head, rich gold under the lamp. She said in a softly pleasant tone. "I wondered if you'd come, Matt."

"You knew all hell couldn't keep me away," Strang said, and stepped into the house.

Dave, pausing on the porch, said: "I'll wait out here for Nan."

Mary hesitated as if balancing her desire against her responsibility. Then, apparently finding her desire the stronger, she nodded and followed Strang inside.

A strange man, this Matt Strang, a tremendous man who outweighed Lacey Markham and Bob Joslyn and all the rest who lived in the valley. He had been here twenty-four hours, but in that short time he had changed everything and he had only started. Dave, thinking of him, was not aware of Nan's presence until she said, her voice sharp-edged: "Nice of him to bring you for me."

Turning, he said: "Yeah, I thought it was."

"They don't want me in the house," she said bitterly.

The two stepped off the porch and walked toward the bridge, Dave disturbed by the tension he felt in the girl. She was thinking, he knew, of her mother and Matt Strang.

"Heard what happened in town?" Dave asked casually.

"No. How would I hear?"

"Thought somebody might have gone by." He told her about it, adding: "Strang could have broken McNair's neck as easy as his arm."

"He's a devil," she cried passionately, "come here to live with other devils." She was still a moment, then asked: "Dave, what happened to your face?"

He hesitated, thinking again as he had in town, that no one else could understand why he would work for Strang after what had happened between him and Clab Holland. Then, making up his mind, he told her the truth and waited for her to say he was a fool.

But she did not. She pulled herself atop the bridge railing and stared down at the water, black under an obsidian sky. She said: "I know how you feel, Dave. Your folks think one way and you think another. We're in the same fix. Mother has her own life. I'm just a caboose that came along to tie her down. She hates this valley and everyone that's in it. I'm the reason for her being here, so I guess she must hate me."

Dave gripped the bridge railing, staring at the pale oval of the girl's face. He could not think of Mary Romney in that way, hating her own daughter. She was an ideal to him, a beautiful matured woman, knowing of a world he had never seen. Her fine house held a part of that world, and because Nan was her daughter, he had associated the girl with those distant places that Mary casually mentioned in familiar terms. He thought of his own mother who had such great capacity for hating, and he found himself again comparing her to Mary Romney. He burst out: "She couldn't hate you, Nan. Ma will hate me for going to work for Strang, but Mary couldn't hate you. She just couldn't."

"Maybe we aren't in quite the same fix," Nan went on as if she hadn't heard. "You're different from your mother. You're the only friend we have in the valley, but she's like the rest of them."

"Lacey Markham's different. You ought to go to school. There's others older than you are."

She took a deep breath. "Mother wouldn't let me. I wouldn't go anyhow. They all think they're so good. Like that Dixie Joslyn who's got her nose in the air. But they aren't good, Dave. They're mean and wicked. Even in a wilderness like this they gossip and lie the same as people in

114

a bigger town do. If I'd been Mother, I'd have let Strang drive them out of the valley."

"Why did she want them to stay?"

"You wouldn't understand, Dave. You don't know what it is to be treated like you had smallpox when all the time you're better than they are. Mother wants them to know what she's really like." Nan gripped his shoulder. "It won't do any good, Dave. No matter what she does, they'll never see any good in her."

"If she's good, she couldn't hate you," Dave said slowly. "Anyway, she wouldn't hate you if she thought enough of you to bring you here."

She took a ragged breath. "I know. I was just talking. She doesn't hate me. Not really. She loves me, or she wouldn't have come to a new country like this. It's just that we ought to be enough for each other."

That was the real reason she did not like Matt Strang. She had been the hub around which Mary Romney's world had revolved. Now she was grown and Mary was pushing her aside so that Matt Strang could be the hub.

"Strang aims to take care of you and your mother," Dave said. "He wouldn't have done what he has about the settlers if he didn't."

"That's just it," she insisted. "We don't want to be taken care of by a man. I don't anyway. We were getting along all right. He showed up and Mother's been walking on stars ever since. Why,

115

Dave? Why did it happen? Wasn't I enough?"

She began to cry. Gripping her arms, Dave pulled her from the railing. He held her against him and let her cry, and she clung to him in a sort of frantic desperation. He had never felt anyone's vital need for him like this before, and it finished what the day had begun. She clutched him, somehow hoping to fill the vacant place in her heart with him, and it was the strange transforming alchemy of this need that changed him into a man with a man's heart and a man's sense of responsibility. Strength was in him, and confidence, and uncertainty was gone. He had taken the right direction today. His mother would never see it. She would not try to understand, for her beliefs were cast in the strongest iron. But the future of the valley lay in Matt Strang's big hands, and Dave Logan would be with Strang. From this moment on he would not be alone; he would never be alone again.

"Nan, listen," he said softly. "Can you hear me?"

She had stopped crying, but still she clung to him, her face pressed against his coat.

"I love you, Nan. I've tried to tell you before, but I couldn't. Seemed like my throat swelled shut whenever I started to say it."

She lifted her face to his then. "Nobody ever said that before. Say it again, Dave. Just the part about loving me."

"I love you," he said simply. "I want to marry you. Not just now. With Pa sick like he is, I've got to look after Ma a little bit. But before long."

"She'd never stand for you marrying me, Dave. She hates me and she hates Mother. She stopped here one time and asked Mother to send you on if you ever came here again. She said I wasn't good for you."

"You're the best thing in the world for me, and she can't stop us. Nothing can stop us. I'm headed my own way now, Nan, and you're going with me."

He kissed her, and her lips were soft and sweet and clinging. Her arms came up around his neck, her slim body was hard against his, and she let him know how much she needed his love. In that moment she could not get enough of him.

A cold wind lifted from the lake and struck at them. A nightbird in the tule marsh cried out, a shrill weird noise, and Dave felt her shiver. He looked at the house, anger touching him. He said: "Let's go over to the barn. It's warmer."

But she didn't move. She stayed in his arms as if it were the only sanctuary where she could find safety. "Dave, let's get married right away."

"We can't. I haven't got any money. Anyhow, the folks need me."

"Your mother can make out. I need you, too, Dave."

He took a deep breath, fighting this temptation.

It would be completely wrong, but it was what he wanted more than anything else in the world.

When he hesitated, she said: "You've got your horse and gear. Other cow outfits will be coming in, so you won't have any trouble getting a job. I've got a horse, too. We'll ride away. I'll get a job cooking. It's a free country, Dave, and I'm not afraid of work. Other people have started like that."

Because he loved her, he said: "We can't, Nan. I've never told you because it was as hard as saying I loved you, but I've had some dreams. You were always in them. So was this valley. A house and a ranch and cattle. It's better to wait so we'll have something when we start."

She gripped him harder. "I can't wait, Dave. I can't stay here. I know how it will be with Mother and Strang. You're all I've got."

There was nothing he could say. For a long time he had built his dreams around Nan, wondering if he would ever hold her in his arms and be sure of her love. Now that she was in his arms, he had every reason to be sure of her love; still he could not grasp what she was offering him. If he could take her to his home . . . The thought died the instant it was born, for he pictured his mother's face.

It seemed a long time that they stood like that while the stars wheeled across the sky and the nightbird cried again and again. Then the front door swung open, and lamplight washed out across the yard. Strang's great voice boomed into the night: "Dave, time to ride."

They walked toward the house, Dave's arm around Nan, and they came into the patch of light falling past Strang and Mary. Suddenly Dave was aware of the pressure of the silence, for Nan had said firmly and in a tone that indicated no doubt: "Mother, we're going to get married."

The silence ribboned on as if both Mary and Strang had been stunned. Dave looked at them— Mary a graceful figure in the star shine, Strang a great square man, both incapable of believing what they had heard.

"It's true," Dave said.

Then Mary found her voice: "No, not my baby. Nan, what kind of crazy talk is this?"

"You've got somebody," Nan answered defiantly. "I've got Dave."

"What do you expect?" Strang asked. "They ain't kids no more. She growed up on you, Mary."

Mary seemed to sway. "She's only seventeen, Matt. And he's just a kid. Not twenty-one. His mother hates us. It wouldn't work. Whatever happens, I want her to be happy. I've had enough unhappiness in my life to do for both of us."

"I'm going to fix that," Strang said. "And I'd say seventeen is old enough for a woman to get married. You weren't any older when you had her, were you?"

"No, but . . ."

"You don't need to stand there and talk about us," Nan protested angrily. "We're . . . not . . . children. We're in love and we're old enough to know it. You've always liked Dave, Mother. What's the matter with you?"

"Yes, I like Dave. I like him very much." Mary put a hand to her throat. "But with things the way they are, and his mother feeling the way she does, it just wouldn't work. Not now."

"Tell them, Mary," Strang said.

She took his arm and cleared her throat. Then, almost as defiantly as Nan had spoken when she and Dave had first come up, Mary said: "Matt and I are getting married. You'll have things a lot easier, Nan. We can send you to Portland to school."

"I don't want to go to school," Nan said sharply. "I just want Dave, and I don't think you've got any right to talk about us waiting when you set an example like this."

Matt laughed. "She's sharp. I was just thinking, Mary. You said Dave was still a kid. I ain't so sure about that right now. Last night he was, but he's done a heap of growing up today. It might not work out so bad."

"No," Mary said. "It wouldn't work at all. Nan, I'll make a promise. If you'll wait, Matt and I will wait."

"No." Strang gripped her arms and turned her

to face him, the lamplight falling across her face. "You just said . . ."

Mary shook her head. "I didn't know about this. Please, Matt."

"All right," he said reluctantly, "if it's the way you want it. What do you say, Nan?"

"How long will you and Matt wait?" Nan asked.

"We'll wait as long as you want us to," Mary said, "or until you and Dave get married."

"We'll make the deal," Nan said,

"Maybe you don't know it, but you just dropped a loop on my life, Nan," Strang said. "Come on, Dave."

Strang strode past Dave to the hitch rack. Dave kissed Nan, and found her strangely unresponsive. He said—"So long."—and walked to his horse, puzzled and a little hurt.

They mounted and rode away. Suddenly Strang said: "Dave, it's the damnedest thing. I never took no stock in miracles. I always figgered that anything a man had that was worthwhile was something he made himself, but finding Mary like this is a miracle. No sense pretending anything else."

Dave nodded, still disturbed.

Strang began to whistle, a tuneless racket pleasing only to his own ears. He was silent for a time. Then he said: "Dave, I'm going a long ways in this country. If you're smart, you'll go along. There's just one thing I ask of a man. His loyalty. That's the size of it. Take Clab Holland. He makes me madder'n hell sometimes, but there's one thing I'm sure of. He'll string with me till the last roundup."

"I aim to go along, Matt," Dave said, surprised that Strang had not known.

VII

Nan did not sleep that night. For a long time she sat beside the open window in her room, staring at the moonless sky. The distant rim was a black shadow against a black sky; the lake and the tule marsh were one, running together into vague space. The wind off the lake, heavy with the dank smell of the marsh and stagnant water, touched her face, but she was not conscious of anything but the bitterness that tightened her nerves until she wanted to scream. She hated the lake and the birds, hated the valley and the wind and the narrow-minded, smug people who closed their homes to her and her mother, but most of all she hated Matt Strang. For the first time since she could remember, there was someone between her and her mother.

A coyote howled from some lonely point on the rim. The nightbird that Nan and Dave had heard still voiced his weird, haunting cry, and the liquid whisper of the Channel was a ceaseless background refrain. Nan shut the window, suddenly conscious of these sounds. It seemed as if this wilderness to which Mary Romney had brought her was shouting at her. Then she closed her mind to the shout, and for a time reality died under a torrent of memories.

There were many things Nan did not understand about her and her mother's lives before they had come to Sage Valley, and some of the memories were vague and mixed-up. If she asked about them, her mother gave her evasive answers that told her nothing. But there were some memories that were clear, so clear that she could live those moments over the details startlingly vivid. She remembered a man she had been taught to call Uncle Ed, a tall handsome man who wore a black suit and a white shirt and a string tie. She remembered his diamond ring that had sparkled like dew under an early morning sun; she remembered his brown mustache that he twisted to fine points and his dark curly hair that was faultlessly combed. There had always been a pleasant smell about him, cologne perhaps. She thought about how he had held her on his lap, jigging his knee and talking about her being his "big girl." Her mother was always there in the room, smiling and beautiful and very slender, and Nan remembered she had brighter lips and cheeks than she had now. Then the man did not come any more, and there was a time when her mother had cried a great deal.

After that they had traveled. Long hours in stagecoaches, dust and heat, or snow and cold. Sometimes there were trains. She liked them better, for she could run in the aisles, and in the winter the coaches were warm. She liked the lights, the boy who came down the aisle with candy and oranges, the clickety-click of wheels on rails, the screech of the locomotive's whistle, the changing flashing pattern outside the car windows—cities and open country, mountains and desert, timber and plains. And everywhere, it seemed, there were men talking to her mother and wanting to hold Nan on their laps. Mining camps. Always mining camps with their crowded streets, muddy or dusty, but never, it seemed, in between. Burros, ore wagons, buggies, saddle horses. The earth-shaking rumble of the great stamp mills. The thin chill air of the high country, the fingers of green spruce that crawled up the steep slopes toward granite peaks, the patches of aspens that sometimes were brilliant gold and orange.

When Nan asked her mother about the colors on the sides of the mountains, she was told: "Every year between summer and winter Jack Frost upsets his paint pot on the hillsides." After that she wondered which one of the men who came to see her mother was Jack Frost. There were many of them, and usually they brought flowers or

124

presents of some kind. She kept a careful watch, for someday, she thought, Jack Frost would spill a little of that orange paint on his pants and she wanted to see what it was like.

There was always music. Sometimes an orchestra, or a melodeon, and her mother would sing. Nan had to be still then. She would sit in one corner of the room, hardly breathing, while her mother practiced. If she was quiet, she was told, she would get some peppermint, but it was unnecessary bribery because she would have been quiet anyhow. She liked to hear her mother sing, and she would have gone to sleep in her chair rather than have done anything that would have exiled her from the room.

There was one memory that stood out more sharply than the others, of a night when she couldn't sleep and she'd heard the music. Getting up, she put on her slippers and a robe, and followed a hall until she came to a door. When she opened it, she looked down into a big room. She had never seen so many men, smoking and drinking and playing cards. Then she saw her mother on a stage at the end of the room, dressed in a long red gown, her hair bright gold under the lights, a bouquet of roses in her arms. Nan had stood very still and listened, but a woman had found her and made her go back to bed. The woman didn't have much on, she remembered, a short-skirted black dress with spangles, and her face was bright with paint. Nan had hated her because she had wanted to hear her mother's song.

Then, for some reason she never understood, they stopped traveling and settled down in Boise, and Nan had gone to school. It was a dull life and she was sure her mother had liked it no better than she had. They'd lived in a nice house with the same furniture they had now, and the years were quiet and prosaic until—and she never fully understood this, either—the girls at school had quit playing with her. She came home and her mother had cried when she'd told her. The next day her mother sold the house.

Nan remembered well the long dusty ride in a covered wagon to Sage Valley, for that had not been so long ago; she remembered the Paiute War and the terror that names like Buffalo Horn and Egan had inspired in her; she remembered the hard, fast ride to Fort Pacific. Her mother had been more worried about the house and furniture than anything else, but when they had returned, they'd found everything exactly as they had left it. The Indians had not gone that way.

It was when they were at the fort that Nan first became aware of the way the other settlers felt toward her and her mother, particularly Dixie Joslyn. Now, trying to think about it with cool detachment, it seemed to her that the moment when she and her mother had been brought so close was there at the fort. It was the two of them against everybody else except Dave. He had been kind even then, and Dixie had not liked it.

Now Matt Strang was here. She knew she wasn't thinking coherently, for Dave was always in the back of her mind, Dave who had suddenly lost his boyish clumsiness and bashfulness, Dave whose kisses had aroused feelings in her she did not understand, and, because she did not understand them, they brought apprehension to her. But Dave was caught in a web of circumstances that made him helpless. That thought turned her mind again to Strang.

She had wangled a promise from her mother, and at the moment she had felt deep satisfaction because she'd won. She had saved her home for the time at least. She could freeze Strang out. But after he and Dave had gone, she knew she hadn't won anything. Not after seeing the strange absent expression on her mother's face, a look of happiness that was close to rapture, as if she was reliving the time she'd spent with Strang. That was the part that was so completely beyond Nan's understanding. *Strang was here!* He was a man who had only to touch another's life to change it.

It was daylight before Nan realized it, and the hushed world burst with life. The sun, tipping up over the eastern rim, spread a thin gold light across the lake and tule marsh. Two swans swam majestically under the bridge, three cygnets behind them, ugly gray and not yet black of bill. Nan raised the window and looked out. She had seen this awakening time after time, but still it thrilled her, for it was one of the few things about the valley that she loved. Nan smiled at a sandhill crane, dancing in his crazy, flapping way. She watched some avocets below her, beautiful birds with slender upturned bills. Suddenly something startled them and they flew away, their melancholy cries floating back to her. A deer that had been drinking beyond the bridge bounded away into the brush. Then Nan saw the rider coming from the south.

For a moment Nan hesitated, wondering if she should awaken her mother. She decided against it, for she was usually the one who collected the toll anyhow. Picking up her coat from the bed, she put it on and tiptoed down the stairs.

When the man came up, Nan was waiting at the tollgate. He was riding a gray mule, and for a moment Nan thought he was drunk. He reeled uncertainly in the saddle, a dirty, bearded man whose yellow eyes came suddenly alive with interest as they fixed on Nan. She decided he wasn't drunk, for both man and mule showed the effect of a long ride, so he was probably bone weary.

He jerked a finger at the bridge. "Sage that-a-way?"

"Yes."

"Well, get the gate open."

"This is a tollgate. The toll is twenty-five cents for a man and mount. When you pay it, I'll open the gate."

He got off his mule and stared at her. She backed away, frightened for she had never seen a man look at her that way before. It made her feel unclean. He was big and a little stooped, perhaps forty years old. His clothes were ragged, and his saddle was patched and worn. Nan had seen other poor men ride through whose gear and mount looked as shabby as this fellow's, but they had been courteous and paid their toll without argument, seemingly well satisfied that there was a bridge to cross.

The man spat a brown stream into the dust at the edge of the bridge and wiped the back of his hand across his mouth. He said: "You own this here place?"

"My mother does."

"What's her name?"

"Mary Romney."

"What's yours?"

"Nan, if it's any of your business. Now if you'll pay your twenty-five cents . . ."

"My name's Walton . . . Rabbit Walton, my friends call me, though why I never made out. I should be Wildcat Walton because I'm sure a wildcat when I go after something I want. Ain't nothing can stop me."

129

"I'll open the gate if . . ."

"I'm gonna settle here, ma'am. I was thinking you and me . . . I mean, you're right pretty and this ain't no place for a girl to live, twenty miles from nowhere. I aim to be a big man in these parts. Bob Joslyn's a friend of mine. He staked me once before, so I reckon he will again. Then I'll be back." He dug into his pocket, found a coin, and gave it to Nan. "Don't you go away."

She took the money and turned toward the gate. A big hand closed on her left wrist. He said: "You can thank me."

For a moment fear froze her. She smelled his tobacco-stinking breath, saw his lips twitch under his mustache. She tried to jerk free and could not. Then in a sudden rush of anger she forgot to be afraid. She doubled up her right fist and hit him on the end of the nose. He yelled and let go, a hand coming up to feel of his nose.

Nan swung the gate open, crying: "Get through there and don't ever come back!"

He climbed on his mule, still holding his nose and blinking the tears back. He rode across the bridge, head bowed. Nan closed the gate and ran back into the house. The anger and fear went out of her, and she laughed aloud as she pictured herself swinging on him with her fist like a man. The fellow was crazy, she thought, as she built a fire in the kitchen range. She wondered if she should tell Dave about it, then decided against it. She knew what would happen if she did. Anyhow, the man was just a saddle tramp who would probably never come through here again.

She made coffee, sliced and fried a pan of bacon and two eggs, listening for her mother's steps on the stairs. She forgot about Rabbit Walton, for Matt Strang was in her mind again. There was no room for anyone else. She was remembering her feeling that he was still here; the house seemed filled with his presence. Desperately she thought: *No matter what I do or what Mother does, it will never be the same between us again.*

Putting dishes and food on a tray, she went up the stairs to her mother's room. This was something she had never done before, and she hesitated in the hall, not sure whether she should go ahead. Then she decided she would, now that she had gone this far.

Mary sat up as a board creaked under Nan's feet. She saw the tray and shook her head at Nan. She sniffed, brushed a lock of hair out of her eyes, and smiled. "You didn't need to do this, honey." She slid a pillow behind her and took the tray on her knees. "But I like it."

"So you and Matt are getting married."

Mary looked at her sharply, but if she sensed what was going on in Nan's mind, she gave no sign of it. "Yes, and before long you'll be marrying Dave. If I'd had a little time to think about it, I wouldn't have said what I did last night. But you are seventeen. I just hadn't thought of you as being grown up. Someday you'll have some babies and you'll know how it is." Mary lifted her coffee cup to her lips, eyes still on Nan. "And I like Dave. You're lucky."

Nan sat down beside the bed. *You're lucky?* Perhaps she was, and she smiled when she thought of Dixie Joslyn. Dixie wouldn't like it a little bit, for Dixie was frankly and shamelessly dragging her rope for Dave. "I guess I am," Nan said.

She was silent, watching her mother eat and thinking of a dozen things she wanted to ask, but she could not find the words. Mary finished her breakfast and, placing the tray on the edge of the bed, got up. She took off her nightgown and yawned, stretching luxuriously. Nan, watching, felt a pang of envy, for alongside her mother's perfectly shaped body, hers was as slim as a boy's.

Mary slipped into her robe and, sitting down in front of her dressing table, began to brush her hair. It was long, falling almost to her hips. Nan, who had watched this morning ritual since she was a child, had always thought of her mother's hair as gold silk. Her own was wheat-yellow, and she wore it in pigtails or knotted on the back of her head. She said in sudden passion: "If I live to be a million, I'll never have hair like yours."

"Yes, you will, but it takes work and time. If I

132

didn't fool so much with it, I'd do more house-work." Mary looked at her hands, frowning. "But I guess I work enough." She went on brushing her hair. Then she said: "Now that you're in love, you'll have the incentive you need to take care of your hair. It's something a man notices. We'll have to fix up some of my dresses for you, too."

"I'd like a new dress," Nan said. "One of my own."

Mary turned to look at her, saying gravely: "We can't afford it."

Nan tossed the 25¢ piece Rabbit Walton had given her to the dressing table. "I let a man through the tollgate."

Mary picked it up. "I made a wrong guess coming here. We couldn't live in Boise any more, and I thought that, when this country developed, we'd get rich from our tollgate, but we won't. It's like Matt says. The valley will always be a cattle country, and cattle countries are never thickly settled." She pulled a drawer open and lifted a metal box to the table top. "This was full of gold when we came here." She flipped the lid back and dropped the coin Nan had given her into the box. "Now there are three dollars in silver and two gold pieces. We've just lived it up."

Nan had not known that, for she had never asked her mother about money, and this was the first time Mary had ever said there was something she couldn't afford to buy. She said with more bitterness than she intended: "I guess Matt Strang is a rich man."

"Yes, and he'll be richer." Mary sat, looking at Nan, the lid of the box still back. "But that's not the reason I'm marrying him, although I'm glad he's well fixed. We'll be able to do things for you I could never do by myself, things for you and Dave."

"Mother, why . . . ?" Nan fought for breath, finding this harder to ask than she had expected. Then she blurted: "Why didn't we stay in Boise?"

"Because I thought it would be different here." Mary took a folded paper from the metal box and handed it to Nan. "That's your father's and my marriage license. It would stop some long tongues if I showed it to every woman in the valley, but I won't. They can go on talking if it makes them any happier."

Nan unfolded the paper. Mary Dorothy Blaine and James Alexander Romney.

"We left Boise because someone recognized me as the Mary Romney who had sung at Silver City, and gossip started like it always does. I didn't care about myself because we were living in Boise so you could go to school, but when I saw what it was doing to you, I knew we had to go. I was sick of all of it. Rebellious, I guess, because there was nothing decent about it. It's the same as it is here, the women who condemn me were no better than I was and their children were

134

no better than you were. We should have gone to Portland. Or San Francisco. We'd have been lost in the crowd in a big city, but I thought we could make our own life out here where we'd be alone. It was a mistake. The fewer the people, the more talk."

Nan handed the license back. Mary dropped it into the box and shut the lid. "Your father was a lawyer. He died before you were born, and I had to make the living, so I went on the stage. When you were five, I met Ed Lowry. That was in Colorado. Central City. He was a gambler, but an honest one. You remember him. We had you call him Uncle Ed because we were going to get married and we didn't think it was right to have you call him Dad."

"You didn't marry him?"

"No. He was shot." Mary was silent for a moment. There was no sound but the whisper of her brush. Then she said: "Ed left me his money. I put it in the bank and kept on singing, but I wasn't good enough for New York. I stayed in the mining camps. It seemed that I made lots of money, but traveling took all I made. Then when you got so big I couldn't put off your schooling, we settled in Boise." Mary laid down her brush and turned her chair so that she faced Nan. "Honey, I've made some mistakes that have hurt you. The worst one was trying to shield you from reality. Now I know I can't. There are a lot of things I've got to tell you before you marry Dave. I should have told you before, but I just couldn't make myself see that you were grown up. There is one thing I want you to remember. I am not ashamed of anything I have done, no matter what has been said."

Nan held her head high. "It doesn't make any difference."

"It shouldn't. The only thing that should make any real difference is whether you know in your heart that what you've done is right, but if you and Dave live here, you'll have to fight it. You will never convince Dave's mother."

"Last night you said it wouldn't work. . . ."

"I know, but I've had a night to think about it since. There's one thing I'm sure of. I've been happy twice in my life and both times men were responsible. One was your father. The other one was Ed Lowry. I ran away from home to marry your father, and I went against a lot of people's advice when I was engaged to Ed. You see, he was a gambler, so they said he was bad." Mary took Nan's hands. "This is what I'm trying to say, honey. If you're sure you're in love with Dave, don't let anything, you hear, *anything* stand between you and him, or you'll be sorry the rest of your life."

Nan was cold. It was a strange coldness inside her that no amount of heat could warm. Her mother had said: "I've been happy twice in my life and both times men were responsible." She thought: *I don't count for anything.*

"I'm glad about you and Dave," Mary said, "and I'm glad about Matt and me. He's a great man, and I'll always be proud to be his wife. He's the kind who makes himself felt wherever he goes."

"He's a cruel, selfish man," Nan stated passionately.

"I love him," Mary said simply. "I know Dave, better than you do, I think, and I'm sure Dave loves him the way a young man loves an older man he can idealize. When you think of Dave's father or Lacey Markham, you can see why he needs a man like Matt. Give Matt a little time, Nan. Try to understand him and you'll love him the way you would a father."

Nan rose, pulling her hands from her mother's. "I never will," she said in her bitter, hurt voice. "He broke George McNair's arm yesterday. That's the way he makes himself felt."

"There's that side of him," Mary said, "but I don't think any man ever does anything worthwhile without hurting someone. There is another side of him, too. That's the side I love. I felt that the minute I saw him." Mary rose, her usually serene face troubled. "I know men, Nan. I've had to. Mining camps have a hundred men for every woman, so I always had more attention than I wanted. I've turned down dozens of marriage proposals. Some were men I liked and some were wealthy, but until you were grown, I kept myself free for you. Now it's different. You have Dave. You'll be making your own home. I have Matt. I love him, Nan. More than any man I have ever known."

"More than my father?"

"Even your father. I know how you feel, and it isn't really right. I've got a big heart, Nan, big enough for you and Matt because you'll fill a different part."

"I guess I will," Nan whispered.

"I don't claim to be a fortune-teller, but I have a feeling about Matt. He's the kind who was born to be shot. That's the way it is with any strong man. People love him or they hate him. Someday a man will hate him enough to kill him." She started to reach out to Nan, and then checked her motion. "I'd like to marry him soon, honey. You see, I waited after I said yes to Ed Lowry. Then he was killed. I don't want to wait too long for Matt."

Nan picked up the tray. She said, her voice dull and distant to her own ears: "Go ahead."

"I made a promise to you last night. I'll keep it no matter what it costs me or Matt."

Nan stood in the doorway, holding her face expressionless. She remembered the promise. "We'll wait as long as you want us to, or until you and Dave get married." She remembered the

138

sense of victory she had felt at the moment. Dave would not marry her now, and she could hold her mother and Matt Strang apart as long as she wanted to. But that thought brought no elation to her. Nor would it ever again. Not after seeing so clearly the feeling that was mirrored on her mother's face.

"I won't hold you to that promise," Nan said in a low tone that barely reached Mary Romney. "You can marry him today."

"I knew that's what you'd say, Nan, and I . . ."

But Nan was going down the stairs, slowly, for she could not see through the tears. She knew Matt Strang well enough to be sure that he would take all of her mother's heart. There would be no room left for her. That was Matt Strang's way. Then Nan thought of Dave, wanting to feel his arms around her again, for his arms were her only refuge.

VIII

Dave ate breakfast with Strang and the others, feeling the difference from the morning before. Today he was respected, a part of the outfit. His fight with Clab Holland and the ride he'd made on the paint had made the difference.

One of the *vaqueros*, Pablo Gonzales, hunkered beside Dave. He said: "A fine morning, *señor*. I have never seen such a morning in California." He waved a hand toward the valley. "I have never seen such grass."

Clab Holland said: "Matt Strang's luck, Pablo. Dab your loop on his star and he'll haul you to heaven or hell. I ain't sure which, but I am sure there ain't no stopping place between."

Matt grinned. "You don't think you'll go to heaven, do you, Clab?"

"I'd sure be plumb lonesome if I did, seeing as you wouldn't be there. What are you gonna call this outfit, Matt?"

Strang chewed thoughtfully for a moment before he said: "I've been working my brain on it ever since we left Nevada. It's going to be S so everybody'll know this is Strang's valley whenever they see a cow hereabouts, and I guess you just gave me the rest of it. Our iron'll be S Star."

"It's a good notion," Holland said. "S for Strang and Star because we're dabbing our loop on your star."

"It's a little more than that." Strang motioned toward Mary Romney's house. "There's my star over yonder and I'm following it."

Holland's mouth gaped open. "Matt, you don't mean that a woman . . ."

"I mean *the* woman," Strang said in a tone that silenced the other. "Dave, I've been looking and I don't find the duds I thought I had, so you stop at Joslyn's today and get what you need. Don't spare the price. Get the best Justins he's got. How you stuck on that paint devil with them boots you're wearing is a mystery to me."

Strang rose and, moving over to the bed wagon, pulled out a gun belt with a walnut-handled .44 Colt in the holster. "I don't let the boys tote their irons unless there's trouble, but I reckon you'd better get used to toting this. Get in a little practice every day. You never know when you'll need to be fast with your cutter, and if you haven't had the practice when that day comes, it'll be too late for anything except the clods they shovel into your face."

Dave buckled the belt around him, suddenly embarrassed, for he felt as awkward as he had the first day he'd worn spike-heeled boots. He looked around the circle of faces, but no one was smiling.

"He's yours, Clab," Strang said. "You're the gunfighter of this outfit."

"Here, I'll show you," Holland said. "You've got it too damned high. See that your hand falls naturally to the butt. Elbow bent a little. Start with the holster too high, and you'll wind up someday with the muzzle getting caught on the holster top. Then you'll be looking for them clods Matt was talking about. Now that looks about right. Let's see you pull."

"I ain't . . . ," Dave began.

"I know," Holland said. "You'll be slower'n molasses in January, you'll be awkward as hell, and chances are you couldn't hit the side of a barn if you was inside and had all the doors closed, but just remember one thing. We all had to start once."

Holland worked with Dave for a time. Then Strang called: "All right, Clab. Dave, what's them grangers going to do to you today when you ride into town?"

Dave slid the .44 back into leather, thinking uneasily about what might happen, and wondering why he was more worried about meeting Dixie Joslyn than anyone else. "I don't reckon they'll do anything much, Matt."

"Scared?" Strang asked.

Dave gave him a flat-lipped grin. "You're damned right I am. I'm not scared of what they'll do, but I'm plenty scared of what they'll say. Like Lacey Markham. He's going to be mighty unhappy about me and I'll hear about it."

"You've got to face it sometime," Strang said.

"I reckon today's as good a day as any." He dropped a hand to the heavy gun. "Maybe I oughtta leave this . . ."

"Wear it," Strang said sharply. "Tell Joslyn I'll be in the last of the week and settle up with him. Get them duds you need and buy all the rakes and mowers he's got. Now I wrote a couple of notices I want stuck up in town where everybody can see 'em. I reckon they'll all get into Joslyn's store or the saloon, won't they?"

Dave nodded, taking the papers. "The men all get into the saloon and the women get to the store."

"Take a look at 'em, Dave. My notion is to keep these folks friendly. No good reason for us to have trouble, and I need a hell of a lot of work done."

Strang's writing was sprawling but legible.

MEN AND TEAMS WANTED TO WORK ON S STAR. HAYING, CARPENTRY, DITCH DIGGING, CORRAL BUILDING. WAGES PAID IN GOLD. MATT STRANG.

"Looks all right," Dave said. "You'll get every man in the valley who's got a kid at home big enough to do the chores. Gold's one thing this valley hasn't got."

Strang grinned. "So I figgered. Now get moving. Tell Joslyn I'll pay him in gold, too. He can have my trade if he wants it. If he don't, to hell with him. I'll haul our stuff from Winnemucca. Get all the lumber from the mill they've got to spare and tell 'em I'm paying in gold. Same goes for the carpenters."

"I'll tell 'em," Dave said.

Dave whistled up his buckskin and saddled him, and, when he had mounted, Strang and

Holland walked over from the fire, Holland's long face dark with suppressed rage.

"I can't figger you out, Matt," Holland was saying. "The kid's all right, but you're sending him on a man's chore that you oughtta be tending to yourself. Once you let this bunch of grangers get the notion we ain't tough . . ."

"If any of them get that notion," Dave cut in, "they'll look at George McNair and change their minds."

"We need 'em, Clab," Strang said. "That's why I'm sending Dave. There's times when a little sugar goes a hell of a lot farther than gunpowder. Dave'll be better spreading sugar than me."

"It's that woman," Holland said sourly. "You ain't been soft like this since . . ."

Strang spun a gold piece up to Dave. "Give that to Mary. I don't aim to cheat her none, but no use stopping and paying every time we use her bridge. Tell her to keep count. When that's used up, let me know." He made a slow turn to face Holland. For a moment their eyes locked, Strang's square body dwarfing Holland's lank figure like a great oak dwarfs a spindly pine. Strang said: "I ain't forgetting that you know cows. Likewise I ain't forgetting that we've come up together. Now here's one thing you better not forget. I play my cards my way. I always have and I always will. If I lose the pot, it's my chips I'll lose. Not yours."

144

Strang moved past Holland to the fire, Holland swinging in beside him like a whipped dog. Dave rode away, the scene burned into his mind as deeply as the scene in Joslyn's store. This time there was no arm-breaking, no violence. Dave wasn't sure how Strang had done it, but somehow he had taken the hide off Holland's back as thoroughly as if he'd used a quirt.

Dave's eyes searched Mary Romney's house for a sight of Nan, but when he came to the bridge, it was Mary who hurried out of the kitchen. She waved to him, smiling, and walked rapidly across the yard to the road. To Dave she had always been the most beautiful woman in the world, but she was more than beautiful today. He raised his hat, an awkward gesture for him, and said— "Howdy, Mary."—wondering what had brought this shining radiance to her.

"How are you, Dave?" She swung the gate open for him. "No charge, you know."

"Matt says there is." Dave reined his buckskin toward her and held out the gold piece. "He says for you to keep count and tell him when it's used up. He says he doesn't want to cheat you."

"I aim to collect off that man." She laughed, but she took the coin. "Tell Matt I'll keep count."

"I can't figger it out." Dave cuffed back his hat. "You look like you'd swallowed a piece of sunshine. I never saw an angel, but I guess one would look just about like you."

"An angel." She started to laugh, then frowned, and the sound that finally came from her throat was close to a sob. "Anything but that, Dave. I'm happy. That's all. I'm like any woman in love except I'm worse. I'm even worse than Nan."

"I guess you are," Dave said soberly, remembering the cool kiss Nan had given him when he'd left the night before. He glanced at the house. "Is she home?"

"She's asleep. She was up all night. Don't ask me why the child won't sleep when she has a chance. It's a bad habit and I hope you can get her over it when you're married."

He mumbled something about hoping he could, suddenly embarrassed, for this was honest talk that was hard for him. Within a matter of hours marriage had changed from a distant alluring dream to imminent reality, and he had not had time to bring his mind into focus so that he could grip the responsibilities that were rushing at him.

He told Mary good bye and rode on, leaving the lakes and the tule marsh behind him, only faintly aware of the meadowlarks that were singing all around him in the rye grass. He rode through a patch of greasewood and came out again into the grass. Sage River lay to the east, its meandering course marked by willows, and beyond it the rim showed, black and forbidding, a natural barrier marking the approximate boundary of Matt Strang's empire.

Near noon Dave swung across the bridge spanning Sage River, and minutes later he reached the settlement. He rode past the schoolhouse and Markham's cabin, hoping he wouldn't see Lacey Markham, passed Joslyn's cottage and hoped he wouldn't see Dixie. He swung across the street to the Gold Bar saloon, racked his buckskin, and went in.

Hambone came out of the back, puffing a little as he moved. He saw who it was and stopped, scowling. He asked: "Where's that tough boss of your'n, Dave?"

"Home."

"Home!" Hambone blew the word out like an oath. "What kind of a home has he got?"

"A campfire and a couple of wagons." Dave handed one of the papers to the saloon man. "Matt wants you to put that up where the boys can see it."

Hambone glanced at the paper, started to crumple it, and changed his mind. He put his pudgy hands down on the rough pine bar and glared at Dave. "I've been around some, sonny. I've seen his kind. I ain't man enough to buck him, so I'll mind like a stepped-on pup. I'll put this where the boys'll see it and they'll go out there and make his ranch for him. They'll take the gold he gives 'em and they'll spend it here or at Joslyn's store. Is that good?"

"Sure," Dave answered, surprised. "Why not?

147

They get jobs, they can buy grub and clothes for their families, and maybe some drinks for themselves. What's wrong with it?"

Hambone wiped his forehead and stared moodily into the street. He said: "Everything. Look what it's done to you. Put you against your own people. I never seen a fellow feel worse than Lacey Markham did after you rode out with Strang yesterday."

It was the way Dave had known it would be. Still, it was worse than he had imagined. To hide the knifing pangs of his conscience, he said sharply: "You don't need to hooraw me about it. My people are wrong and Matt Strang's right, and we'll all be better off for his coming. Now hang that paper up."

The saloon man stared down at the pencil-scrawled capital letters. "Yeah, I'll hang it up. You know why? Because I don't want my arm broken or a gun barrel bent over my head. You knew why Strang broke George's arm? I'll tell you. So we'd see the light and see it damned fast." He leaned across the bar. "Dave, I tell you I've been around. I can see the handwriting on the wall. It'll go for a while, but there'll come a day when Matt Strang will get shot. Then where'll you be?"

"I'll be here shooting the man who got him," Dave said, and, swinging out of the saloon, crossed the street to the store.

Dixie was not in sight. Dave was glad for that. Bob Joslyn was fussing with some bolts of gingham on the dry-goods side of the long room. Dave stopped inside the door, calling: "Howdy, Bob!" Slowly Joslyn turned, saw who it was, and stepped around the counter.

"How are you today, Dave?" Joslyn said, coming forward.

For a moment Dave stood motionlessly, smelling the mixed odors of freshly ground coffee and leather and new cloth in bolts and vinegar. Usually it had pleased him. He had liked to come here when he was staying in town for school; he liked Bob Joslyn almost as well as he liked Lacey Markham. On any previous day he would have joshed Bob a little and gone on back to the cracker barrel and grabbed a handful. Today he waited until Joslyn came up, and although the storekeeper was as gentle and pleasant as always, Dave sensed that a barrier had risen between them.

"Matt wants to buy your mowers and rakes," Dave said. "He'll pay in gold. He said to tell you that, if you wanted it, you could have all his business. If you don't, he'll freight his supplies up from Winnemucca."

"I see," Joslyn said. "So he sends you to threaten us. Why doesn't he come and break my arm?"

For a moment anger pressed Dave, then it

faded, for he was remembering, as Bob Joslyn and Lacey Markham and Hambone were remembering, the cool, machine-like way in which George McNair had been punished. Still, McNair deserved it, for his filthy mind had put filthy words on his tongue.

"If you speak about Mary like George did," Dave said flatly, "I reckon Matt will break your arm, but you won't."

"No," Joslyn agreed. "I may think a lot, but I won't say it."

Dave handed Joslyn the paper. "Matt wants that put up where everybody can see it."

Joslyn glanced at it, and nodded. "All right."

"He didn't find the duds he thought he had. I'm supposed to get some. He'll pay when he comes in at the end of the week."

"All right," Joslyn said again. "Where'll you start? Reckon you don't need a gun and belt."

"No, Matt gave me this rigging. Let's see if you've got any Justins that'll fit."

Dixie came in through the back. Whether she knew he was there or not was a question Dave never settled in his mind. She seemed surprised when she saw him, but he remembered from their school days that she was always a good actress.

"Why, Dave, this is almost as bad as the way you treated me yesterday." She came quickly along the counter to him, pouting. "It was scandalous the way he treated me yesterday, Dad."

"It's scandalous the way he's performing yesterday and today," Joslyn said with less gentleness than his voice usually held. "The lines are drawn and he's on the other side."

"I'll fetch him back to our side." Dixie winked in a conspiratorial manner. "It just so happened that I made a cake this morning, Dave. You'll eat dinner with us, won't you?"

"Sure," Dave said absently, looking at Joslyn. He was thinking of the storekeeper's words: *The lines are drawn and he's on the other side.* It sounded like Lacey Markham, for Joslyn lacked the talent for handling words that Markham had.

Dixie sniffed. "You'd better show a little more interest than that. It's a good cake, if I do have to brag on it myself, and I'll bet you eat two pieces."

"Run along," Joslyn said. "Dave's buying an outfit."

She started to leave and would have if a man hadn't come in then. She stood rooted, staring at him rudely, and Dave turned to look. He was a stranger, a dirty man who filled the room with his smell. Joslyn said sharply: "You might as well get on that mule and keep riding, Rabbit. I staked you once. Now you can starve for all of me."

The man sidled along the counter, yellow eyes on Dixie. "That any way to treat an old friend, Bob? Why, we knew each other for years in the Willamette Valley. Only reason I came was

151

because I hear you had a store hereabouts."

"Won't do you any good," Joslyn said bluntly. "Why you haven't been hung is a mystery to me. Now get out of the valley, or we will hang you."

Dixie whispered—"Come over as soon as you're done, Dave."—and fled through the back door.

The stranger dipped a hand in the cracker barrel and drew it out, filled. He stuffed his mouth and chomped hungrily, glancing briefly at Dave. Then he asked: "That your filly, Bob?"

Joslyn said: "Give me your gun, Dave."

The man scratched his whiskery chin. "You won't shoot me, Bob. You ain't mean enough." He picked up the paper from the counter Dave had given Joslyn. "So they pay wages in gold. Where is this S Star, Bob?"

Dave handed the gun to Joslyn. The storekeeper pronged back the hammer. He cried out in a ragged voice: "I've got a girl I aim to keep safe, Rabbit. Get out of the valley. You aren't working for Matt Strang or anybody else around here."

"Think not?" The man filled his pockets with crackers. "I'm pretty damned sure you won't stop me."

Joslyn lowered the gun and passed a trembling hand across his face. "I can't kill him, Dave. I'd do all of us a favor if I did, but the Lord gave him a man's body. I don't know whether He gave him a soul or not, but He gave him the body."

The stranger's laugh was a high giggle. Dave

thought: *The fellow's crazy*. He looked at Joslyn. "Want me to throw him out?"

Joslyn nodded. "If he stays here, we'll have to hang him or build a jail to put him in."

Dave strode toward the stranger. "Get out."

The man's yellow eyes flicked uneasily to Joslyn. "Bob, call him off. I ain't done nothing."

Dave grabbed his coat collar, yanked him around, and, gripping him by the seat of the pants, carried him to the door. The man began to kick and thresh, cursing with a steady flow of obscene oaths. Dave reached the door and threw him out into the dust. He skidded on his face, stirring up a white cloud around him. He lay flat, groaning as if trying to arouse sympathy, then sat up and wiped his eyes.

Dave said: "Stay away from S Star. Matt Strang don't want your kind around there."

The man got to his feet, lurched to the hitch pole, and gripped it. He wiped his hand across his face. He said in a whimpering voice: "I ain't gonna forget this, kid. I ain't gonna forget it."

Dave went back into the store. "Now about them Justins, Bob."

Joslyn handed the gun back to Dave, his face thoughtful. "It's a strange thing the way life goes along peaceful for a while. Like a stream flowing across the plain. Then something happens that changes everything so that the stream becomes a torrent thundering down a rocky channel."

153

"You've been listening to Lacey," Dave said.

Joslyn smiled. "That's right. Lacey said something of the sort after you and Strang left yesterday."

"Who was that fellow I heaved out?"

"We used to call him Rabbit Walton. He's dangerous. If he can get his hands on a gun, he'll shoot you in the back. He was a neighbor of mine in the Willamette Valley. I made the mistake of giving him credit. He kept telling me about his bad luck. Finally he stole some money and sloped out of the country, leaving a wife and shack full of kids. A lot of other things he'd done came out later. He isn't safe to have around a woman." Joslyn turned to the shelves. "I was going to say, Dave, that nothing much has happened in the valley since the Paiute War until Strang got here. Now everything's happening. Watching you throw Walton out let me see something I didn't like. If you don't watch out, you'll be just like Matt Strang when you get a little older."

IX

It was the first meal Dave had ever eaten at the Joslyn table, and it was a good meal, the best he'd eaten anywhere for a long time. He was not surprised that Dixie was a good cook, for she had kept house for her father since she was twelve

154

when her mother had died. Still, it was better than he expected.

When he finished a second piece of cake and drank his third cup of coffee, he leaned back and rolled a cigarette, conscious of the bright expectancy in the girl's eyes. He busied himself with his smoke, knowing he had to say something, and failing to find the right words. He sealed the cigarette as Dixie asked hopefully: "You could eat another piece of cake, couldn't you?"

"No, but it sure was good." He reached into his pocket for a match. "You're sure a good cook."

Bob Joslyn rose, masking his amusement. "I've got to get back to the store. I wouldn't want to miss a customer if one did walk in."

After he left, Dixie got up from the table and moved to a window. Dave thumbed his match to life, holding his gaze away from the girl. He remembered the first time he had kissed her. It was at a party here in the Joslyn house. She'd wanted him to come into the kitchen with her and help with something. Then she'd closed the door and asked him to get some cups down from a high shelf. She'd stood beside him, her lips lifted to his just as they had been yesterday. He'd kissed her and dropped the cups with a terrific clatter that had brought the rest rushing into the kitchen. For months afterward the memory of that kiss had been a fire burning his adolescent body.

Beside Dixie's small, rounded figure, Nan seemed straight-lined and almost unattractive. Compared to Dixie's face with its red full-lipped mouth and sparkling black eyes, Nan's features were plain. Still, and this was the part that he did not understand, every plan he'd made, every dream he'd dreamed, had included Nan. It had been that way for months.

"Those clothes change you a lot, Dave," Dixie said. "New boots, new Levi's, new shirt. And look at the Stetson. It was the best one in the store. You must have robbed a bank."

"Your dad gives the stuff away." Dave rose and dropped the charred match into the stove. "I've got to go."

"No, Dave." She crossed the room to him. "I expected you to stay here this afternoon. There's a lot of things we've got to talk about."

"Are there?" he asked stupidly.

"Why, of course. We're engaged, aren't we? I mean, being on opposite sides like this doesn't make any difference, does it?"

He turned back to the stove and threw his cigarette into it, his tongue glued to the top of his mouth. He had never asked Dixie to marry him, although he had long been aware that his mother and Lacey Markham and probably Bob Joslyn expected him to. He turned back to her, blurting: "I'm going to marry Nan Romney."

For a moment he thought she was going to

faint. She sat down suddenly as if her knees could no longer support her weight, her face pale. Her chin began to quiver and she lowered her head so he couldn't see her tears. He looked at the door, wanting to make a run for it and knowing he couldn't. She breathed: "You wouldn't marry a girl who doesn't even have a right to the name she uses, would you?"

A sickness crawled into him. This was what Mary was talking about that morning. His mother's venomous tongue had given voice to the same thing. It was what George McNair had tried to say in the store before Strang had broken his arm. He looked at Dixie, feeling first disappointment because he had thought she was different, and then he knew he hated her. If there was any one thing that had turned him from his people to Strang, it was their willingness to believe evil in two women he loved.

He said nothing. Dixie hurried on: "You've lost your mind, Dave. You know I love you. I've loved you since we were kids in school. Look at me, Dave? Is she prettier than I am? Is there anything she can do for you that I can't? You said I was a good cook, you know."

Still he said nothing.

"Why, Dave?" she cried. "Why?"

"Don't ask me why," he said. "You had better ask me what I'd do if you were a man and you said that about Nan."

Turning, Dave walked out through the front room and left the house, slamming the door. He stalked across the dusty street to his horse and, mounting, rode out of town. It was a long time before the pain left his chest, and he could breathe easily.

A mile east of Sage, Dave swung north, leaving the well-traveled road to Fort Pacific and followed the wagon tracks through the sagebrush, a rude hint of a road that passed Cotter's sawmill and eventually reached Cañon City. The country lifted and broke into the foothills of the Blue Mountains, and by late afternoon he was in the first scattering pines. Stopping, he watered his horse, for here the road paralleled the east fork of Sage River, a clear brawling creek that bore no resemblance to the meandering stream that curled across the valley as if reluctant to reach its destination.

Dave loitered for a time, smelling the dry tangy air of the valley, not liking the chore ahead of him. There was no tangible reason. He only knew he hated the mountains, for there was always a strange uneasiness that gripped him when he found himself pressed between two cañon walls with the weight of the pine forest laid against him. Finishing his cigarette, he toed it out and, swinging back into the saddle, turned his buckskin upstream. Once he looked back, had his last glimpse of the tawny sweep of the valley, then the cañon gave a sharp eastward twist and his world was narrowed to the pines and the slopes on both sides of the creek.

Later, near dusk, he smelled smoke from the burning sawdust pile, and presently rode into a clearing. A pond lay beside the gaunt frame that housed the machinery; logs floated on its surface, and there was a solid chop of little waves that the wind had raised. Abe Cotter, who ran the mill with his two younger brothers, stepped around a pile of lumber and raised a hand in greeting when he saw who it was.

"Light and rest your saddle, Dave!" Cotter called. "Damned if I didn't think you was a real buckaroo the first time I saw them duds. What you doing?"

"A fellow named Matt Strang bought the valley from the state. I'm riding for him."

Cotter looked skeptically at Dave, a finger digging sawdust out of an ear. "Bought the valley, did he? Now just how in hell could he buy a valley?"

"It's marked as swamp land. You know what the deal is. He ain't bothering the folks that's in the valley already. Fact is, he's giving 'em a patent to their quarter-sections."

"That's right kind of him," Cotter murmured. "I'd like to meet that fellow."

"You'll have a chance. He wants to buy all the lumber you've got on hand. He'll pay you in gold."

"Well, now," Cotter crowed, "I will be glad to meet him. It's about time something was happening hereabouts. I was beginning to think we'd made a mistake setting up in these parts. Pay in gold, will he?"

"That's right. He's pretty well fixed, I guess. Fetched a herd up from Nevada and he's sending back for another bunch. Now he's aiming to build a ranch and he needs lumber."

"He'll get it." Cotter waved a big hand to the piles of lumber, much of it recently sawed and not yet darkened by weathering. "We sawed the lumber for the fort and we sawed what they used in town. Then we went back into the woods and fetched down more logs, believing that fool Markham's gabble about the settlers flocking to the valley. They didn't come, by hell. Someday I'm gonna shove a plank down Markham's throat. Then his tongue will stop wagging."

"I guess he had the wrong notion," Dave said dryly.

"Did for a fact. Well, get down off that horse. We've et, but I'll rustle something for you."

"Thanks, Abe, but I've got to get back. How about hauling the lumber to Strang?"

"We've got horses. No sense sawing any more lumber till we see whether we'll need it or not, so I reckon we can do the job. We might be a little slow. It's a long ways across the valley."

"He's building on the other side of the lakes.

Right where Logan Creek comes out of the Pocket."

Cotter groaned. "He's as far away as he can get and still be in the valley. Get down, Dave. You can't do anything tonight."

Dave looked at the big man, smelling of pitch and sawdust and sweat, his great muscles swelling under his shirt. Cotter wouldn't understand, for this was his home. Dave wasn't sure anyone could understand. He only knew he could not stay here.

"No, I've got to get back. Matt wants me to fetch some carpenters and I suppose I'll have to go to hell-and-gone to find 'em. Get that lumber rolling tomorrow. Matt ain't a patient man."

Dave turned his buckskin down the cañon, the smell of the burning sawdust a stain in the air. Darkness crowded twilight out of the timber, and night lay all around him, relieved by only a few stars in the wedge of sky above the pines. Something scurried across the trail ahead of him. Then there was silence except for the rustle of water and the creak of the trees in the wind. Even the hoofs of his horse made no sound in the needle blanket that had been built up through the centuries.

He was out of the timber before he realized it. He made camp, the sky a starry sweep above him, and built a fire and cooked a meal. Later he slept soundly.

161

He woke in the morning and looked across the valley carpeted by sage and grass and greasewood; he watched the early morning shadows slowly retreat beneath the east rim, and he felt the rush of returning confidence. Now, standing here between earth and sky, he could forget the fears that had plagued him the night before.

He cooked breakfast, saddled, and rode eastward, keeping outside the fringe of timber, a long treeless slope breaking away to his right. Near noon he came to Fort Pacific, the long row of officers' quarters, soldiers' barracks, and guardhouse making a conspicuous white line in the sunlight.

Dave found Captain Lawford, the same officer who had commanded the post at the time of the Paiute War. Dave shook hands, asking about the carpenters. For a moment Lawford said nothing, his face marked by surprise. Then he burst out: "Damn it, Dave, you don't look like the spindle-legged kid who was trying out the bad ones for us last summer. Spend all you made on the duds you're wearing?"

"No." Dave smiled thinly. "We ate up what I made. I'm riding for Matt Strang."

"Who's Matt Strang?"

"He owns the valley." Dave told Lawford about him, adding: "I'm supposed to fetch the carpenters."

"They aren't here now. Last I heard they were

in Gouge Eye." Lawford gave Dave a quizzical look. "So the cows finally got here. For once the settlers beat them, but it'll take more than shirt-tail settlers to make a farming country out of this valley. Nature's got a way of deciding some things that no government order can settle."

"They've hung on," Dave said.

"It's Lacey Markham's fine words that's held them, but there comes a time when words and fine prophecies wear thin. Look at them, Dave. I don't mean your folks. I never met them except during the Indian ruckus, but I know some of the others pretty well. Take that saloonkeeper. Calls himself Hambone. Probably got chased out of some mining camp and settled down here where his past would never catch up with him. And Joslyn. He had money, or he couldn't have started his store, but why would he settle here? And Markham." Lawford threw up his hands in disgust. "He may be a good teacher, but he's got some kind of a kink so he's not satisfied just to be a teacher. He thinks he's a leader."

"He is," Dave said quietly.

Lawford smiled. "Perhaps, if you want to be polite about it. Anyhow, I'm glad the cows are in the valley. This'll be a cattleman's paradise, but it'll never be anything but a settlers' hell. We proved that here at the fort. Couldn't raise anything. Sagebrush and grass. That's all."

"And greasewood," Dave added.

163

"And greasewood," Lawford agreed. He swung a hand to the lines of barracks. "We won't be here much longer. They can settle their troubles themselves. Uncle Sam finally heard the Indian ruckus was finished, so he's opening the reservations for settlement."

"When?"

"Next spring, I suppose. Nothing definite yet. Most of the land is worse than it is here in the valley, but the damn' settlers will come a thousand miles because it's free. All but the agency farm. The government will hold that back. Maybe sell it later at auction."

"Strang could use the agency farm," Dave said thoughtfully.

"Tell him about it. I hope he gets it." Lawford's gaze dropped to the gun on Dave's hip. "This Strang aiming to make a gun hand out of you?"

"No," Dave said sharply. "Nobody will do that, but it's like Matt said. Someday I may need some gun speed. If I'm not fast then, I won't need anything but the clods they shovel into my face."

As Dave stepped back into the saddle, Lawford said: "I'll be over one of these days to see your Matt Strang."

"Won't be long till you can dance at his wedding."

"Bringing a woman up from Nevada, is he?"

"No. Him and Mary Romney are getting hitched."

Lawford's leathery face showed surprise, and then envy. "He's a damned lucky man. You know, Dave, when we were having that Indian trouble, I did my best with Mary, but she wouldn't even look at me."

X

It was a week before Dave rode back into Sage. He had found two of the carpenters in Gouge Eye, two more working on a barn north of the settlement, and the fifth one on his way out of the country, convinced that it would be another generation before Lacey Markham's words about Sage Valley came true. The fifth man returned to Gouge Eye with Dave, promising to come out with the other four once their jobs were completed. They would all be on hand by the end of the month, they said, and Dave returned to Sage, satisfied with what he had accomplished, although at times he puzzled over what Strang had said about sugar and gunpowder, and wondered if he had spread the sugar Strang wanted.

Darkness had settled upon Sage when Dave watered his buckskin and led him into the shed behind the hotel. He fed the horse, and Tildie Fields, hearing him, came out of the back door, a lantern held high. When she saw who it was, she said with some asperity: "Dave Logan, you have more gall than a brass monkey, putting your horse into my shed without asking me about it."

Dave came out of the stall, grinning. "That's me, more gall than a brass monkey. I've ridden a thousand miles, Tildie. Maybe a million. Now I want a meal and a bed."

Tildie sniffed. "Well, come on in, but let me tell you something. Your Matt Strang doesn't need to think he owns the country and everybody in it just because he fetched a lot of cows into the valley."

"I don't reckon he claims he owns the people," Dave said, "but he owns the country. You sure can't deny that, Tildie."

She sniffed again. They had reached the back door and she paused in the patch of light, defiantly eyeing Dave. "I'll deny that, too, if he gives us the patents he promised. Here, blow out this lantern while I warm up something."

Dave jacked the chimney up and blew out the flame. Hanging the lantern on a nail outside the door, he went in and dropped into a chair at the table. It had been warm, and the kitchen, even with the doors and windows open, still held much of the day's heat. Dave rolled a smoke, watching Tildie stir up the fire and trot from pantry to kitchen and back in her quick, bird-like way.

Tildie dropped a piece of salt side into the frying pan and, without warning, whirled on

Dave. "I'm feeding you on one condition. You've got to go over and see Lacey as soon as you finish eating."

Dave had missed the teacher on his way north, and he hoped he might miss him this time. Still, he knew that sooner or later he'd have to listen to Markham. Shrugging, he said: "I ain't in position to auger about it Tildie. I'll go see him."

She turned to the stove and set the coffee pot on the back. "You can tell that Matt Strang something else, too. All the gold he's got won't make folks love him. He's got men working out there. He bought some stuff from Bob Joslyn and paid for it. He rented a room from me so he'd always have a place to sleep when he was in town. You can sleep there tonight. He's paying for it." She whirled to face him again, anger stinging her cheeks. "Sure he wants to be friends with us and he wants us to be friends with the Romney woman, but he won't get anywhere. You'll see."

Tildie dished up the beans and salt side, and set a plate of warmed-over biscuits on the table. She poured a cup of black steaming coffee and returned the pot to the stove. Then she watched him eat, her back to the stove.

Dave finished quickly and reached for tobacco and papers, covering his embarrassment with the motion. For some reason Tildie was close to crying. Dave knew her well, and should have, for he had stayed with her when he'd gone to school. Still, she had always held him at a cool distance so that he had never been able to talk to her in the way he talked to Lacey Markham and Bob Joslyn. Tildie was like the saloon man, Hambone, insofar as she never mentioned her past. Dave suspected that her name was as fictitious as Hambone's, and like the saloon man she did not want anyone who had known her previously to find her here. In other ways she was unlike the rest, for she possessed a stubborn pride that set her apart from her neighbors. By many subtle hints she had let it be known that there was both money and good blood in her family. In all the months he had stayed in the hotel, Dave had never seen Tildie Fields worried or excited; he had never seen anything ruffle the cool mask under which she hid her feelings. Now she was silent for a moment, watching him seal and fire his cigarette, and when he raised his eyes to her, he saw her proud little chin quiver.

"Dave," she burst out, "if you're big enough to talk about getting married, you're big enough to take a man's responsibility. Do you know what you'll do to your mother if you marry the Romney girl? Do you know what you've already done to Dixie?"

So that was it. He rose, reaching for his Stetson. "I guess I'll get over to Lacey's."

"Not for another minute, Dave Logan." She

stepped in front of him. "Times are changing. I know that. There's nothing but trouble ahead, shooting trouble and dying trouble. I won't run from it. I ran once, but never will run again. Shame is like a cancer that gnaws at your vitals, Dave. It's the kind of shame that's in Lacey and Hambone and Bob Joslyn because they sat with guns on their hips and watched your Matt Strang break George McNair's arm and they didn't raise a finger to stop him. It will go on and on, gnawing in them until they can't sleep and they can't breathe. Perhaps they'll go away and forget it. If they don't, they'll stay here and shoot themselves. Or shoot Strang."

He stared at her, his cigarette cold in his mouth. For all of her pride, Tildie Fields was uncovering her soul to him.

"I know about men like Strang," she hurried on. "He's like a wall of mud oozing down over the valley. You can't fight it, you can't hold it back. You just stand and let it run over you and bury you. Then you belong to him, but the shame is still in you." She turned away, not wanting him to see the nakedness of her feelings. With her back to him, she said: "There are some things we can't change, Dave. We hold to our pride if we're old and we die with the shame in us, but you're young and you're strong and there's a touch of greatness in you. That's what Lacey Markham says." Tildie whirled, small chin thrust defiantly at him. "Don't marry Nan Romney, Dave. What-ever you do, don't marry her. The taint of her mother is in her and she'll never scrape it off. Never. She will only bring you sorrow and regret. Then you'll hate yourself because you'll think of Dixie who loves you."

"I'll get over and see Lacey," Dave said, and, walking past Tildie, left the kitchen.

Dave paused in back of the hotel and lit his cigarette again. Looking through the door, he saw that Tildie had not moved. He walked around the building to the street, passed the front of the hotel and Joslyn's house. There was a light in the front room, and he saw Dixie sewing, dark head bent over her work. He went on and turned up the path to Markham's house, stirred by what Tildie Fields had said and a little angry. He tapped on Markham's door, and when the teacher opened it, he stepped in without invitation.

"Lacey, what the hell has hit everybody?"

Smiling thinly, Markham shut the door behind Dave. "So you wonder what's hit everybody. Take the blinders off your eyes, Dave. Then you could see for yourself."

Markham moved back to the table where he had been reading. The flames of two kerosene lamps flickered uneasily inside smoky chimneys. A volume of Emerson's essays lay spread out, face down on the table. Lifting it, he slipped a bookmark into place, and laid it back. He blew out one lamp and, sitting down in the straight-backed chair, rubbed his eyes. Markham's house, like most of the others in Sage, was a one-room cabin. He cooked his own meals; he did his own washing and ironing and mending. Judging from the odor that lingered in the room, his evening meal had consisted of sauerkraut.

"I've been putting this off, Lacey," Dave said, "figgering you'd peel my hide off, but Tildie wouldn't feed me till I promised I'd come over."

Markham reached for his pipe and tamped tobacco into the bowl. "I'm going to have to clean those chimneys out one of these days." He dug a match from a shirt pocket. "No, I'm not going to take your hide off, Dave, but I have been wanting to talk to you. I'm glad you dropped in. I presume you're on your way back to S Star."

Dave nodded. He went, opened the door again, flipped his cigarette stub into the yard. After closing the door, he came back, sat down, and waited.

Markham fumbled with his pipe, the murky lamplight falling across his narrow face. Then he lit his pipe and blew out the match. "I can tell you mighty quick what's hit everybody, Dave. It's hit the whole valley. The best illustration I can think of is to compare the valley with a pool of water. Somebody throws a big rock in. What happens?"

Dave was used to these illustrations. He said obediently: "You get waves."

"Exactly. Big ones maybe, and you don't know how much destruction they'll do along the banks or how long they'll last. All right. The Lord just threw in a big rock named Matt Strang."

"Everybody can . . . ," Dave began rebelliously. He stopped, staring at Markham, a new thought striking him. "Nobody around here puts words together like you do. But lately I've heard some pretty fine ones come out of Hambone. Then Bob. Now Tildie. Maybe you've been drilling them like you used to drill us before graduation."

Markham puffed silently for a moment. "Maybe I have, Dave. You see, you're the key man, although I'm sure you never thought of it that way. You were a seed capable of tremendous growth, the soil and weather being right. It was right the moment Strang came. A number of things were responsible. Your feelings about Nan, for instance. Your discontent with the way things were at home. And perhaps you were tired of waiting for the day of development that I have prophesied and still do. So, in the few days since Strang first saw Sage Valley, you have sprouted and begun your growth. Unless I am greatly mistaken, the day will come when you are the big man in this country."

"Why are you telling me this stuff?" Dave demanded.

"To let you see your own possibilities." Markham took the pipe put of his mouth and pointed the stem at Dave. "You can believe that or not, but you must believe this. We're facing an issue that's bigger than you or me or Matt Strang. It's a problem of the land and its people and the people who will yet come. In a hundred years from now it will be still a bigger problem because there will be more people, but no more land."

"That's their problem," Dave said irritably.

"No, it's ours to look ahead. It's right here in our hands. Sage Valley is one big chunk where a lot of families could make a living, but, if Strang has his way, there will be many cows and few families. What you do and what I do may decide which way it goes. Cows or people, Dave. Which do you want?"

"The same old argument," Dave said irritably. "I'll take cows. Looks to me like it's better for a few people to do well than for a lot to starve. I was over to the fort the other day. Captain Lawford said something about your fine words. He said they'd wear out and cattle would stay after the settlers were gone."

Again the thin humorless smile touched Markham's lips. "I'm afraid Lawford and I disagree on the fundamental issue, Dave. He tried to raise some grain and vegetables and failed. Therefore he says the valley is not fitted for agriculture. Perhaps part of it isn't, and I'll admit we have no prosperous settlers, but the failure is

173

not in the valley. It's partly the people who have to learn by trial and error, but it's largely the primitive conditions under which we must live. A railroad will bring prosperity. Settlers who have something to ship will bring a railroad. It's that simple. But Strang will fight a railroad as long as he's able to fight anything." Markham fired his pipe, puffing hard for a moment, blue eyes bright with the zeal that burned in him. "Dave, I have nothing to make from this myself. I'm not a farmer. I have never even staked out a quarter-section. What I cannot do with my hands I must do with my mind. Here in this valley there were a dozen families before Strang came. Small people. Inarticulate people. I shall be their voice. I cannot beat Strang with a gun or my fists. You saw that in Joslyn's store. It was something Strang knew all the time. He's a smart man, Dave. Make no mistake about that. Look at the way he's using you. He's an opportunist, and a brilliant one."

"He owns the land, Lacey. You forget that."

"By the robbers' act only. We'll change it. Settlers will pour in once they start. I'll bring them, Dave. We'll fight in the courts until the land goes back into the Public Domain and is open for entry."

"How will you bring in settlers?" Dave asked curiously.

"I shall start a newspaper. I will call it the Sage Valley *Sun* because it's the sun in the sky that gives light. I will see that the Sage Valley *Sun* gives light to the world on what is happening in this isolated corner of a great state. The only way Matt Strang can put that light out is to kill me. Then he'll make a martyr out of me and my death will call attention to what is happening here. I will be the voice of the small people, Dave. I want you with me. I'll give you a job. You won't have to work for Strang."

Dave rose. "I've picked my side, Lacey. I thought you'd understand."

Markham stood on the other side of the table, the light fading from his thin pale face. "No, I don't understand, Dave," he breathed. "I thought it was merely a case of your understanding the issue. I was sure you would not be a traitor to your own people."

Dave's mouth tightened. "That's an ornery word, Lacey, a damned ornery word. I haven't sold my saddle, and I reckon I've got the right to do some figgering on my own account. You don't need to talk about my people, either. If I let everybody else run me, I'd marry Dixie."

"She's a fine girl," Markham said heavily. "She's your kind."

"If gossiping about Mary Romney for no reason at all is the way my people are," Dave said bitterly, "I don't want anything to do with them. I've heard too much of it at home."

"You say no reason?" Markham shook his head.

"We're a strange assortment of people, Dave, but we're fair. There's plenty of reason to talk about Mary Romney."

"Then what is it?"

"Mary Romney sang in saloons in mining camps. Hambone saw her in Silver City. As far as what she's done here is concerned, the situation on the face of it is enough, settling twenty miles from town the way she has, just the two of them, letting men stay there overnight. Human nature is human nature, Dave. There is very little traffic over her toll bridge, but she isn't starving. Figure it out for yourself."

"Human nature's the same in Sage as it is on the Channel," Dave said hotly. "Tildie keeps men overnight. You figger she's the same?"

"Of course not. Tildie lives where everyone can see. She has nothing to conceal. If Mary Romney was the same, she would have settled here in town." Markham spread his hands. "I'm not condemning anyone, Dave. I just want you to see that evil and good are on separate sides in this trouble. Strang and the Romney woman were in town last week, asking when the preacher would be here. Two of a kind, Dave."

"If it hadn't been for Mary, you and Bob and Tildie and all the rest would be off Matt's land by now, but I suppose that doesn't make you like Mary any better."

"No, even if it is true."

"And you don't suppose that Mary, being prettier than the other women, has anything to do with the way they feel about it, do you?"

"Certainly. I told you human nature doesn't change. There is some jealousy in all of us. But that doesn't change the facts."

For a moment their eyes locked. Lacey Markham must have seen in Dave's face the contempt that was in him, the disappointment, the sense of outrage that had grown in him since he had been old enough to understand vaguely the talk about Mary Romney. He understood it more clearly now, for these last days had taught him many things he had only sensed before. These last minutes had taught him something more, too. For all of his artistry of words, Lacey Markham could not make himself a bigger man than Matt Strang. He had only succeeded in demonstrating his own size. His artistry was in words, not in action.

"You're a good teacher, Lacey," Dave said quietly. "You ought to stick to it. So long."

Dave went out, leaving Markham looking after him, the lamp throwing its murky light across his thin, zealous face.

XI

Dave left Sage the next morning as soon as he had eaten breakfast. Tildie had been her prim distant self again, serving him efficiently and saying nothing about what had happened the night before. When Dave left, she said coolly: "Give my regards to your mother."

"I will when I see her," Dave said, and left the hotel.

It was another hot day. By the time he reached the tule marsh, his shirt was sweat-pasted to his back. Coming to the bridge spanning the Channel, he let himself through the tollgate, dismounted at the kitchen door, and knocked. No one answered. It worried him, for it was not like Mary to leave and take Nan with her. He cut wood for a time, thinking that Mary or Nan might be upstairs, and the racket of his chopping would bring one of them out of the house, but no one came. After half an hour, he rode on, leaving a sizeable pile of split juniper.

Near noon Dave reached camp, surprised by the activity that was all around him. Strang had staked out the shape of his buildings. Two wagons were hauling juniper posts for the corrals from the rim, three mowers were working in the meadow between the camp and the lake, and four men were setting corral posts. Judging from the pile of lumber on the ground, Abe Cotter and his brothers had come and gone.

"Where's Matt?" Dave asked the cook.

The cook jerked a hand toward the rim. "Yonder. Him and Mary Romney and Nan. They'll be down for dinner, I reckon."

Dave reined his horse toward the men who were setting posts, noting with some surprise that none of them was a Strang buckaroo. They were settlers, all but the bearded man who gave his back to Dave as he rode up. Dave spoke to the men he knew, and turned his horse toward the bearded one. He swore in sudden anger, for the fellow kept tamping dirt around the base of the post with the end of his shovel handle. His head was lowered and he had the brim of his battered hat pulled low over his forehead, somehow contriving to circle the post as Dave rode around him so that his back was always to Dave.

"Hey you!" Dave called. "Ain't you got that post tamped yet?"

"Not yet," the man said, and kept on pounding.

The other three had stopped work to watch, grins curling their mouths. One said: "Maybe he ain't proud of his face, Dave."

"If he's who I think he is, he's got nothing to be proud about." Dave swung down, grabbed the man's shoulder, and jerked him around. "Yeah, he's who I think he is, all right. Walton, Joslyn told you to get out of the valley and I told you Matt didn't need the likes of you."

"You're just an upstart kid," Walton jeered. "When Mister Strang fires me, I'll know I'm fired, but who in hell do you think you are?"

Dave glared at the man, knowing he'd started something he couldn't finish. Walton had called his bluff and there was nothing he could do except tell Strang what Joslyn knew about the fellow.

Without a word Dave mounted and rode off, Walton calling after him: "Just an upstart kid too big for his pants."

Strang was in camp with Mary and Nan when Dave rode back. Strang called: "How are you, boy? Glad you got in."

Mary smiled, and said: "We've been expecting you, Dave."

He muttered something, eyes on Nan who was blushing and trying to smile. He wanted to kiss her, but there were too many people watching, so he said: "I got back as soon as I could. Seems like it's been a year since I left."

For a moment Nan stood motionlessly, struggling with her pride. Then she rushed to Dave, crying: "It *has* been a year, Dave!" He held her hard and kissed her. She drew back, whispering: "You're breaking my ribs, Dave."

Strang whooped a laugh. "Never regret you've got a strong man, Nan."

The cook, watching from the tailboard of the chuck wagon, grunted: "What'n hell is this outfit coming to, Matt, all this billin' and cooin' goin' on?"

"It's spring," Strang said.

"Spring, is it?" The cook sleeved sweat from his face. "Then I'm lookin' for a cool summer day 'cause hell won't get no hotter'n this."

Stepping back, Dave jerked his head at Strang. When the cowman came up, Dave said in a low tone: "I ain't trying to tell you your business, Matt, but you've got a fellow down there you don't want around. Joslyn knew him in the Willamette Valley and he says they'd hang him if he went back. Joslyn says that's what we'll have to do or else build a jail for him."

Strang scowled. "Who?"

"Walton."

"Aw, Joslyn's an old woman," Strang said contemptuously. "Lot of work to be done. Lot of work to be done for the next ten years. Walton smells like a sheepherder, but he ain't afraid to earn his wages. Forget it. What about the carpenters?"

For a moment Dave fought his anger. "They'll be here by the end of the month." He motioned toward Walton who was coming with the others for his dinner, and his words were hot: "You're changing the country, Matt. You're changing everything, but I want to know one thing. Are you fixing it so a coyote like Walton can live with human beings?"

Surprise touched Strang's craggy face briefly. "Easy, boy," he said evenly. "I told you he was a good worker." He swung toward the women. "Dave says we'll have carpenters by the end of the month. A double wedding and a house warming. How does that sound, Mary?"

"Perfect."

The light had gone out of the day for Dave. He hunkered beside Nan while they ate, dourly silent, and Nan, as if feeling his mood, said nothing. There was a good deal of coming and going around the camp, a hurly-burly of motion that Dave was dimly aware of, for he kept his eyes on Walton. The man emptied his plate, filled it, and emptied it again, eating with wolfish relish. He carried his plate and cup to the wreck pan, walking sideways so that he could keep his eyes on Mary. When he returned, he circled behind her and dropped a hand to touch a curl of her hair.

Mary screamed and jumped away from Walton, dropping her plate and spilling coffee on her ankle. At that moment Strang was at the creek, talking to the men who had just come off the rim with their loads of posts. He wheeled and lumbered toward the fire in a rocking run just as Dave lunged at Walton. Dave swung twice, short chopping blows that had the effect of an upswinging axe handle, Walton went down and stayed on his back, a hand coming up to feel of his jaw.

"What'd he do?" Strang bellowed. "What'd he do?"

"Nothing!" Walton cried as if outraged. "I didn't do nothing, Mister Strang."

Mary picked up her plate. "It's all right, Matt."

"It's not all right," Dave said, standing over Walton. "I told you, Matt."

"What'd he do?" Strang asked again.

"I touched her," Walton said in the same outraged tone. "I just touched her. That's all."

"Get out." Strang threw a gold coin at him. "That's more'n you've earned. Get out of the valley."

Walton came to his feet, still rubbing his jaw. "You don't treat Rabbit Walton that way. Nobody does."

"Get out!" Strang threw each word like a blow of his fists. "Get on that mule and dust."

Walton picked up his money and scurrying toward his mule, threw on the saddle and rode off as fast as he could make the animal go. Strang watched until Walton disappeared toward the Channel, then he turned and said: "All right, Dave. All right."

"He rode in from the south," Nan said, "the morning after you and Dave were over there. Real early. He gave me twenty-five cents and I

183

opened the gate. He grabbed my hand and said Bob Joslyn was his friend. He wouldn't let me go, so I hit him."

"Nan, you didn't tell me." Horror was in Mary as she put a hand out to Nan. "And I was asleep."

"Why didn't you tell me?" Strang demanded.

Nan faced him, very grave, her eyes defiant. "You wouldn't have believed me. You're a stubborn, bull-headed man, Mister Strang. You didn't even believe Dave."

"It's all right, Matt." Mary reached out, one hand holding to Nan's arm, the other to Strang's big one. "I shouldn't have screamed. It just surprised me. He'll leave and everything will be all right."

Strang softened under her smile. "I reckon, Mary."

Dave, watching, sensed a weakness in Matt Strang, the first since he had known him, the weakness of a strong man who cannot admit a mistake.

"Sure, everything will be all right," Strang said. He gave Nan a quick, probing look, then nodded at Dave. "Done eating?"

Dave said: "Yes. I lost my appetite."

"Lot to be done," Strang said. "Lot to be done for the next ten years. Get up on the rim and chop some juniper posts. The boys'll be up there for a load pretty soon."

Refusal was on Dave's tongue. He had not

signed on with Strang to cut juniper posts. Still, if he worked for Strang, he would obey Strang's orders, or he wouldn't work long. He said—"All right, Matt."—and turned away.

"I'll ride with you," Nan said.

"No, you'll go to the house with your mother," Strang ordered.

Nan flounced around to face him. "I'm not working for you and I'm not marrying you. Let's understand that now, Mister Strang."

"You'll take this order," Strang said curtly. "Let the posts go, Dave. Fetch Hanna. Tell him to take Walton out of the valley. I reckon a look at his star will do the job."

Nan stared at Strang, wildly defiant, pushing her hate at him, but she made no move to go with Dave, no sound to call him back.

Dave stepped up. He lifted a hand to Nan, forcing a smile, but he did not think Nan saw him. Splashing across the creek, he took the trail to Hanna's place. For the first time doubts of Matt Strang had entered his mind and had taken root there. If Rabbit Walton had felt a blacksnake across his back and been conducted out of the valley, he would have kept going. It would not have taken the sight of Hanna's star, but the feel of Dave's fists might not be enough.

It was the middle of the afternoon when Dave and Hanna rode down from the rim and passed

185

Strang's camp, Hanna grumbling about the heat and his hard saddle. Dave ignored him, for he was used to Hanna's grumblings. Strang, Dave saw, was working with his men, digging post holes.

"We'd better stop and see what Strang's got on his mind," Hanna said.

"We've got to find Walton," Dave said impatiently. "This is your first job, Bill."

"More riding," Hanna said gloomily. "Why'n hell didn't Strang keep Walton when he had him?"

"He's probably wondering that himself," Dave said.

Dave knew, but there was no sense telling Hanna. Matt Strang had realized his mistake in not listening to Dave, but because he was Matt Strang, he had refused to admit that mistake, so he had continued the same line by paying Walton off and firing him. After that Nan had defied him, and Strang, only then understanding the possible consequences of his error, had realized what might happen if Walton remained in the country. That, Dave thought, must have been the way Strang's mind had worked.

Hanna said: "I reckon he wanted the law to handle that fellow. Mighty smart gent, Strang is. Always safer to let a legally appointed official take care of things like this." Hanna sighed, wiped sweat from his forehead. "But I sure wish he'd hung onto Walton. Would've saved a pile of riding. Where do you reckon he went?"

"Dunno."

Hanna sighed again. "Hell of a big country to hunt for one man."

Walton would not go back to Sage. Dave was sure of that. Even a gentle man like Joslyn could be pushed into violence, and fear was a powerful compulsion in Rabbit Walton. Nor was it likely he would stay around camp. How far he would go was a question. Dave, remembering the look on his face when he had touched Mary's hair, felt a sickness crawl into him. Walton would not be far from Mary Romney's house. "He might be hiding in the tules, Bill," Dave said at last.

"Then he'll hide till he gets hungry enough to come out," Hanna growled. "You couldn't root a man out of them tules if you hunted till hellfire got cold."

Dave held his silence, for he knew it was true. Later, they reined up in front of Mary's house and dismounted. Nan must have heard them, for she ran out through the front door, crying and talking in an incoherent babble. Dave caught her, asking: "What is it, Nan? What is it?"

Hanna came up, flushed face heavy with worry. "Where's Mary?" he asked.

But Nan was past the point where she could talk. Dave held her, her hands clutching his shirt, her face buried against his chest, slim body trembling. Dave jerked his head at the house. "Take a look, Bill."

Nodding, Hanna moved up the path to the porch, pulled his gun, and went in. Then Nan began talking, wildly, bitterly. "He killed her. I'm to blame. I didn't stay here like Strang said. I rode off. I wouldn't take his orders. I had to show him."

Hanna came out of the house, calling: "Come here, Dave!"

Something tightened around Dave's chest, choking him. One thought hammered at his brain like a ragged pulse beat: *If Matt had listened to me, this wouldn't have happened.*

"I can't go in," Nan whispered. "I can't go in."

Dave put an arm around her and forced her to walk toward the house. He said: "Sit down. I'll go in."

"Come on," Hanna said irritably. "Bring her inside. Mary wants her."

Nan stiffened. There was no sound from her except the choking pull of her breath. It was Dave who asked: "Mary all right?"

"Sure, sure," Hanna said, "but damn it, she needs Nan. Get her in here."

Nan lunged past Hanna, stumbled, caught the door casing, and ran on. Hanna scowled, muttering: "Women sure dive in over their heads. Easiest way to live is to do without 'em."

Dave crossed the porch and went inside. Mary

was lying on the couch; Nan was on her knees beside her, crying in soft moaning sobs. Mary had an arm around Nan, whispering: "I'm all right, Nan. I'm all right." She raised her eyes to Dave. "He knocked me out, or I fainted. I'm not sure which, but, when Nan found me, I was lying on the floor."

Dave came to the couch. "What happened?"

Mary said nothing for a moment. She kept patting Nan, making soft crooning sounds as she would to a weeping child. It was then that Dave saw the red bruise on the side of her face, the marks on her neck where she had been choked. Her dress was torn along one shoulder, her hair had come loose and spilled to the floor in a long golden curve. Then Nan was quiet, but she still kneeled with her arms around her mother, her face buried. Mary brought her gaze to Dave again. "Walton must have been hiding in the barn. Nan went for a ride and he came in through the back door. He surprised me and I didn't have time to get a gun. Matt didn't think there would be any danger until night. I talked to him a while and he kept saying he was a better man for me than Matt. He told me I was beautiful and he wanted to touch my hair. He said it was like cobwebs of golden dew at sunup. I got panicky and tried to run. He caught me. I don't remember that he hit me, but he may have."

Nan raised her head, staring defiantly at Dave.

"It was Strang's fault. Don't you say it was mine."

Mary reached out with a handkerchief and wiped Nan's eyes. "Don't blame Matt, honey."

"He knew Walton was crazy. Didn't he, Dave?"

"I think he did," Dave answered. "I think he did."

"But, Nan, you should have stayed here like Matt said," Mary remarked softly. "He knew that as long as we were together, there was no danger."

"I won't take his orders," Nan said rebelliously. "I'll tell him again."

"What scared Walton off?" Dave asked.

"I did," Nan said. "I rode in behind the house and I saw his mule. I ran in and he must have heard me. He slammed into me and knocked me down . . . I guess I fainted."

Hanna, still standing in the doorway, said: "We'll hang him, Mary. Come on, Dave."

"We can't leave them alone." Dave rose, pulled between two decisions. "But he's getting farther away all the time."

"We'll be all right," Mary said. "He won't come back. Matt should know about it. One of you better go after him."

"You go, Bill," Dave said. "I'll go after Walton."

Dave pushed past Hanna and left the house. Hanna followed, saying angrily: "You ain't the one giving orders hereabouts. I'm the deputy. Hod dang it, I'll go after Walton."

Dave swung into the saddle. "This is a big man, Bill. Now that he's done this, he'll be crazy. You go get Matt." Ignoring Hanna's sputtering, Dave swung his horse away from the house and crossed the road.

The tollgate was closed. It seemed to Dave that a panicky man on the run would not take time to open the gate. He would not go back toward Strang's camp. That left only one other way, west around the south side of the lake.

The tule marsh was a vast green sea extending for miles along the southern fringe of West Lake, a wilderness more difficult to pierce than the densest forest. A steep bank rose above the waterline. Faint wheel tracks wound along the crest of this bank, a hint of a road that Hanna had used to haul wood to Mary Romney. The townsmen, coming from Sage to hunt ducks, had dug the ruts a little deeper. Dave followed it for a time, riding slowly as he watched for tracks. It was unlikely that anyone except Walton had used it for several days.

Dave rode half a mile before he found a track. Walton had not lost his head completely, for apparently he had kept close to the talus slope in the high grass south of the road. But there was no mistaking this track. A mule had made it, and there was no mule in the valley except Walton's.

Swinging down, Dave kneeled in the soft earth. There was a seep here ten feet wide that was entirely without grass, only a faint crust of alkali. Apparently Walton had thought he had gone far enough to throw off any pursuers who might follow. Now, intent on the best speed he could get from his mule, he had turned into the road. Dave was no expert tracker, but as he studied the deep marks across the seep, it struck him that Walton was spurring his mule like a crazy man. Now he was thinking of nothing but escape. Handled this way, his mule could not last.

Dave stepped back into leather and crossed the seep. His buckskin, heavier than Walton's mule, sank deeper into the muck and was floundering badly by the time he reached the solid turf on the other side. Then, quite unexpectedly, Dave came upon the mule. It lay to his left among the rocks below the rim. Swinging down, Dave saw that the mule had a broken leg. From the tracks, he judged that Walton had tried to make it to the top here. There was a break in the rimrock, and a man who did not know the country would think he could gain the plateau above the valley, but Dave had tried it and knew better.

Walton, Dave thought, could not be far away. He laid a hand on his gun butt, looking at the mule and knowing that a shot would warn Walton. He turned toward his buckskin, put a foot in the stirrup, and pulled it out. Drawing his gun, he returned to the mule and shot it. He thought: *Matt wouldn't have done this with Walton so close.*

Dave rode on, eyes searching the space between the rim and the edge of the tule marsh. Walton was nowhere in sight. Dave pondered this for a moment, certain that his man had not climbed to the rim and equally certain that there had not been time for him to get out of sight by walking base of the rim, making a stream that left the tule marsh. Dave reined to the left.

A spring boiled out of the ground that wound in looping meanders across the flat meadow to the tules. This was Bill Hanna's and Bob Joslyn's favorite duck-hunting place, and both had flat-bottomed boats they had built for that purpose. Dave rode on to the creek, thinking of the boats and deciding that Walton, not knowing the marsh, would not try anything that desperate. Dave had been in the tules once with Hanna, and he knew it was as trackless a jungle as a man would find in the state. But when he reached the stream, he saw that Hanna's boat was gone. Reining left, he crossed a wide loop of the creek, and found Joslyn's. Walton, in his haste, had not looked for a second boat. A less panicky man would have found it and destroyed it.

Dave swung down, leaving his buckskin ground-anchored, his heart hammering sledge-like blows in his chest. At such a time Rabbit

Walton would be dangerous, for he undoubtedly knew the West well enough to be certain of what lay ahead for him if he were caught. It was a question, then, whether his panic would drive him into the marsh so far that he would never find his way back, or whether he would draw just far enough off the road to be hidden until dark. Stepping into the boat, Dave shoved it into the stream. He heard the chattering of a pair of sora rails, saw a mallard go after something in the bottom of the water, leaving only his wiggling posterior above the surface. Then Dave was in one of the serpentine twists among the tules, and the fear left him, for he was remembering Mary Romney, the bruise on her face, the mark Walton's fingers had left on her throat.

The tules were eight to ten feet high here, the open water of the lake more than two miles to the north, so it was an unmapped jungle of hundreds of floating islands around which channels flowed in seemingly aimless fashion. There was no landmark of any kind, one channel looked like another, and only occasionally could Dave glimpse the sun that was now well over to the west. It was an impossible task. Dave stopped the boat, knowing he would be lost if he kept on. He sat motionlessly for a time, considering this. Ahead blue herons stood fishing, ignoring him. Redwings and tule wrens swung on the swaying stems. Suddenly the herons took wing and sailed out of sight.

There was no sound, nothing tangible that warned Dave. He slapped at mosquitoes, then tried to remain motionless while the feeling grew in him that Walton was not far away, perhaps watching him. Unless the man had gone completely crazy, he would not risk going any deeper into the marsh, and he would more than likely have followed this same channel that Dave had used. A muskrat paddled by, tail waving. Dave watched him until he was out of sight. Slowly he followed, rowing as silently as he could. He pointed the nose of the boat around the island and at once used his oars to stop. Just ahead was a big muskrat house. Lying belly flat on the roof was Rabbit Walton, yellow eyes staring malevolently at Dave from under the brim of his dirty hat.

XII

For what seemed an endless moment they stared at each other, neither speaking, neither moving. Here was the man Dave wanted, but now that he had found him, he didn't know what to do. He didn't even know whether Walton had a gun. If the man tried to draw on him, he would have no choice but to get his out as fast as he could. He remembered Strang's words: *You never know when you'll need to be fast with your cutter.* Then he thought of Nan. He had never known until that moment how important it was to stay alive.

Dave had no notion how long they faced each other, both as frozen as pointers at work, Walton's eyes shining like the eyes of a cornered animal. Suddenly he broke, his voice sounding like the bleat of a scared sheep: "Go way. Let me alone. I didn't do nothing."

Dave thought—*If he had a gun, he'd have tried for it by now*—and exploded into action. Using the oars, he shot the boat forward, straight at the muskrat house. Walton tumbled off the roof and Dave jumped out of the boat on him, both going belly flat into the alkali water and muck. Walton may have had the wind knocked out of him, or it may have been a trick. Dave was never sure, but when he straightened up, Walton was still under the surface, apparently out cold. Thinking he was drowning, Dave hauled his head and shoulders out of the water. Walton gained his footing and clawed mud out of his eyes. Then he pulled a knife from his boot, and his right hand struck upward out of the muddy water, the blade aimed at Dave's throat. Dave bent sideways so that the steel ripped his shirt and scraped an inch of skin off his shoulder. He caught Walton's wrist and twisted, left fist coming through to Walton's jaw.

For a time they strained that way, Walton pawing at him with his left hand, and cursing in a shrill frantic voice. Dave hit him again and again, but he was handicapped by the water and mucky footing, and his blows lacked any real power. The arm-twisting was more effective. Walton was a bigger man. Still, he lacked Dave's strength and staying power, and in the end he let the knife go.

They wrestled across the channel and back, working the water into muddy foam. Walton rammed a thumb at Dave's eye, attempted to knee him in the crotch, and finally tried to bite his ear, but nothing worked for him. He had no fighting skill and his only real asset was his animal-like cunning. It was that cunning that prompted him finally to sob between his labored breaths: "Take me in. I can't fight no more." Walton put his hands up to protect his face, whimpering like a dog.

Dave said: "Climb into the boat."

Walton obeyed. Dave followed and took the oars. For several minutes he sat, not moving, only then realizing how thoroughly the struggle in the muck and water had sapped his strength. He began rowing slowly, nosing the boat around the turn and into the channel he had followed coming in.

It took a long time to get out of the tules and into the clear water of the creek. Dave pushed the boat against the bank and ordered Walton out. The man climbed to the bank and stumbled and fell. He lay as if utterly exhausted.

Dave stepped out of the boat and pulled it

from the water. Kneeling on the bank, he washed the dried muck from his face and hands, still watching Walton who seemed to have lost consciousness. Then the man came alive just as Dave leaned over the creek and sloshed his face. Somehow, when Dave hadn't been looking at him, Walton had got a hand on a rock. Now he lunged at Dave, the rock clutched above his head in his right hand, ready for a down-sweeping blow. Dave spilled forward into the creek, the rock striking within six inches of his head. He floundered out of the stream and, pulling his gun, rushed Walton just as the fellow was stooping for another rock.

Walton dropped to his knees, holding his hands over his head, once more setting up his dog-like whimper. This time Dave brought his gun barrel slamming down across Walton's head. The man went slack. Dave toed him in the ribs. Sure that Walton was out cold, Dave went after his horse. He led the buckskin up and, taking down his rope, tied Walton's hands and feet. Half an hour later Strang and Hanna found him stretched out beside Walton, still bone weary.

"Well, looks like you got him," Strang said with satisfaction. "Gave him a bath, too."

"In mud," Dave said, "but I guess he's cleaner than he was."

Walton, conscious now, sat up and bobbed his head at Strang. "Get these ropes off me, Mister

Strang. I haven't done anything to be treated like this."

Hanna said: "Took a boat, did he? Hell, Dave, you should have left him in the tules. He'd have starved to death, or he'd have come out for grub."

"I thought we'd better get it over with," Dave said. "Your boat's back there."

"It won't go nowhere." Hanna shot a glance at Strang, then asked: "Dave, why didn't you shoot him?"

Dave kicked at a rock. "I thought Matt would want him alive. Anyhow, I reckon I couldn't just shoot him."

"That's right," Strang said quickly.

"Well, damn it, what'll we do with him?" Hanna demanded. "There ain't no tree hereabouts big enough to hang him from."

"We won't hang him here," Strang said curtly. "We'll take him to town. Even Walton has the right of a trial. Good thing for you to remember. Good thing for the valley to remember."

Dave took his rope from Walton and limped toward his buckskin. He was cold and stiff, and the depressing aftermath of his struggle with Walton still gripped him.

"Where's his mule?" Strang asked. When Dave told him, Strang said: "We'll get a horse at Mary's place. I sent a man to town to let Joslyn and the rest know, and Clab and the boys are

199

hunting around the north side of the lake. We'll pull them in and get on into town. Hanna, let Walton have your horse. You get up behind Dave. If he makes a run, kill him."

Walton pulled himself into the saddle, peering at Strang's face. "You ain't gonna let 'em do nothing to me, are you, Mister Strang? I worked hard for you. Remember?"

"You'll have a trial," Strang said evenly, "and you'll get a chance to say anything you want to. All right, Hanna. Climb up."

They stopped at Mary's place for a horse, put Walton on him, and set a faster pace. Neither Mary nor Nan was in sight. A mile beyond the bridge Strang said: "I'll swing off and pick up the boys. We'll catch up before you get to Sage."

Strang disappeared into the dusk, and presently Dave heard a shot. Another came answering from the lake shore, then a third distant one, and presently Strang, Holland, and a half a dozen other riders swung in behind Dave and Hanna. A ragged cloud slid off the moon, and the pale light was all around them. There was no talk as they rode, no sound but the beat of hoofs in the soft soil, the occasional squeak of saddle leather, the clink of bits of metal. Now and then someone fired a match, the flame flaring up to light the man's face. They all looked the same, stern and grim and a little sick.

A mile from town they met another band of

horsemen, Bob Joslyn leading. They swung off the road, Joslyn calling: "Get him?"

Strang said: "Dave pulled him out of the tules."

"Good boy," Joslyn said in a hard, biting voice that seemed strange coming from him. "Take him in back of the blacksmith shop. There's no tree in Sage big enough to hang a man from, so we put some wagon tongues up before we left."

Dave and Hanna went on with Walton, and as they passed Joslyn's party, Dave peered at them, recognizing all but two. Markham, Hambone, George McNair with his arm in a sling, and the three Cotter boys. The Cotters, Dave judged, were on their way south with loads of lumber. The two men Dave did not know were at the end of the line, strangers, Dave guessed, who had stopped at Sage on their way through the country.

It was nearing midnight when they came into Sage and turned between the Gold Bar saloon and the blacksmith shop to the cluster of wagons. There was no livery stable in town, so McNair had built a feed corral and made a business of taking care of the animals that belonged to the few outfits that came through the country.

The rest of the party had dismounted and tied in the street. Now they crowded through the opening between the buildings, lighted lanterns swinging in their hands. Strang and Joslyn were in front, Joslyn saying in his strange biting tone: "We have no jail and they wouldn't believe us if we took him to the county seat. We have the job to do, so why wait for the farce of a trial?"

It was Lacey Markham who usually did the talking; it was Lacey Markham who fancied himself the leader of the settlers, yet now at a time like this it was Bob Joslyn who was accepted as the leader. As they came on to where Dave and Hanna waited with Walton, Dave saw that Markham loitered behind the others, his thin face looking as if he were jaundiced. Then he came on, slowly, as if his legs were uncertain. It was Hambone who remained in the shadows.

There were almost twenty men who formed the circle around Walton. He sat his saddle like a half-filled sack of grain, head dropped forward so that his beard fanned out upon his chest. Ahead of him the tongues of three wagons slanted upward to form a tripod. A rope dangled from the center.

Strang stepped toward Walton, stared at him for a moment, then swung to face Markham and the Cotters. He said: "This is a new country without regular officers to enforce the law, so we must do our own enforcing. What is done here tonight will never be forgotten in this valley. Bob Joslyn says we should do it without the farce of a trial. I say this trial will not be a farce and even Rabbit Walton deserves the right to state his defense."

They shifted uncertainly. It was Lacey Markham who said at last: "That's right, Strang."

One of the strangers walked across the circle

until he faced Strang. He said: "I rode into town this afternoon and asked for work. They told me I'd find work on S Star. I aimed to go out there in the morning. Then I heard about this Walton and was told there'd be a hanging. Now I aim to find out one thing. Are you damned sure this is the man, or is it your way of getting rid of somebody?"

"This is the man," Strang said.

"I know what he did in the Willamette Valley," Joslyn broke in. "If they had him over there tonight, there'd be a hanging. I was the fool because I took his part, not knowing what he was and believing his stories of being abused. After he left just one jump ahead of a posse, they took it out on me because I'd given him credit. I'm not sorry I did. I kept his family from starving, and when the judgment day comes, I believe I'll have a star in my crown for doing it." Joslyn made a wild sweeping gesture with his hand. "The other day Dave asked why we were here. Walton's the reason I came to Sage Valley. He's the reason I lost a store and a good living in a settled part of the state where my daughter could have had an education. He's the reason we almost lost our hair to the Paiutes. I settled in the most primitive part of the country to get away from Rabbit Walton and away from anybody who knew him." Joslyn choked. He bowed his head, fighting his rage before he could say: "Now he's followed me.

Somehow he heard I was here and he's followed. I should have killed him the minute he rode into town."

There was a silence for a time. Joslyn stood with bowed head, his body trembling, a gentle man who had bared his soul and showed the violence that was hidden there. Then Strang said: "We're hanging him for what he's done here today, not for what he done in the Willamette Valley and not because of anything personal you've got against him."

Joslyn raised his head to stare defiantly at Strang. "I'm not asking that you hang him because of anything he's done to me. I'm telling you what he was. What he's done before, he'll do again. I say hang him and get it done with."

"No," Strang said. "You men will be the jury. Do you want someone to act as a lawyer for you, Walton?"

"It's no use!" Walton cried passionately. "You're bound to hang me, but you'll never forget me, Strang. None of you will. As long as you live, you'll remember me and you'll remember you hanged me. Not on account of what I done. It's 'cause you ain't got a jail to put me in. Go ahead. Hell won't be no worse than living with your kind. Maybe down there I won't be chased and kicked around and driven from one place to another. Maybe I won't have to be riding a damn' mule."

It was not what they expected to hear from Walton. Again there was a period of silence, no sound at all except the breathing of the men, the stomping of horses in the street. A man coughed, a brittle break in the stillness.

Strang turned his back to Walton. He said: "Dave, tell what you know about this man."

Dave had never seen a hanging, but he had seen the marks on Mary Romney's face and neck; he had come close to losing his own life to Walton when he had brought him out of the tules. That may have been the reason he was able to talk coolly when he told what he knew about Walton from the time he had seen him in Joslyn's store until he knocked him cold with his gun barrel at the edge of the marsh.

"Tell your spiel, Hanna," Strang ordered, and when Hanna finished, Strang told what Nan had said about Walton's action when he had crossed the bridge the first morning he had come to the valley. He asked then: "Anybody else got anything to say?"

"I have," Joslyn said in his hard, biting voice, "but I won't say it. They've heard enough."

"Walton, you admit all this?" Strang asked.

"Sure I done it, but it ain't nothing that deserves a hanging." Walton held out his hands. "I worked hard for you, Mister Strang. Awful hard. If you hang me, I'll haunt you till you're crazy. Nothing to hang a man for, I tell you."

Again Strang turned his back to Walton. "Those of you who say he's guilty and has got to be hanged, step up one pace."

They moved forward at once, all of them in the circle from Joslyn on around to dark-skinned Pablo Gonzales, dour, harsh-faced men who, by taking that one step, recognized the inexorable demands of the frontier, hating this thing yet accepting their part of the responsibility.

Strang swung back to Walton. "Do you want to pray?"

"Why should I pray?" Walton shouted. "You think I'd pray for you? I'll be in hell before you will. I never lived like a man, but I'll die like one. You'll see."

"Don't hang him." It was the saloon man shoving between Joslyn and Markham. He had been the only one failing to vote for Walton's hanging. Now he reeled like a drunk, and he would have jammed against McNair's broken arm if the blacksmith had not jumped back. "Don't hang him. Whatever he did was my fault. Hang me, but let this fool go. He's just a saddle bum."

"Let him go so he can do something worse on another range?" Strang shook his head. "Where'd you come from that you'd let a man like this go?"

Hambone faced Strang, hatless, his oiled hair rumpled, soft body shaking. "All right," he breathed. "All right, but I say I'm to blame. If you've got to hang him, hang me beside him."

Joslyn had his arm then. "Come away. No sense blaming yourself."

Hambone jerked free. "Hang me, Strang. Damn you to hell, hang me. You broke McNair's arm. You want us all to bow and scrape like you and that Romney woman was something holy. You ain't. Neither one of you. I ain't ashamed of what I said to Walton. I just didn't know what he was."

Strang grabbed a fistful of his shirt and shook him. "You told him what?"

"Don't, Strang." Joslyn was there, clutching Strang's arm and shaking it to get his attention. "Forget what he said. He's out of his head."

Something burned through Dave Logan's mind as he saw Strang's square face darken, saw fear in Joslyn as he tried to shake the big arm. It was the memory of Tildie Fields's words: *Shame is like a cancer that gnaws at your vitals. It's the kind of shame that's in Lacey and Hambone and Bob Joslyn. It will go on and on until they can't sleep and they can't breathe.*

Markham and McNair were there, trying to crowd in between Strang and Hambone. Clab Holland and the S Star riders were moving up from the other side. The strangers and the Cotters watched, frightened and not understanding.

Walton shouted: "Sure it was his fault. He told me about her. Hang him, Strang. Hang him and let me go."

Strang struck the saloon man with a back-handed sweep of his hand. He said thickly: "Get out. Hanna, put the rope on Walton."

Holland and Abe Cotter stepped up, Cotter saying: "I'll tie his hands."

Hanna said: "Stand up on the saddle, Walton."

Then, with his last blue chip down, Rabbit Walton forgot his resolve to die like a man. He fell out of the saddle and began to scream, begging for his life, twisting and babbling as he struggled in Cotter's grip.

"Shut up!" Hanna shouted.

But there was no shutting Walton's mouth. He kept on babbling while Cotter tied his hands. They got him back into the saddle. Hanna mounted and rode in on one side, Dave on the other, and while Dave held him upright, Hanna fitted the loop around his neck. Abe Cotter tied his ankles and stepped away. Dave let go and dropped back into saddle. Walton slumped, the rope tightening around his neck. He straightened at once, his belly contracting and pushing a scream out of him that ran in trembling echoes across the flat. Then it died, and there was silence except for Walton's panted breathing.

Strang asked: "Want anybody to pray for you?"

For a moment Walton seemed past the point where he could talk. His mouth sagged open, his tongue filling it. Then he cried out: "You're the one that's doing this, Strang! Joslyn ain't mean

208

enough. Hanging me ain't gonna make nothing better out of your woman . . ."

"All right," Strang said.

Clab Holland had been holding Walton's horse. He stepped back, the men in front scattered, and Strang laid his quirt against the horse's back. The animal jumped out, leaving Walton dangling, killed, Dave thought, by the fall. For a moment the men stood watching the body turn and sway like a great ghastly pendulum. Markham lurched away, emptying his stomach.

Strang said: "Cut him down before your womenfolks and the kids see it, Joslyn."

Joslyn said tonelessly: "We'll attend to it."

They turned toward the street, lanterns throwing weird, shifting shadows along the ground and against the sides of the buildings, boots stirring the dust. They crowded between the saloon and the blacksmith shop, and as Strang and Joslyn reached the street, a gunshot slammed out into the night, cannon-loud in the tense silence.

"The Gold Bar!" Joslyn shouted, and lunged toward the saloon, Strang and the rest crowding behind.

Dave, still on his horse, had waited with Hanna for the others to get into the street. It took a moment for the opening between the buildings to clear so that he could get through. He swung down, leaving the reins dangling, and shoved into the saloon and through the tight circle. Hambone lay on the floor between the bar and a poker table, a bullet hole in his forehead. The gun lay a few inches from his outflung hand.

"What'd he do that for?" Strang demanded of nobody in particular.

"I can tell you," George McNair said. "I'll be glad to tell you, Strang. He figgered it was better to shoot himself than wait for you to break his neck. Remember the promise you made?"

Without a word Strang wheeled, jerking his head at Holland, and left the saloon, the building trembling under the weight of his stomping feet. He mounted and rode out of town, Holland beside him, Dave and the other S Star riders strung out behind.

Later, after they had crossed the bridge over Sage River and turned southward toward the lakes, Strang said: "Dave, come here."

Dave touched his buckskin to move forward and Holland dropped behind. Strang said nothing for a time. The moon was in the clear now, and by its thin light Dave could see that Strang's face held a bleak tightness around the mouth and eyes that was not like him. "I don't savvy," Strang said at last. "Not about that fellow. He blowed his brains out before I ever had a chance to find out what he'd told Walton."

"I don't know what he told Walton," Dave said, "but he was the one who knew Mary had sung in saloons in mining camps and he told the others.

I guess that's how the talk got started in the first place."

"Hell," Strang said savagely, "there's nothing wrong with singing in saloons. I'm gonna marry her and I'm damned lucky to get her."

"You're not like these people," Dave said. "They figger a woman who would sing in a saloon would do anything, so she's a bad woman and they'd lose their souls if they had anything to do with her."

"I should have run every damned one of 'em out of the valley," Strang said passionately. "Every damned one."

Then he was silent for a long time. A cloud slipped over the moon and shadow ran across the grass. It had rained somewhere on the desert, and the wind was cool and damp and weighted with sage smell.

"I guess," Strang said at last, "it was a good thing that fool put a bullet in his head."

Strang said nothing more until they reached the Channel. Dave opened the tollgate, and Strang rode through and reined to a stop on the south side of the bridge. When the others were over, Strang said: "Won't be long till sunup, Clab. You and Pablo and Dave get a little sleep. Then light out for Winnemucca. Close everything out down there."

Holland and the others rode on, but Dave waited. Strang said impatiently: "I'm staying the rest of the night here. You want something?"

"I'll be gone a long time. My folks ain't got no money but that gold piece you gave us. I don't reckon . . ."

"Here." Strang handed Dave two gold eagles. "I'll see that Joslyn sends out some grub. Your ma don't need to know who's paying for what Joslyn fetches her."

"I'm paying for it," Dave said sharply.

A long sighing breath ran out of Strang's great chest. He rubbed his face. "We're all paying, Dave. You and me and Mary and Nan. The devil's got my tail in a crack, and I don't know how in hell I'm gonna get it out. Nan needs you and that means I need you."

"Tell her good bye for me," Dave said.

"I'll tell her."

Dave rode on, thinking of the rest of Tildie Fields's words: *Perhaps they'll go away and forget it. If they don't, they'll stay here and shoot themselves. Or shoot Strang.*

But Hambone had lacked the courage to shoot Strang. He had only the courage to shoot himself. As long as Lacey Markham and Bob Joslyn lived, they would not forget the sight of George McNair standing with his broken arm dangling at his side. They would not forget Rabbit Walton's body, swinging like a giant pendulum. Walton had been right when he'd said it was Strang and not Joslyn who was doing the hanging. And they would not forget Hambone, lying on the saloon floor, one hand flung out toward his gun. For the first time since he had signed on with Matt Strang, Dave realized he had been wrong in his judgment of the man. He had thought of him as power, as one who decided destiny. But Matt Strang's strength was his weakness. Lacey Markham might outlast him, for Strang had no talent for making his enemies love him, and in hate there was the seed of self-destruction. Then Dave thought of Strang's words: *The devil's got my tail in a crack, and I don't know how in hell I'm going to get it out.*

XIII

The first skim of ice had appeared around the edge of the lakes and in the quiet pools of the streams when Clab Holland and his trail crew brought Matt Strang's second herd north and choused it through Logan Pocket and over the rim. Wagons with supplies, furniture, and grain had gone on ahead, so Strang would know the cattle were not far behind. But Strang had not come to meet them. Too busy, Holland said.

Holland had been riding point. When the herd was lined out across Logan Pocket and up the trail to the rim, he rode back to Dave who was on the drag. He said: "Looks like your folks ain't living here now."

Dave nodded, staring at the few scraggly cornstalks, the beaten-down patch of rye, and on to the cabin with the door swinging open. "Gone to town, likely." He glanced up at the wedge of ducks flying south. "Winter ain't far off. I'm glad they've moved into town."

Holland said: "I'll tell Matt you've stopped here if you want to take a look around."

"Thanks, Clab," Dave said. "I'd like to."

Dave reined over to the corn patch and swung down. He dragged the toe of a boot across the hard soil. Probably it had not been watered since he had left. Maybe now his mother knew this was not farm country. He shook his head. No, she probably wasn't convinced. Nothing could convince her. He remembered the look on her bony face when he'd stopped on his way south and told her he was sticking with Strang.

Dave had said: "Bob's going to fetch some things out from town." He laid the two gold eagles Strang had given him on the table. "I've made arrangements about paying for the stuff. You keep this."

There had been no approval in his mother's face. "I don't believe Strang's fool enough to pay you that kind of money for less than two weeks' work. Where did you get it?"

"Strang let me have it. I'll earn more'n that before I get back."

He had looked at his father who lay very still on the bed, his eyes closed. He would never get up. Dave had known that, and for a moment he had doubted his decision. Then the doubts had fled. He should be here when his father died, but the old man might live for months, and, before winter was over, his mother would need all Dave could earn.

His mother had gone to the stove and stirred the pot of lambs' quarter greens. They would make their whole meal off the greens just as he had done with them many times. He said: "I'll be working for Strang all winter. I'll see you get more to eat than we've had the last few years."

"We've made out," she said dully. "The Lord has given us food just as He gave manna to the children of Israel. It was honest food, Dave, earned honestly and not by working for a man who would destroy your people." She had put the lid back on the pan and turned to face him. Woman-like, she had wanted to cry, but the fountain of her tears had dried up long ago. "Next week you'll be twenty-one. After that I have no authority over you. I . . . I have no authority now, it seems. If I had, you wouldn't be working for Strang. I've tried to raise you as a moral, God-fearing boy. You were until you took up with the Romney woman and her girl. Now it's Strang.

You'll never be the same after you go on this trip. You'll just be another cowboy, drinking and gambling and throwing your money away on floozies. Go on, Dave. I can't stop you, but I'll pray for you. Remember that. I'll pray for you, and someday I'll plead at the throne of eternal grace for your soul."

He had kissed her cheek, awkwardly, not knowing why except that he might never come back, or, if he did, she might be dead. Her skin had been sere under his lips, crepe-like, and he had the feeling that she was dying outside, and, like his father, was waiting to die inside. Then he had walked out, mounted, and caught up with Clab Holland and Pablo within the hour.

The hopeless battle of wringing a living from this reluctant soil had finally been lost just as he had always known it would be. He walked toward the cabin, depressed by the emptiness of a place that had been his home. He went inside and at once wished he hadn't. There was dust everywhere. The furniture was gone—just four walls and a door sagging open and two dirty windows, that and the dust.

Quickly he swung around and left the cabin. He shut the door, propping it with a stick, and crossed the hard-packed earth of the yard to his horse. This was where his mother had thrown countless buckets and pans of dishwater and wash water. There was the chip pile where he had cut wood, in both heat and cold, dry weather and wet. There was the clothesline, the one thing his mother had left.

Dave would have mounted if he had not heard a horse. Stepping away from his buckskin, he laid a hand on his gun butt, a habit that these last weeks had firmly entrenched in him. Then his hand dropped away, and something sang inside him. It was Nan on a brown gelding, riding easily and gracefully, and when she saw that he had seen her, she waved to him.

He ran toward her, awkwardly in his tall heels, and a moment later she reined up and fell out of her saddle into his arms, laughing a little and crying a little and wildly hungry for his kiss. He held her in his arms, swinging her off her feet, and for a time they were in their own world, a crazy and delirious world that blotted reality from their minds.

"Oh Dave, Dave," she said, pulling away from him and looking into his face. "I thought you'd never get back."

She was wearing a man's flannel shirt and a brown riding skirt, and a gray Stetson dangled from her neck by its chin strap. He had never seen her wear clothes like these before, nor had he seen her hair, thicker and darker than he had remembered it, pinned as it was now in a coronet on her head. "You're pretty," he said. "I'd forgotten how pretty you were."

She laughed, pushing away from him. "You've got dust in your eyes from the drive."

He took her hand and they walked down to the creek. He said: "Seemed like a long time getting back, but we came as fast as the cows would go."

He was silent then, for she was looking at him with probing intentness. Frowning, she said, "You've changed, Dave."

"I just need a shave and some clean clothes. It's a long ways from Winnemucca and I ate a lot of dust. Then on this side of Denio we had a rain that was a wowser. We had gumbo running out of our ears."

She laughed, and sobered immediately. "I don't mean that. You're bigger and maybe kind of . . . hard. No, that isn't it. You just look different. What did you see, Dave? Is Winnemucca much of a town?"

"Quite a burg," he said.

They sat down beside the creek, and he idly tossed a rock into a pool and watched the dark, darting shadows of the trout as they flashed downstream. He couldn't tell her. Not really tell her so she would know what he had seen and what he had felt. He was different. A trail drive would make any man different. It was a life in itself and he lived a lifetime in the weeks since he had left Logan Pocket.

He had seen new country, some of it good

and much of it bad. He had seen Winnemucca, popping at the seams, wild enough, as even Clab Holland had admitted. But how could he tell her what he had seen and what he had felt? The saloons, the gambling layouts, the girls tinseled like Christmas trees, girls who were easy with their hands and made Dixie Joslyn seem as retiring as an old-maid schoolteacher. How could he describe his feelings when he'd stood at the ornate bar in the Hoof and Horn Saloon, nothing like the rough pine bar in Sage, and downed a drink with Holland and Pablo? Or when he'd watched Holland lose $200 to a slim-fingered gambler, and Holland had caught him with an extra ace and beaten him to the draw? Or how Pablo, a little drunk perhaps, had got into a fight with a Nevada cowhand over a red-headed girl and slit his throat from ear to ear? Or how could he tell her about eating the dust of the drag day after day, beating the laggards along, living in the saddle, taking the edge off a strange horse, feeling the cut of a knifing wind, or on another day the hammering heat of the sun? Of getting half the sleep he needed, of eating sand in his grub, of hearing the *vaqueros'* soft-toned Spanish songs, of riding night herd while lightning fired the sky and thunder boomed like great boulders rolling off the rim, and all the time the fear that the restless cattle would bolt lay in his stomach like an undigested flat iron? Of the rain that knotted men's tempers and turned the trail into a gumbo sea so that every mile of travel seemed like a hundred?

No, he couldn't tell her about those things, but they were a part of him, and Dave Logan would never be the same Dave Logan who had gone south weeks before, riding between Clab Holland and Pablo Gonzales. It was as if some miracle of chemistry had poured new elements into his soul and fused the old and the new together, and he was not yet familiar with the combined product. Because he was puzzled about himself, her probing eyes embarrassed him and he got up. "Clab made me practice with my gun," he said like a small boy showing off before his girl. "He says I'm pretty good."

"Let me see," she said.

He motioned to a tin can upstream, and when she nodded, he pulled his gun and fired, his shot kicking the can into the air. He emptied the .44, keeping the can bouncing until he'd shaken out the last bullet. Then he dropped down beside her, pleased by the admiration that was honestly given. "Of course, shooting at a man is different than shooting at a tin can," he said.

"You aren't going to start shooting at men, are you?" she asked incredulously.

"Hope not, but Clab expects trouble. He thinks Matt should have run everybody out of the valley but you and Mary and my folks and Bill Hanna.

He said as long as Matt's let a few stay, more will come in and try it."

He was surprised by the way her pleasure went out of her. She cried out: "Are men always looking for trouble, Dave? Are they all like Strang, pushing and crowding and shoving and talking about what they're going to do?"

"There's nobody else like Strang," Dave said quietly.

"I hope not," she breathed.

He took her hand. "How about the house-warming and the double wedding?"

She tried to smile and failed. "There won't be any double wedding. Mother married Matt a week after you left. He's been sleeping at our house. I guess it will be spring before his house is finished."

"What about us?"

"I don't know. I've thought about it ever since they were married. Your father's dead, Dave, and your mother's living in town."

He nodded, showing no expression of surprise. He said: "It's been a long time since he wanted to live."

"We went to the funeral. Mother and Strang and I. They didn't know we were there. And a month before the funeral Mother invited them to the wedding. No one came but Joslyn. Maybe that's the part I'm not sure about. I don't think I could live here a lifetime without having a few friends."

He pulled her around so that she leaned against his chest, her head under his chin. He said: "I'll tell you one thing about Winnemucca. There were girls. Lots of them. Some good, I reckon, who just danced or maybe sang, and a lot of them bad, but I didn't forget I loved you."

"Were they pretty, Dave?"

"None as pretty as you by a long shot."

She laughed. "You learned some blarney on this trip. I know I'm not pretty, but it's wonderful to hear you say I am."

He dug his chin into the top of her head, grinning. Pablo had lectured him all the way to Winnemucca about how to talk to a woman, and, judging by the way he had handled the redhead, Pablo understood the art.

"I'm damned if I know how he does it," Holland had said, "but they'll forget he's a Mex every time. He'll sing 'em a song and tell 'em they've got eyes like the blue in the rainbow and a face that makes the sun hide itself 'cause it's ashamed. Then he just holds out his arms and they'll fall into 'em as sure as hell's hot."

Suddenly Nan turned to look at him. "What are you grinning about?"

"I was just thinking," he said. "About all the times I used to try to talk to you and couldn't."

"It's time you were getting able to talk." She sat up so she could face him. "Dave, Strang and Mother will want us to get married now. Your mother is working for Tildie Fields, so she won't be any responsibility to you. Strang's going to offer you a deal. I've stuck my ear out a few times and listened."

"Why, then we'll have a single wedding."

"No, Dave," she said miserably. "It won't do. But I love you. Don't ever doubt that even when you see the pretty girls in Winnemucca or when that Dixie Joslyn comes around, all smiles with her rope laid out ready to drop it on you."

He scratched a stubbly cheek, puzzled. "I always had a notion that if a couple loved each other and the man could make a living, they got married and had a family and were happy ever afterward." He grinned. "Lacey had some books that told it that way."

"I'd like if it was that way, Dave. I'd like it awfully well." She leaned back on her hands, staring at the creek that twisted like a looping silver ribbon until it disappeared into the gorge that it had cut through the rimrock. "I'd like to live here, Dave. It's beautiful. I hate the valley, but I like it here." Turning, she lay on her stomach, face upturned. "Couldn't we make a living here? You could fix up the cabin. It wouldn't be so bad. Later you could build more rooms on if we needed them."

"That's crazy," he said. "I've tried to raise grain, corn, wheat, and such, but you know how it's been."

"You don't have to raise grain, do you?"

"How else can a man make a living on a quarter-section if he don't farm?"

"Grass grows, doesn't it? There's plenty of summer range in the Steens, isn't there? You can raise enough hay to feed through the winter."

"I reckon, but . . ."

"Look, Dave." She pointed upstream to the spring. "I ride up here a lot because I like it. Strang gave me that gelding. I call him Skeeter. He's the best horse I ever owned, but it's not enough to make me love Strang. Anyhow I come here, maybe, because it was your home. I've been thinking. If you'd throw up a dam and take a ditch out just below the spring, you could irrigate almost all of the Pocket."

He stared at her, surprised. He had thought of the same thing. With a little money and the right kind of stock, a man could make a good living for a family here, but the Logans had had neither money nor the right kind of stock. "You're smart," he said, "except for one thing. Even if you have land given to you, it still takes money to start. Outside of the wages Matt owes me, I ain't got a plugged nickel."

"Let's wait until we have it, Dave. You can save. Maybe I can find some work to do, even if it means I've got to go away."

"But if Matt's got a proposition to offer us . . ."

"No, Dave." She jumped up, suddenly furious.

"I love you. I've told you that, but I don't love you enough to marry you and live on money Strang gives us."

He rose, not understanding her and seeing no reason for the wild fury that had suddenly burned through her. "All right, Nan. We'll wait. Only I was thinking about what your mother said one time. About taking the thing you wanted. She said not to wait."

"I know, Dave," she said softly. "I don't want to, either, but there's one thing I'm sure of. We've got to make whatever we have with our own hands."

They walked back to the horses, Nan beside him with her hand on his arm. He should feel good, he told himself, for there had been no holding back in Nan when she had kissed him. It was all he had hoped for. Still, the warmth that had been in him a few minutes before was gone.

Her feeling about Matt Strang might be right or wrong. That was not something he could or should pass judgment on, but it was wrong, he told himself, to let that feeling come between the two of them. Perhaps that was not the way she intended it, but it was what she had actually done. It would take ten years for a man working for buckaroo's wages to save enough to make a start for himself. At that moment Dave Logan was not of a mind to wait ten years, even for Nan.

XIV

When Dave and Nan reached the valley floor, she said: "The crew eats here at S Star, but Strang always comes to the house for supper. You come over with him, Dave. Mother wants to see you." She blew him a kiss, smiling. "So do I."

Dave turned toward the flat east of Sage Lake where the new herd had been driven. S Star, he saw with surprise, was nearly ready for winter. The big house was up and roofed, a bunkhouse and cook shack stood behind it, and a small barn had been built between the other buildings and the creek. As he passed, he heard the hammers of men working inside the house. It was bigger than Mary's house, Dave saw, and he thought with some amusement that it was like Strang to build a bigger house than anyone else had, even Mary.

Ditches had been dug, pastures fenced, and between the house and the lake were the haystacks, long rounded mounds disturbing the monotony of the flat. When Dave rode up to Holland and the trail crew, he saw that Strang was with them. Strang reined his big black around and held out his hand.

"Clab said he spotted Nan on the rim, so he left you to catch up on your sparking," Strang said. "How are you, boy?"

"I'm fine, Matt." Dave gripped Strang's hand and dropped it, eyes swinging to Holland. "Why'n hell didn't you tell me you saw Nan? I thought you told me to take a look around because . . . well, because I'd lived there."

Holland winked at Strang. "I figgered she'd like to surprise him. Now he's plumb graveled about it. That's gratitude for you, and me not even hanging around to watch him kiss her."

"Let it go," Dave said stiffly.

Strang studied him, craggy face very grave. He said: "Don't look like trail grub hurt you none." He turned back to Holland. "If we have an open winter, we'll make out slick as goose grease. Another year I'll have ten times as much hay."

"Going down we met up with a gent named Hartzel," Holland said. "He was fetching a herd up to a place east of the Steens that he'd spotted last year. He allowed we were crazy when I said we was putting up some hay. Said there never was enough snow here to cover the grass."

Strang shrugged. "We'll see who's ahead in another ten years, me or Speck Hartzel."

"You know him?" Holland asked.

"He rode up to see what was doing," Strang said. "Likewise a couple more outfits moved in west of the Steens, Rafter L belonging to a gent named Jim Lundy and Hat belonging to Ben Kane." Strang shook his head. "Funny thing. One fellow hears about something good and everybody else gets word at the same time."

"Maybe it's a good thing to have some neighbors," Dave said, "if they've got cattle."

"Some ways," Strang agreed. "Well, you brought 'em through in good shape, Clab. Ain't gaunted up like I figgered they'd be. Now I've got to get over to the house for supper." He jerked his head at Dave. "Coming?"

"Nan said something about it, but I don't know . . ."

"Come on," Strang said impatiently. "I'll be back after supper, Clab. I want to talk to the boys you brung up the trail. I'll keep 'em on if they want to work."

Strang wheeled his black and headed away. Dave reined in beside him, saying: "You've done a lot of work, Matt."

Strang rubbed his forehead, looking out across the flat to the lake. "And a lot more to do. Work for the next ten years. I ought to be twenty men, Dave. I've looked the valley over and I know how it's got to be done. Too big for one ranch. I figger to lay out several, this one to be the home ranch. Number two will be around on the other side of the lake where Sage River comes in. Lot of good hay land there."

Dave nodded and waited for Strang to go on.

"I figgered to drain some of the tule land and burn the tules off. Trouble is I can't be everywhere. I need more men. Some drifted in from Cañon City. Next year there'll be more." He rubbed his forehead as if to relieve the pressure there. "This is one time a man's got everything he could dream of, but getting it all done takes so damned long, and I ain't one to wait." Strang lifted a cigar from his pocket and fired it. "See any girls in Winnemucca you liked?"

Dave shook his head. "I haven't changed my mind about Nan if that's what you mean."

Strang looked at Dave, and Dave sensed what was coming. Anger flared in him when he thought of Nan. Any sane man would grab the chance of landing a permanent job with Strang, but he would have no choice. Not if the job depended on him marrying Nan.

"I figgered you wouldn't change your mind," Strang said. "You ain't built that way. Now a man don't learn the cattle business overnight, so I aim to give you a chance to learn it right. I've got Cotter's sawmill cutting all the lumber it can and my men are doing the hauling now. Figgered I'd build a small house where I want my number two outfit. Fact is, I've got it started. You and Nan can get married and move into it in about a month. I thought I'd have Pablo stay with you. He knows cows, Pablo does. I'll pay you enough to support Nan. Soon as my house is finished and we get our furniture fixed around, there'll be some extra you and Nan can use." Strang chewed on his cigar, glancing at Dave again. "I told you once

I was going a long ways and if you was smart, you'd go along. Well, here it is, handed to you on a silver platter. Soon as you're ready, you'll be running my number two ranch. Might even be a partnership in it for you someday." Strang pulled on his cigar, covertly watching Dave who was staring ahead at Mary's house. Strang asked: "What do you say, lad?"

Without looking at him, Dave said: "I'd give my right arm if I could take it, Matt, but I can't."

"Why not?"

"That job depends on Nan going with me, and she won't go. She says we'll wait until we've got something saved. Then we'll start on our own."

It may have been what Strang expected. Dave never knew, for Strang kept his face clear of expression. He said: "Maybe she'll change her mind."

But Nan would not change her mind. Dave was sure of that, and he was equally sure that there was nothing Matt Strang could do that would make her change her mind. It was Nan's will against Strang's, rapier against cutlass. For the first time in his life Strang had found a problem he could not settle with fist or gun.

Mary met them at the door. She kissed Strang, and then she kissed Dave, laughing as she said: "I should welcome my prospective son-in-law home, shouldn't I?"

230

Red-faced, Dave mumbled—"Sure."—and followed Mary and Matt in.

"You don't need to get bashful just because your mother-in-law kissed you." Strang winked at Mary. "How is it when Nan kisses you?"

Nan came out of the kitchen in time to hear what Strang said. She crossed the room to Dave, saying: "Let's show him how it is."

She moved with the same grace that was always in her mother and, boldly putting her arms around him, kissed him. Again he felt the hunger that was in her, the urgency as if she had been starved for his love, but still, now that she had him back, he was not quite enough.

"Better let him take a breath," Mary said, as if amused.

Nan let him go, holding her head back to look at him, then turned. "You see? It just takes the right woman." She walked back to the kitchen, hips swinging as if suddenly conscious of her power to stir him.

Nan had changed from her riding clothes into a freshly starched dress that rustled as she walked, white with red dots. A new dress, Dave thought, with a skirt that made a snug fit around her hips. She had worn it for him, and he liked that, but he didn't like her kissing him in front of Mary and Matt just to show off.

Dave saw Mary glance at Matt, saw that she was troubled. She said—"I'll help finish supper."—and turned into the kitchen.

Strang cleared his throat. He laid his Stetson on the table and fumbled among some papers until he found the one he wanted. He handed it to Dave, saying: "Your friend Markham is spoiling for a fight."

It was the Sage Valley *Sun* with heavy black type across the top that announced: *THIS IS NOT A MONOPOLIST NEWSPAPER.* Below it, set in a box, was the paragraph: *The* Sun *wishes to make its policy known in its first issue, and by making its policy known it will shout a clarion call for justice. It believes in the small people, the farmers whose hands are bent to the plow handle, women whose hearts hold the courage it takes to follow their men across the continent to the frontier. It believes that men who make their living from the soil have a right to own that soil, and it believes that only disaster can come to a nation that allows a privileged class to buy thousands of acres under the robbers' act, thereby depriving worthy men of a chance to inherit their part of the nation's wealth. For that reason the* Sun *will fight this evil power of monopoly until it is destroyed. Next year the reservation lands will be open, but it is safe to prophesy that there will be more people than available blocks of land. Some will come to Sage Valley demanding their rights. What will you do then, Matthew Strang?*

Dave dropped the paper on the table. "He told me he aimed to start a paper."

"I'll kill the son-of-a- . . ."

"Supper!" Mary called. "Wash up."

"He won't put on a gun to fight you," Dave said as they walked through the kitchen to the back porch. "If you kill him, it will be murder. How does that jibe with your notions of law and order?"

Matt soused his face, rubbing briskly and threw the water over the porch railing. He dried and combed his hair, saying: "It don't. I didn't mean it, but it's a hell of a system that lets a man do what he's doing and keeps me from shutting him up."

Dave washed and dried. Then he said gravely: "I think Lacey figgers you'll kill him. He said his death would call attention to what is happening here."

"Yeah, it sure as hell would," Strang muttered. "We'd have special agents out here asking why sagebrush grew on swamp land."

Dave grinned. "You'd have a tough time telling 'em, Matt."

Nan called: "Come on! Everything's getting cold."

They went into the kitchen, Strang saying: "The man ain't just a fool who knows pretty words. He's an anarchist. There's money circulating in this valley for the first time. There's work to be done. Wages to be earned. Who done it? Me, that's who, but you think that slick-tongued yahoo gives me any credit? Not by a damned sight. I'm the monopolist. I keep worthy men from inheriting their share of the nation's wealth. Hell's bells, if that ain't hogwash, I never heard any."

They sat down, Mary passing the platter of meat to Matt. "It's wonderful to have you back, Dave," Mary said. "Your mother is working for Tildie Fields, and a hotel is not a home." She handed the plate of biscuits to Strang. "So consider this your home until you and Nan have your own."

Dave took the biscuit plate from Strang, helped himself, and passed the plate to Mary, looking down at the table because he did not want Mary to see the emotion her words aroused in him. He had never admitted it to himself, but actually it had been a long time since there had been any real understanding between him and his mother. Without knowing it, Mary Romney— Mary Romney Strang now—had taken the place in his heart that his mother should have held. "Thanks," Dave said, still looking at the table. "Sure is good to be here. Kind of funny, having a roof over my head again and putting my feet under a table."

"Felt the same way myself," Strang said, "when I ate here the first time."

Nan's plate was empty. She sat with her hands

folded on the table, looking squarely at Strang. Now she said: "I think Mister Markham is right."

"Nan." A fork dropped from Mary's hand and clattered to the floor. "You have no right to say that."

"I have a right to think it, anyhow," Nan said, "but I guess I didn't have the right to say it. Consider it unsaid, Mister Strang. It was just what I thought."

"I ain't surprised." Strang's face betrayed nothing as he reached for the syrup pitcher. "Dave, you'll want to see your mother tomorrow. Drop in on Markham and talk to him."

Dave nodded, and they went on with the meal, but the good feeling that had been with them a moment before was gone. Nan filled her plate, smiling often at Dave while she ate. He thought: *She doesn't know what she's doing.* But he knew she did.

XV

Dave rode to town next morning. He had gone back to the bunkhouse to sleep and had eaten breakfast with the crew. Now, as he passed Mary's house, he looked for her and Nan, but he saw no indication of life about the place. Nan's gelding was in the corral, and, as Dave went by, Skeeter lifted his head and whinnied.

Dave crossed the bridge, the buckskin's hoofs cracking pistol-sharp on the planks. The tollgate, he saw, had been taken down, but once he was beyond the bridge, it was more like returning home than coming back to Logan Pocket had been. Snowy egrets, avocets, rails, and snipes—all were familiar birds to him. As he came into the higher grass flat north of the lakes, a band of antelope flashed across the road ahead of him. The grass had been untouched by cattle and was belly-high on a horse. Here were the upland birds, quail and sage hens and owls. It was exactly as he remembered the valley the first time he had seen it when his father, ailing even then, had driven a wagon south from Joslyn's store, Mrs. Logan on the seat beside him. Dave had been following on a gray mare, amazed by everything he saw and already dreaming dreams of the day he would own the valley. No, there had been no change here, but there would be. Strang would have a ranch somewhere north of West Lake, there would be fences and haystacks and grazing cattle. It was the way it should be, still the thought brought regret.

He turned across the bridge spanning Sage River, heard the rattle of chain harness, and saw dust raising from the road just west of town. Presently he passed three heavy loads of lumber, shouted a greeting to the men, and rode on. They were all settlers he knew, content to work for

Matt Strang, and Dave wondered if Markham would be able to stir them into quitting.

Dave came into Sage, change striking him like a blow in the face. The town was twice the size it had been the last time he had seen it. There was a barbershop between McNair's house and the hotel, a livery stable across the street from it beside McNair's blacksmith shop. A new cabin had been built beside the church house, and when he rode on down the street, he saw that there was a bank across from Joslyn's house. Beyond the bank were two more buildings, one marked *Al Dillon, Attorney-At-Law*, the other *B.J. Whitley, M.D.*

Dave swung back to the hotel and racked his horse. The night crispness had gone from the air, and now, near noon, there was a pleasant lazy warmth about the day. Dave saw that his mother was in a rocking chair on the porch, and when he called—"Howdy, Ma!"—she waved to him, a listless motion that surprised him, for she had always been a vigorous woman.

"How are you, Dave?" She rose when he came up and kissed him, and dropping back into her chair, began to rock again.

He sat down on the porch and, leaning against a post, took off his Stetson. "Everything's changing, Ma. Sage'll be quite a burg."

"I suppose it will." She kept looking at him as if trying to fill her mind with the picture of him, his long-boned body, his wiry sandy hair, his sun-and-wind darkened face with the wide chin and gray eyes. "You've changed, too, Dave. Maybe it's just being gone for a while." She glanced at the gun on his hip. "Or maybe it's because I'm seeing you as the man you've become instead of the man I've tried to make out of you."

He looked at her more closely then, observing how much she had aged since he had seen her. Again he had the feeling that she had died on the outside and was merely waiting for time to bring death to the rest of her. "Winnemucca's quite a town," Dave said finally. "I guess Sage will be like it if we ever get a railroad."

Again there was silence except for the creak of her rocker. Suddenly she got up. "I'll get your dinner, Dave. Tildie's ailing today." She went inside, leaving the chair rocking.

Dave ate alone, his mother fussing between the stove and the table until he was done. Then she went into her room and returned with a small canvas bag.

"I'm ready to die, Dave." She placed the bag in front of him. "As long as Pa was alive, or as long as I had to live to prove up on the place, I had something to live for. Well, Pa's gone and Strang's given me the deed to Logan Pocket. You've got a job and you'll never come back home." She cleared her throat. "When are you marrying the Romney girl?"

"I don't know."

"They came to Pa's funeral." The old bitterness was in her voice again. "Strang and Mary Romney and the girl. They told me they was sorry. Maybe they was. It ain't for me to judge, but I had a notion they just came out of curiosity."

"You're wrong," Dave said quietly.

"Maybe." She sat down across the table from him. "But I'm not wrong about the evil that's in them. Mary Romney wanted everybody to come to her wedding. Preacher Naylor lives here now and we have preaching every Sunday. Well, Tildie says everybody told him not to marry 'em, that a wedding wouldn't undo all the sin that's gone on before, but he's mighty stubborn, Naylor is. He just went ahead and tied the knot. Nobody much went. She should have known."

"I never liked Naylor much," Dave said. "I reckon I do now."

She looked at him sharply and he saw that his father's death had not softened her, but she must have decided that argument would gain nothing, so she said no more about the preacher. "I told you I was ready to meet my Maker." She touched the bag. "I sold the team and milk cow and Tildie bought our furniture. I never spent the wages you gave me before you left, and I kept the gold Strang gave us that first time he brought his cattle into the Pocket. It's all there, Dave. Over three hundred dollars. It's yours and I'm having the new lawyer deed the place over to you."

Dave rose. "I don't need this money. I'll put it in the bank for you."

"All right," she said wearily. "It will help you get a start after I'm gone. Pa and me always wanted to leave you something. It ain't much, but it's the best we could do."

"It's a fortune, Ma."

"A mighty small one judged some ways. I guess we were failures, but I'd rather be our kind of failures than successes like Matt Strang. It wasn't our fault the panic wiped us out and we wasn't afraid to start again." She rose, hands gripping the edge of the table. "I don't reckon we were really failures, Dave. We worked hard and we was honest. We always knew the difference between right and wrong. That's why Pa wasn't afraid to die and it's why I'm not. I've asked the preacher to talk to you about your soul. I'd like to know you're saved before I die."

Dave dropped the bag into his pocket. "I'll get over to the bank."

"Maybe I won't see you again, Dave." She gripped his arm, the back of her hand as sere and brown as a last year's leaf. "I wasn't going to say this, but you're my flesh and blood. I want you to be happy, but if you marry the Romney girl, I know you won't be. It's just like when her mother married Strang. No one came to the wedding.

The women will never take her in. It will be the same with Nan. Marry Dixie, Dave. She's a fine good girl."

"Don't worry about not seeing me, Ma. If you get to ailing, send somebody after me."

Dave pulled away from her grip and stumbled out, as miserable as when he had lived at home and had heard this same kind of talk day after day. He would have gone his own way even if he had never known Mary and Nan, or if Strang had not come along.

Looking up at the sky, Dave felt the cleanness of it, felt the wind touch his face. He thought of Strang's words: *I ain't sure about this business of being right.* Then he thought of his mother who was always so certain in her judgments. He wondered, a sour smile touching his lips, how soon Preacher Naylor would start working on his soul.

Stepping into the store, Dave shook hands with Joslyn. The old warmth was gone. Just as when he had come that time to buy his clothes. Joslyn was friendly, but still the barrier was there. He asked courteously about Strang and Mary, about the drive, and what was going on in Winnemucca. Still, it wasn't the same, although there was nothing Dave could put his hands on. Joslyn, he thought, was like the man who knew all the words of a song, but he could not find the right tune for them.

Dave turned to go, then remembered the supplies that had been taken to Logan Pocket just after he had gone south. He swung back, asking: "How much do I owe you for the load of grub you took to the folks?"

"Nothing. Strang paid for it." Joslyn came along the counter, letting his face show the intensity of his feelings. "Strang pays for everything now, Dave, or so it seems, but in the end it will be us who do the paying. You'll see."

"I don't savvy."

"Just look around. New bank. A doctor. A lawyer. Livery stable. Preaching every Sunday. Who do you think did all that?"

"They just came in, I reckon."

Joslyn shook his head. "Not by a jugful. Strang fetched them in here. Hired a Prineville man to run his bank. Talked a sawbones and lawyer into coming. Likewise a barber and someone to run a livery stable. He got it all fixed up for Hanna to be deputy. Now he's working on getting this end of the county cut off so it'll be a county by itself."

Dave cuffed back his Stetson, irritation stirring him. "Well, what's wrong with that?"

"Anybody with eyes can see. He's fixing it so we're all beholden to him. Now I'm not fighting him like Lacey is. If I did, he'd start another store and run me out of business, but I say it's a damned poor thing when one man gives the orders and the rest of us jump through the hoop when he whistles."

"I ain't ashamed to jump. Been more happening since Strang got here than in all the years before when you were in the valley."

"That's right," Joslyn admitted, "but I liked it the way it was when the country was open for the small people Markham talks about. George McNair's sold out and he'll be leaving in the spring or sooner. Tildie's going to sell. Maybe that's it. I just liked things the way they were."

Dave nodded, not wanting to quarrel with Joslyn. "How's Dixie?"

"She's not happy," Joslyn said morosely. "Why don't you go over and see her?"

"Reckon I'd better not," Dave said.

"Maybe you're smart at that." Joslyn smiled, a hint of malice on his face. "You know, Dave, Strang's quite a man except when it comes to handling women. He wanted folks to come to his wedding. Nobody did but me and Hanna and his own men."

Suddenly angry, Dave said—"So long."—and left the store. What Joslyn had said was true. Strang possessed no weapon that could bend women to his will.

Troubled and still angry, Dave walked past Joslyn's house, holding his eyes straight ahead and half expecting to hear Dixie call to him. He turned up the path to Markham's cabin, knocked, and stood motionlessly when Markham opened the door and said: "How are you, Dave? Come in."

"No." Dave looked past Markham at the Washington hand press and the cases of type. He said: "I told you that you'd better stick to teaching."

Markham asked soberly: "You mean I'm not a good editor."

"I mean you're a damned careless one," Dave said hotly.

"I take it you read my clarion call."

"Yeah, I read it. Strang didn't like it."

Markham stepped into the sunlight and looked along the street. Watching him, Dave felt the tension that tightened the man's nerves. He was, Dave thought, like a fine spring that had been too tightly wound.

"I didn't think he'd like it, Dave. Take a look at our town. Doubled in size, but it's not a healthy growth. Not the same as if people had come to settle and farm and make their homes." He took a long breath. "Even the air isn't sweet any more. It isn't free. I suppose we'll be paying Strang for it before long."

"Lacey, get hold of yourself." Dave shook his arm. "You're plumb crazy. Keep on writing stuff like you had in your paper and you'll make Strang do something."

"I aim to make him do something. I'll tell you how. They've had a grasshopper plague in

244

Kansas and Nebraska. Before spring I'll see that those farmers know about Sage Valley. They'll know about the reservation land and some will come on across the ridge and see what this valley is like. Then Strang will resort to violence, but I have an answer. More violence. All we need is a man to lead the new settlers." He waved a hand toward the eastern horizon. "You can't see the clouds yet, but they're gathering. The storm is on its way."

Dave stared at the man, not understanding the change that had come to Lacey Markham, for this was not the Markham who had taught him, had read to him, had stayed up half the night talking to him. He said: "Lacey, when you see the first man die, you'll be damned sorry you ever thought gunsmoke would settle anything."

"No. I tell you I'll lick Matt Strang. He doesn't want anything but fifty thousand acres of land. He wants the kind of law that favors him. He wants all of us to look to him for our daily bread. Why? So nobody will go to the Secretary of the Interior with evidence that this valley was placed on the swampland list by false and fraudulent representation. But I'll give them that evidence because Strang can't buy my soul. Tell Strang that."

"I will," Dave said, and wheeled away.

It was dusk when Dave rode back across the bridge spanning the Channel, the air knife-sharp,

There would be a freeze again tonight, Dave thought.

Strang flung the kitchen door open and stood there, square body filling the open. He called: "That you, Dave?"

"Yeah, it's me."

"Mary's waiting supper for you."

Dave loosened the cinch and fed and watered his buckskin. He went around to the back porch and washed. Then Nan was there, waiting for his kiss, and he held her a moment, her slender body trembling in his arms, her lips hungry for his, and, when at last she drew back, she whispered: "I love you so much, Dave. A little more every day."

"Let's not wait. Matt said . . ."

Stiffening, she pushed him away. "I know what he said. It doesn't change anything, Dave. I'm thinking about tomorrow and all the tomorrows after that." She gripped his arm fiercely. "They've got to be ours, Dave. Just ours. Not ours and Matt Strang's."

"Supper's waiting!" Mary called.

They went in, Dave's arm around her. Strang asked at once: "You see Markham?"

"I saw him, but talking to him is like talking against the wind. He's fixing to prove to the Department of the Interior that your dry land was placed on the approval list by false and fraudulent representation."

Strang shrugged. "He won't get far."

"Likewise he says you'll use violence, and his answer is more violence. He says that all the new settlers will need is a man to lead them."

Strang scratched his cheek, gaze swinging to Mary. For a moment there was no sound but the scrape of his fingernail against the stubble. Then he said: "He's finally going to make us trouble as sure as the Lord made little apples."

XVI

Fall was the dying season with the grass turned brown and the birds flying south, so many at times that the earth was shadowed. But it was not a season of idleness, not on Matt Strang's ranch. He worked like a man hard-ridden by the knowledge of his own destiny, like a man whose time is short and he has much to do. There was more juniper posts to haul down from the rim, more lumber from Cotter's mill, finishing work inside the big house. The first coat of red paint was on the outside, the windows in place and the doors hung, and a stove had been set up in the house so the carpenters could work on into the winter. There were willows to cut, for Strang built stockade corrals, claiming they were the strongest that could be made. It was a new kind of corral to Dave. The juniper posts were set close together, willows were interlaced between them and tied into place with leather thongs. A lot of work, it seemed to Dave, but in this, as in all things Strang did, S Star was being built for generations yet unborn.

Strang worked with his men, for he made it a rule never to ask a man to do a job he wouldn't do himself. No one carried a gun, and for weeks nothing was heard of Lacey Markham or his plans. But there was a good deal of practicing around the bunkhouse in the evenings. If Mary heard the shooting and understood, she gave no indication of it. She was content with her bargain.

It turned cold in the middle of December, and a storm that brought a skiff of snow to the valley floor laid a deep blanket in the Blue Mountains. The cattle drifted toward the lake, seeking refuge in the tules and coontails and willows, for the wind blowing off the high desert cut like the slashing tip of a blacksnake. Dave stayed at the bunkhouse and ate with the crew, but Mary always asked him over for Sunday dinners. When it wasn't too cold in the afternoons, he went riding with Nan. If it was cold, they sat in the front room, alone, for Strang and Mary always found something to do in another part of the house.

For the first time since he could remember, Dave had plenty to eat, the kind of clothes he needed for winter, work that he liked, association with men he respected, and love that he talked about to no one but Nan. This love seemed like a delicate wildflower, blooming in the rocky waste of the high desert, unexpected, beyond logical explanation, and altogether delightful. There was another thing, too, something he was ashamed of and tried to kill in his thoughts, and could not. Dixie Joslyn loved him. He knew she would marry him the day he asked her. Then his thoughts would return to Nan, and he could not help wondering whether she really loved him, or whether she was trying to hold him while she searched for the thing her mother found in Strang that had made her so completely happy.

Two weeks before Christmas Mary announced after a Sunday dinner that she wanted to have a big Christmas celebration. "I don't suppose there's a turkey within two hundred miles," she said, "and I know I couldn't find a pumpkin for pies, but I guess we can make out with beef and plum pudding and dried peach pie."

"I guess we could make out," Strang said. "How does it sound, Dave?"

"Fine, if I'm invited." He grinned at Mary. "How about it?"

"Even if I didn't want you, which I do, I'd have to invite you to keep Nan peaceable." Mary cleared her throat, fingers tapping on the table. "I thought we'd ask our new neighbors."

"Sure," Strang said. "They'd come just to look

at a couple of pretty women. Dave can ride down next week and invite 'em."

"We could have Doc Whitley and Al Dillon out from town," Mary went on. "And Bill Hanna, of course. What about your banker, Symonds?"

"He's hiking out to Prineville to fetch his wife back," Strang said.

They were silent then for a moment, but Dave knew what they were thinking. There were other people they would like to ask but Mary could not bring herself to give them the opportunity of ignoring her invitation again.

Then Nan, tight-lipped and a little pale, looked across the table at Strang: "I'd like to go to town and ask Doc Whitley and Dillon."

Surprised, Strang said: "Sure, if the weather ain't too bad for you to ride."

Nan turned to her mother. She said timidly as if she were doubtful of Mary's answer: "I'd like to ask the Joslyns. I think they'll come."

Mary and Strang looked at each other, both too stunned to say anything for a moment. Mary recovered her poise first. She said in her serene way: "Why, certainly, Nan, if you want to."

Dave never knew what was said between Nan and Dixie, but when he returned to S Star, Strang said: "The Joslyns promised Nan they'd come." His lips tightened. "But if they hurt Mary again, I'll put a rope on Joslyn's neck and drag him." He scratched his cheek, glaring at Dave. "Damn it, what kind of people are they, sticking their noses so almighty high? If anybody ought to do any snubbing, it's Mary, not them."

It was warmer Christmas morning. Kane, Lundy, and Hartzel had ridden in the night before, and Joslyn, Dixie, Doc Whitley, and Al Dillon came out from town in a two-seated hack, arriving before twelve. Bill Hanna rode down from his shack shortly after noon. It was the biggest crowd Dave had ever seen in Mary's house, and he felt awkward and embarrassed when he came in and heard their shouted: "Merry Christmas!"

Dixie came quickly across the room to him, saying: "I haven't seen you for months, Dave. How are you?"

He shook hands with her, hoping Nan wouldn't run in at that exact moment and kiss him. She did not, probably, he thought, because she was too busy to get out of the kitchen. Dixie excused herself, saying she was trying to help out, that it was a wonderful dinner, and it was going to take all hands to get it on the table.

Strang introduced Dave to Doc Whitley and the lawyer, Al Dillon. He liked them just as he instinctively liked the cattlemen, Kane, Lundy, and Hartzel. When he sat down beside Joslyn, he could not help comparing him to the other men in the room, and for some reason he could not define Joslyn seemed like a pygmy in a company of giants.

251

There was no strain at any time during the meal. Mary asked the blessing, and that was a strange thing to Dave. He had never heard her or Nan talk about religion, and he had not known Mary to ask a blessing before. But when he listened to her voice and her prayer, simple and direct, he could not help thinking how different it was from the long and often cold prayers he had heard so many times at home, how thoroughly Mary Romney Strang understood that this, of all days in the year, was a time when hate and bitterness should be laid aside.

Mary and Nan waited on the table. Dixie sat beside her father, saying nothing, eyes demurely on her plate. Now and then she raised her head to look at Dave, a small smile touching the corners of her mouth. It was a gentle, unspoken invitation. That was all. If Nan understood it, she gave no indication. She did not need to. When she had time to sit down, she took her place beside Dave as naturally as Mary sat down beside Strang at the head of the long table. Without saying a word, without touching Dave, Nan established a bond of possession.

There was small talk about the weather, the price of beef in Omaha, when the Red House would be finished, the need for a new county. Speck Hartzel, a lanky bowlegged man who wore heavy glasses, prodded Strang about his hay, and Strang came back with a request for Joslyn to have twenty mowers on hand by the next 4th of July because he was going to have haystacks all over the valley.

Ben Kane, a small aggressive man with a booming voice, said he aimed to start alfalfa, but Strang shook his head and argued that the best thing to do was to improve the native grasses, that the wild hay would beat any other kind. Jim Lundy, an older man than the others, changed the talk to cattle, saying that the Steens were a little rough for his cattle and that a strain of mountain goats was desirable. Everybody laughed but Hartzel who apparently lacked a sense of humor. He said immediately that the practical answer was to bring in some Devon and Hereford bulls. Then they'd have stock that would go after feed wherever it was to be found.

Later, when they were back in the front room, Mary played and they sang familiar hymns that many of them had not heard for years. For a time there was a strange hushed silence as the minds of the older people dipped into childhood memories to Christmases long forgotten.

It was Bob Joslyn who destroyed the feeling of gentle nostalgia that lay upon them, whether by design or accident Dave did not know. Ugly clouds had been working across the sky. Joslyn, looking out, said suddenly: "If we're going home tonight, we'll have to start." He nodded at Doc Whitley. "You and Al coming now, Doc?"

"No hurry," Strang said.

"There is for me," Joslyn said. "I know what can happen in this country when a blizzard cuts loose."

"We'll go now, I guess." Doc Whitley turned to Dave. "Your mother isn't well. May turn into pneumonia. Better get into town before long."

"I'll ride in tomorrow," Dave said.

Dillon put on his coat. "Matt, this is a bad time of year to travel, you'd better hike over to Salem."

"Too busy, Al."

"Let it go and maybe you won't be busy at all," Dillon said pointedly. "It's time you had a talk with the governor and told him just what you have done for the country and what you're going to do. He's had some letters from Markham asking that he set aside the report of the government agent and request the commissioner of the Land Office to stop all action so the claimants can have a hearing to prove the character of their entries."

"Why, hell," Strang said belligerently, "there ain't any claimants. The settlers that were here when I came have sold the land back to me, or they're working on S Star. Nobody else has come in."

"There will be," the lawyer said gravely. "You'd better go see the governor before they get here."

"All right," Strang said doubtfully, "but there's

a lot of work to do. A lot for the next ten years."

There was a flurry of putting on coats and thanking Mary for the dinner. Dixie acted as if Nan had done her a great favor in inviting her. Dave, watching, sensed that it was more of her acting and she meant none of it, a falsity he had never felt in Nan.

Joslyn had almost reached the door when he turned as if only then remembering something. "Here's the last issue of Markham's *Sun*. It isn't much of a paper, but you'll want to see this copy."

They left then. Dave helped them hook up. He waited until the hack clattered over the bridge, heard Dixie's final good bye, and waved a parting salute. He hurried into the house, shivering, for he had not put on his coat and the temperature had dipped sharply since noon.

"Say, Bob was right. This is going to be a wowser of a storm. . . ." Dave stopped, only then feeling the strained atmosphere that was upon them.

"Read that," Strang said, tossing him the paper.

Dave, glancing over the *Sun*, saw that Markham had run his challenge in a black box as he had in his first issue. The first paragraph was similar to what Dillon had told Strang. It was the second that hit Dave. *There are thousands of acres of fertile land south of Sage Valley that are waiting for the homesteader, but this land is now*

255

claimed by two stockmen who drove herds on it last summer. What will these men do when their range is settled? What will Matt Strang do when the homesteaders turn south with their wagons? The only means of reaching this country is over the toll bridge that Mary Romney Strang has operated for years. The eyes of all justice-seeking people are on you, Matt Strang.

Dave threw the paper on the table. Speck Hartzel was not directly concerned, but both Kane and Lundy were, and they kept staring at Strang. It was Lundy who said: "Generally speaking, nesters ain't hard to handle, but there's no way of knowing what will happen with this man Markham stirring them up."

"I'll kill that loud-mouthed son!" Kane shouted passionately.

"No." Strang rose and slid a cigar into his mouth. "Whatever we do will be legal. I don't know how you can legally kill Lacey Markham, so we'll wait. Nature takes care of things like this. It won't be long till all the fools unlucky enough to grab reservation land will sell out for a song. No man can drive as far as we'll have to drive to get to a railroad and make a living off cattle if he's in a settled country and don't own nothing but a quarter-section. Same with you boys. They'll come down there and they'll starve out."

"Sure," Lundy said hotly, "but what happens

to us while they're starving? We get our grass ploughed up, our beef eaten, and maybe some wild-eyed yahoo will start shooting at us from the rimrock." He motioned toward the bridge. "You can stop 'em right here."

"How?"

"Close the road to the public. Or raise the toll so high nobody can pay it."

"It was Mary's bridge a long time before I ever saw the valley. I guess this is kind of up to her."

Mary stood beside the melodeon, very straight. She said: "No, it's your decision, Matt. I told you I didn't believe in violence, but this isn't like giving the early settlers land like I asked you to."

Strang walked the length of the room and back, pulling on his cigar. "I'd do these people a favor by keeping 'em out, but with Markham egging 'em on, they won't see it." He faced Lundy and Kane. "All right. I'll close the road at the junction. Meanwhile you boys buy all the swamp land you can that's been classified, and you and your buckaroos can file on any land that's open to entry. Now maybe we'd better vamoose. Mary was up before daylight. I reckon she's pretty tired."

Nan gripped Dave's wrist. "I've got a present for you."

She led him into the kitchen and handed him a small package. He opened it, fingers trembling. It was an orange neckerchief. Nan whispered: "Merry Christmas."

He looked down at her, feeling his love for her rush over him in a wave of tenderness that made it hard for him to talk. He said slowly: "I found out something today. I know why you asked Dixie to come."

She winked at him, tongue in her cheek. "All right. Tell me if you're so smart."

"Dixie used to be prettier than you are. You didn't fuss with your hair and you didn't care much about your clothes. It's different now. You're prettier'n she is."

There was more he could have said, that her slim body had filled out into womanly maturity almost unnoticed. Today, when he had seen her standing beside Dixie, he had become acutely aware that there was nothing boyish about Nan's figure, that she could let her face and form and personality be compared to Dixie's and come out ahead. But he said none of those things, for he could not at the moment find words for them.

Her hands came up along his arms. She breathed: "It wasn't just who's the prettiest, Dave. I wanted you to see us together. I want you to know which one you're in love with."

He looked at her indignantly. "I knew that a long time ago. Here. I got this for you in Winnemucca. Now we'll see who's in love with who."

He drew a diamond ring from his pocket and slipped it on her finger. She looked at it a long moment, then, for no reason that he could see, she began to cry. He held her in his arms, wondering, as all men do, why women cry when they are happy. She stopped crying presently and pulled away to look at the ring again. "I'll wear it, Dave. Always. And I'll always love you. But I can't marry you now. I just can't."

"If it's Matt . . ."

"No. It really isn't Matt. I've said it was and I've tried to make myself believe it was, but it's something else. Something I don't understand. But I love you, Dave, and I'll marry you someday. I promise."

She gave her lips to him again. Then he held her in his arms, her head against his chest, and she was very still. Outside, the first snowflakes were coming down from an ugly steel-gray sky, drifting lazily as if they were in no hurry to reach their destination.

XVII

It was a long winter with snow clinging in the cracks and crannies of the rimrock for weeks after the Christmas blizzard, and it was, on the surface, a quiet winter, but only on the surface. Time was like a quiet pool with a gently bubbling spring at the bottom. It would be late spring before the first bubble reached the top.

There was a break in the cold weather in February, and Matt Strang took the long trip by stage to The Dalles, by boat down the Columbia to Portland, and by train upvalley to Salem. When he returned late in the month, he would say nothing except that he'd talked to the governor and he thought everything would be all right. Then he added with a good deal more enthusiasm that they'd have their new county and Sage would be the county seat.

In that Strang was right. Sage County came into being, Bill Hanna was appointed sheriff, and a jail with a small office was built at the west end of Main Street. The county officials were named, Matt Strang and Ben Kane among them as county commissioners, Joslyn as county judge, and Al Dillon as district attorney. A small courthouse was built across the street from the jail.

Lacey Markham had little to say in his paper about the organization of the county except that the governor was apparently backing the powers of monopoly, but he did add that the cattlemen's victory was only temporary. As soon as the reservation was settled, the settlers would be in the majority and in the first election they would turn the appointed officials out.

The McNairs took advantage of the February weather to move to Prineville. Tildie Fields left in April. And on the first day of May Matt and Mary moved into the Red House. A row of Lombardy poplars had been planted across the front of the yard, a picket fence had been built, and a ditch had been brought down from the creek so that a stream of clear water ran past the house.

"We'll get a lawn in next year," Strang said. "Be less dirt tracked into the house, and when we get some kids around, the grass will be a good place for 'em to play."

Mary said nothing to that. But when she was outside, she would look at the barn-red house and shudder. "Matt, if you don't change that, I'll have indigestion."

"I'll change it right away," Strang would say blandly. "Just as soon as I get some white paint."

"You're an old faker," Mary would say then. "You don't intend to get any white paint. You like that horrible color."

And then Strang would scratch the back of his neck and grin like a kid caught in the sugar bin. "You've changed this old horse in most ways, Mary. Ain't you gonna leave him one little thing?"

Mary always let it drop then, for it was a minor matter. On all important points she had her way. Her furniture was moved over from the house on the Channel. Most of the things Strang had freighted north from Winnemucca were stored or used in the house on the number two ranch where Pablo and a man named Clark stayed, but there was one small room in the northeast corner of the house that was strictly Strang's. It was to be

261

his office, and he laid down the law to both Mary and Nan that it wasn't even to be swept unless he was there. Within a matter of days a weird collection of tally books, catalogs, odds and ends of leather, and half a dozen guns had appeared and were piled in a haphazard arrangement on the floor and over his spur-scarred desk and the ancient leather couch.

"I don't see how you can stand this mess," Mary said in exasperation. "Why, if I let the house go . . ."

Strang stopped her with a wave of his big hand. "This chair," he patted the arm of his swivel chair, "that desk, and the couch all started with me in California when I didn't own no more than ten cows and a bull. We fetched 'em to Nevada and we've fetched 'em to Oregon, and hod dang it, if you don't like the looks of 'em, you go sit in your room."

That was a second point Mary could not argue about, for Strang had arranged the house to give her a small room in the back. Her favorite rocking chair went there, a walnut table for her sewing, and a velvet-covered orange love seat that she particularly liked.

There was no place for Nan except her bedroom upstairs. "I guess Matt didn't build the Red House for me," she told Dave. "You know why?"

"Sure. He figgered we'd be in our own house by now."

She must have sensed the intensity of his feeling, for she was suddenly contrite. She crept into his arms, her hands slipping up along his back and pressing hard against him. Then, with the side of her head against his chest, she said: "Dave, I love you. You won't forget that, will you?"

"I try to keep remembering it," he said a little grimly, "but it ain't easy with you telling me we're going to get married someday. Here we are, getting old . . ."

She giggled. "We are getting old, aren't we? You're almost twenty-two and I'm over eighteen."

"Old enough to have a family and start making our own lives."

She was very serious then. "Dave, I've never told you, but last summer when you were gone on the drive, I was riding north of the lakes and ran into Lacey Markham. He was nice, just like you always said he was. I talked to him a while, and since then I've seen him several other times."

"I reckon he convinced you that Matt had no right to buy the swamp land and the small people he talks about are being cheated."

She stepped back, eyes searching his face. "That's right, but don't say I think that because of Matt. I like him. I mean, kind of. Mother's changed him a lot just like she does everybody who knows her well. She's good and fine and sweet, and Matt isn't as rough as he was."

Dave knew it was true. He'd heard Strang say: "Mary winds me around her finger, but why not? It's a damned pretty finger." But he was surprised that Nan could speak of Strang with anything except bitterness. "Well then, you and me . . . ," he began.

"Listen, Dave." She put a hand up to his cheek in a soft caress. "I want you. Sometimes I lay awake at night thinking about you and wanting you so bad it hurts. But I tell you it isn't enough. Marriage is for a long time. I want to know we've got some common ground."

"We've got plenty."

"I'm not sure. It would be simpler if Matt was a thieving killer like I've tried to make myself see him, or if Markham was a hypocrite who wanted Matt out of the way because he hated him."

"I'm beginning to think that's the way it is with Lacey," Dave said grimly.

"You're wrong about him. But the trouble is that both are a little right and a little wrong. You agree with Matt. I think Markham's got most of the right. Can't you see what that would do to us someday?"

He thought of what Tildie Fields had said about the shooting trouble and the dying trouble. It was coming as surely as the spring had followed winter. For the first time he understood some-

264

thing, at least, of what was keeping him and Nan apart.

"I reckon I do," he said tonelessly.

"I don't hate Matt like I did. I tried to. You know how it was with Mother and me. There was that Walton trouble and I kept blaming him. I'm ashamed of some of the things I've said, but he's been patient. I swear I'll never open my mouth again to make him mad, but it seems like I always do."

He grinned. She had a way with him just as Mary had with Matt. He wasn't fooling himself. That's how it would be all their lives, but he wouldn't change it if he could. "All right," he said. "Only one of these days I'm going to quit asking. Then you'll have to come to me."

"And beg?"

"You bet."

So Dave waited, and because it was spring, there was more work than all of them could do, and the waiting didn't seem so bad. The snow edged back on the Blue Mountains to the north and the Steens to the south. The birds returned to the lakes and the tule marsh—Canadian geese, a dozen kinds of ducks from mallards to blue-winged teals, avocets, grebes, sandpipers, pelicans, and all the rest. The meadows turned green with a sudden surge of life, and the dry wind, roaring in off the high desert, ruffled the sage and turned it silver.

There was a good calf crop, so good that Strang was jubilant. He was enthusiastic about all of it. He said several times: "Never seen a healthier bunch of cattle. Another year, and we'll have steers to drive back the way they came, the biggest damned steers them buyers ever saw."

Spring saw one ditch-digging crew at work in the tules draining the marsh and another running an irrigation ditch from the creek to the higher land between Sage Lake and the rim.

"What a country," Holland complained. "One place you got so much water it ain't good for nothing but bogging down a cow critter, and up yonder it's so dry it won't raise right good sagebrush."

Spring saw the poplar trees showing leaves and shooting out tender branches and days when the air was still and rich with the smell of the moist soil and growing things. On those days Mary and Nan felt the urge to garden, and someone, usually Dave, was pressed into spade and hoe duty.

Branding time. Swinging reatas and the smudge of smoke from the low-burning fires. Bawling cattle and cursing buckaroos and taunting laughs when a loop missed, a tragedy that seldom happened. They were good hands, these riders who had come up the trail, and pride of their craft was in them the same as there was pride in their expensive center-fire saddles with the fancy stamping and their silver-mounted bridles, spurs, and bits. It was a two-man job to throw a calf, both working on horses. One roped him by the neck, the other picked up his hind feet, and they stretched him out between them as the horses came back on the ropes. Then a man on foot— and this was Dave's job—flopped the calf on his side and slapped on the iron. There was the smoke cloud, the stink of burned hair and flesh, and always the bawling that caused Mary to ask plaintively: "How much longer are you going to abuse those poor things, Matt?"

Then it happened, the first bubble to break the surface of this quiet pool of time. It was noon of the last day of branding. Strang had left the cook shack and turned toward the house when Clab Holland called: "Take a look, Matt! Company."

Strang swung around. Three men were riding in from the Channel. Dave, hearing Holland's call, stopped to look. He recognized the gaunt figure of Lacey Markham in the middle, Bob Joslyn on the right, but the third rider was a stranger.

"They ain't here just to look at our mugs," Holland said. "Maybe we better get our guns."

"No," Strang said sharply. "Come on, Clab. You, too, Dave."

Strang strode past the barn, tall heels stirring the dust, his craggy face looking as if it had been hewn out of granite. Holland glanced at Dave and shook his head, cursing softly. They followed Strang to the creek, Holland muttering: "There'll come a day when he'll wish to hell he had a gun."

Strang waited at the creek, Holland on one side of him, Dave on the other. The three riders reined up, the stream between the two parties. Joslyn said courteously: "Howdy, gents."

"Howdy, Bob," Strang said. "Markham, you ain't welcome here."

"I am not surprised, Strang," Markham said evenly. "How are you, Dave?"

Dave nodded, saying nothing, his eyes on the stranger. It was Joslyn who motioned to him. "Matt, this is Beans Poe. Beans, meet Matt Strang, S Star's owner. That's his ramrod, Clab Holland. The other one's Dave Logan."

The three of them nodded, all making the same cool appraisal of the stranger that he was making of them. He sat his horse easily, a rangy roan, hands folded across his saddle horn. He was as tall a man as Markham, but there the resemblance ended, for he had a good pair of shoulders, a lean-jawed face burned to an old leather brown, and long-fingered hands. His eyes were pale blue and entirely expressionless. Only his mouth held a faint smile as if he were enjoying a silent laugh. He carried two guns, butts forward, and even Dave, knowing little about such men, immediately pegged him as a hired gunman.

Poe cuffed back his sweat-stained Stetson to show a lock of white hair. The color surprised Dave, for the man was in his early thirties or late twenties. "You ain't real friendly," Poe said in a drawling voice. "Lacey told me you wouldn't be."

"Looking for work?" Strang said.

"Sort of. Looks like I've got it cut out for me. We had a couple reasons for riding out. One was to size you up. I don't mind saying, Strang, that I've seen your kind all the way from here to the Pecos, and I never met up with one I couldn't take."

Holland took a step forward, throwing out a fierce oath. Strang grabbed him by the arm and hauled him back. He said: "I've seen your kind, too, Poe, from here to the San Joaquin, but you're the first that's stunk up this range."

"We didn't come to jangle," Markham cut in. "We had another reason. We want to know what your intentions are concerning your road and toll bridge."

"I'll close 'em if we get a nester invasion. I won't have 'em crossing my range."

"Why?"

"They'll stop and camp, eat my grass, and maybe rustle my beef. Likewise they might get a notion to stay, and then I'd have the job of boosting 'em off. It's just easier to keep 'em off in the first place."

"What about the roads in the north end of the valley?"

"They'll be kept open."

"The county court can declare this road open," Joslyn said.

Strang nodded. "Then it'll be open. This is my valley, but I don't consider myself above the law. Remember that, Markham."

"Neither do I," Markham said, "but, according to my lights, a law is for two purposes. It should protect a man's property and it should protect the man. Both are important."

"We won't auger on that," Strang said quickly.

"But it's foolish to talk about the county court opening this road," Markham went on, "with you and Ben Kane commissioners."

"I expect it is," Strang agreed, "so if your nesters get here, just tell 'em to keep moving."

"One more question. Are you closing this road to keep settlers from moving in on Kane and Lundy?"

"That may be," Strang said laconically.

"I don't like this business," Joslyn broke out. "I've tried to tell Lacey it's better to let sleeping dogs lie."

"These dogs have been sleeping too long," Markham said. "I'm simply making the public interest my interest, Strang. If there is trouble in this valley, it will be because you insist on what you call your rights."

"They are his rights," Joslyn said. "He don't owe nothing to any raggle-taggle bunch of farmers who come in now."

"Do you see this Strang's way," Markham asked coldly, "or are you siding him because his trade has made money for you?"

Joslyn withered under Markham's cool stare. He lowered his gaze, muttering: "I see it his way."

"Let's ride, gents," Poe cut in brusquely. "I'm a fighting man, Strang. Markham's long on words, but bullets are my suit. All I see around here is land, too much for one man. I aim to fix it so these settlers can get what's coming to them."

"Why?" Strang demanded.

"Because I've hated monopoly all my life. I've fought it everywhere I've found it. I'll fight it here."

Without another word, Poe wheeled his horse and rode away, Markham following. Joslyn hesitated, his sour face showing how much Markham's questions had torn his pride. He asked: "What can I do, Matt?"

"Nothing," Strang said curtly. "You'd best stay out of this."

Sighing, Joslyn turned and rode after the other two.

"Now we'll have fun," Holland said. "Did you see Poe's eyes, Matt?"

"Yeah. He's a killer." Strang reached for a cigar. "A cross-draw man riding a double-fire saddle. Texan, I reckon."

"Got out one jump ahead of the Rangers," Holland said, "or I miss my guess."

"Hell, might be here because he figgers no sheriff will bother him." Strang fired his cigar, staring thoughtfully at the backs of the three men. "Or Markham may have sent for him."

"I've seen his kind," Holland said. "Killing a man ain't nothing more to them than beefing a steer, but they do their killing for pay. Now who would be paying him?"

"He's looking ahead maybe," Dave said.

"Maybe," Strang agreed. "He figgers a new bunch will pay him to worry us."

"We gonna start toting our guns?" Holland demanded. "Or are we gonna buy some pea-shooters so we can swap peas for his lead?"

Strang's craggy face reddened. He opened his mouth, closed it, and glanced at the house. He said—"We'll try the pea-shooters first."—and walked up the slope to where Mary was working in the garden.

XVIII

They came that summer, from Kansas and Nebraska and Iowa, came in covered wagons, singly or in pairs, hundreds of them with bony horses and a few cows and plows tied on behind their wagons. These were the men and women Markham had called "the spiritual descendants of those who followed the Oregon Trail." Some secured reservation land; the rest came on across the ridge into Sage Valley, lured partly by Lacey Markham's letters to the Midwestern news-papers, and partly by stories they'd heard of a great valley owned by one man. They camped on Joslyn's land around the town site, and because Markham's name was familiar to them, they talked to him first. Beans Poe was there to fan a smoldering fire and talk about their homestead rights, to point to the valley that could, he said, be taken. Bob Joslyn was there, listening uneasily. Doc Whitley visited wagon after wagon knowing he would never be paid for what he was doing, but sickness was among them, and the danger of an epidemic was a constant threat.

It was late in July that the lawyer, Al Dillon, rode out to S Star. He said bluntly: "You haven't been in town for a month, Matt. It's time you were doing something."

"I have been doing something," Strang said mildly. "We've got a lot of hay put up. . . ."

"Oh, hell." Dillon waved it aside. "You don't hold land with hay. They're pouring in like ducks in the spring. Markham has agitated so much that the commissioner of the Land Office has granted time so a claimant can have a hearing before the Registrar and Receiver concerning the agricultural character of any given quarter-section, but that's on the disputed land Kane and Lundy are claiming. As far as this valley's concerned, I think it's settled. Your visit to the governor did some good."

"If I'm out of the woods . . ."

"I'm a lawyer and I don't like a saddle," Dillon said shortly, "so I didn't come out here just to visit. I'll fight like hell for you in the courtroom or with the Land Office, but handling a bunch of claim-jumping settlers is your problem."

"There hasn't been any trouble."

"There will be," Dillon said grimly. "If all the settlers camped around Sage decided some morning to move in on you and stake out their claims, you'd have a job. Markham is talking sense to them, which surprises me, but that Beans Poe is raising hell with them. He's even talking about riding out here and burning you out."

"They'll get hot lead if they do that."

"So will you. A hundred men with scatter-guns and Winchesters can stir up quite a mess. I don't know what you can do, Matt, but you'd better come in and take care of Poe."

"I'll send for Dave," Strang said. "He knows how them kind of people think. We'll be in tomorrow."

Strang sent Nan south to the cow camp on the north shoulder of the Steens. She returned with Dave late that evening. As long as Dave lived, he would never forget the hour spent with Mary and Nan and Strang in the big front room of the Red

House. Mary had baked a cake, and when she heard the horses, she heated up the coffee. When Dave came through the front door in answer to Strang's call, Mary had cut the cake and poured the coffee.

"I didn't figger on this," Dave said.

"A little sugar to sweeten a sour job," Strang said. "Tomorrow we do the job." He looked at Mary. "We'll be packing our guns in the morning."

"I know," she said.

"I can't understand Markham sending for this Beans Poe," Nan burst out. "It isn't like him, is it, Dave?"

"No, not if he's anything like he used to be."

Strang laid his plate down on the table, his cake half eaten. "It's a funny thing," he said in an oddly gentle voice, "how a country changes a man. Or maybe he's changed by the people he finds in that country." He smiled at Mary. "You. And Dave." He turned his heavy shoulders, craggy face very grave. "And you, Nan."

Nan looked down at her plate, her chin quivering. It was Mary who said quietly: "Do what you have to do tomorrow, Matt."

"I'll handle it without cracking a cap," Strang said. "Now, I'm going to bed."

Dave rode out with Strang early in the morning before Nan was up. Dave had never seen much show of affection between Strang and Mary, but he had been aware of its existence from the first day they had been together. It was different this morning. Mary walked beside Strang to his horse, his arm around her. Dave looked away when Strang kissed her. Then he heard saddle leather squeak as Strang lifted his big body into the hull. He turned in time to see Strang look down at Mary, her gold-blonde hair almost red under the sharp morning sun.

Strang said: "We may stay in town tonight."

"Good bye, Matt," Mary said, her face composed.

"So long."

They clattered across the bridge and set a steady pace northward, a brooding silence upon them. When they came to the junction with the Prineville road, Dave saw the sign:

NO TRESPASSING SOUTH OF THIS POINT
UNLESS YOU HAVE BUSINESS AT S STAR
—MATT STRANG

Ahead of them the buildings of Sage made a break in the monotonous sweep of the flat, and all around the town were the weathered, canvas tops of the settlers' wagons. They came into Sage, Strang watchful now, and rode the length of the street to Markham's cabin. The town appeared deserted.

Strang called: "Markham!"

Markham stepped out, a dab of ink streaking his forehead. It was not a hot day, but Markham was sweating. He wiped a hand across his face, and asked: "What do you want, Strang?"

For a moment they faced each other, Markham tall and gaunt and a little stooped, Strang scowling, square face hard-set with none of the softness that had been in it when he'd left Mary that morning. Here they were, opposite poles to two ways of life.

"Dillon was out," Strang said. "He claims you're talking sense to these fools. Are you seeing things my way?"

Markham's smile held little humor. "I'll never do that, Strang."

Strang made a sweeping motion with his hand. "What are you going to do about these people?"

"What are *you* going to do?" Markham returned. "You're the one who could do something."

"How do you figger that?"

"You could sell them land without hurting your prospects."

"They haven't got any money," Strang said curtly, "and I sure wouldn't give it to them."

"No, I guess you wouldn't."

"I asked you what you were going to do. You fetched them here."

"I made a mistake," Markham said evenly. "I've seen you use violence, so I thought the answer was more violence. That was my mistake. I can't undo it. I've asked Poe to leave the country, but he won't go."

"You paying him to kick up a ruckus?"

"No. The settlers are. He's worked up an organization. Some of them have a little money, and before he's done, he'll get all of it. It's just a job with him."

"You'd better think up some way to move 'em on before winter hits the valley."

Markham shook his head. "I can't move them, Strang. They came for land and there's land in Sage County for them, you know. Open your road if you want them off your range."

"Not by a damn' sight. Where's Poe?"

"They're having a meeting north of town. Poe's talking to them."

"Come along," Strang said.

Markham shook his head. "No. I'll do all I can to stop violence because I'm to blame if it comes, but I will not stand beside you again while you break a man the way you did McNair just for the effect it has on your audience."

Without a word Strang reined his black around sharply and rode across the street to the jail. Hanna was waiting for him. He said with satisfaction: "I knew you'd be along. Want me to throw Poe into the jug?"

"Not unless he starts something. Come on."

Hanna got up behind Dave, and they rode around the courthouse and on into the maze of wagons. It took a moment to find the meeting, and when they did, they heard Poe's great voice beating into the noon stillness: "I tell you he can't hold public land he's secured by fraud. Go out and stake your quarter-sections. He can't do anything to you."

Strang rounded a wagon and reined up. He said—"You're wrong, Poe."—and stepped down. He moved straight toward the gunman, tall heels stirring the white dust, Dave and Hanna a pace behind him. Poe stood his ground, a hand moving toward his gun butt. There it stopped, his Colt remaining in leather. Dave was never sure why Poe did not make his play then, unless it was as Clab Holland said afterward: "Nobody ever looked Matt in the eye and pulled a gun on him."

Strang was a pace from Poe when his right fist swung up. Poe started to duck and took the blow high on the side of his head as he frantically clawed for his gun. It was too late. Strang's left caught him squarely on the point of the chin. He went down in a curling fall and lay still. Strang stooped, pulled his guns, and tossed them aside.

For a moment Strang faced the men Poe had been talking to, lips curling in distaste, for the age-old antipathy between stockmen and settlers lay between them. There were fifty or more in the crowd, some with rifles, some with shotguns, a few with Colts stuck inside their waistbands. No one moved and no one said anything for a long moment.

"You folks don't belong in this country." Strang said finally. "You're looking for something for nothing, but you won't find it. If you're hunting for land to farm, keep going. If you want to work, I'll give you a job. There's plenty of work in this valley, but you'll be working for me. For S Star. No matter what Poe told you, this is my land." Strang jabbed a finger at the unconscious Poe. "He's buttering his own bread, stirring up trouble to get himself a job. He's a killer, and you men don't strike me as being his kind. Unless you want to die trying to steal land that ain't yours and never can be yours, fire this fellow. Sage Valley ain't made for the plow. No sense of you starving two, three years to find that out."

Dave forgot to breathe. The hardness had dropped away from Matt Strang. Now there was something magnificent in him, in his strength and courage and determination. They felt it, these men who faced him, many of them in ragged clothes, many with the sunken cheeks of fathers who had shared their portion of the family meal with their children, many with the beaten look of men who had followed the rainbow, always to find the pot of gold just out of their reach. Now, too tired to go on, sick of eating dust, sick of jolting wagons and turning wheels, they could only stare at Strang and hate him because

280

he had kicked the pot of gold out of their reach again.

"I have never let a man starve on my range," Strang said, "but if a man ain't willing to work, he deserves to starve. I've got fifty men working for me. I could use fifty more. I pay wages in gold and I'll buy you lumber to build a winter shelter if you're willing to work on it evenings and Sundays. I'll be at the Gold Bar till ten. If any of you want to stay in this country, come over and have a talk with me."

Strang stalked to his horse, mounted, and rode away, Dave and Hanna following. They left their horses in the livery stable and took the path beside the street to the saloon. They stood beside the pine bar, poured their drinks, and downed them, Hanna saying: "Here's mud in your eye."

Dave said then: "Matt, I don't savvy why you sent for me."

"This ain't finished," Strang said. "For one thing, I figgered I'd need you and Hanna to watch my back. Besides, I wasn't sure Markham would talk to me and I knew he would to you." He poured another drink and stood staring at the liquor. "Markham's sure a queer duck, and he's got a damned funny kink in him, but I respect any man with guts and who's willing to admit a mistake. I never could."

Fourteen men came in that afternoon and evening to see Strang about work. Eleven said they'd sign on. The other three said they'd talk it over with their wives.

At 10:00 Strang said: "Reckon Poe ain't coming gunning for us. Let's go to bed."

The next morning they left the hotel at sunup, and as they stepped through the front door, Markham called: "Strang!" They waited, Markham crossing the street in his long-legged stride. When he was close, he said: "You did a better thing than I thought you would."

"I need men," Strang said laconically.

Markham shrugged. "Maybe that was the reason. What I wanted to tell you was that when Poe came to, he told the settlers he was going to settle on your land to show them you wouldn't bother them if they staked out their claims. He borrowed one of the wagons and left before dark. I was afraid he planned to ambush you."

"So you're worrying about me getting beefed," Strang said skeptically.

"No," Markham said sharply. "I don't care if you fall out of your saddle dead, but I don't want Poe bushwhacking you. These are good honest men, Strang. They've got wives and kids to look out for, but if you're shot, your buckaroos would take it out on them no matter who did the shooting."

"You don't know me or my men," Strang said.

"I know you."

"No, you don't. I've always lived within the

law and I always will. If Poe shoots me, my buckaroos will let the law handle it. I've taught 'em that."

Strang wheeled away toward the stable. Dave said—"Thanks, Lacey."—and caught up with Strang.

They saddled and rode out of town, the morning sun hot upon their backs. They crossed Sage River, swung south at the junction, and then Dave, looking west, saw the wagon. He took a long breath, uneasiness working down his spine.

"I reckon that'll be Poe," Dave said.

Strang, deep in his thoughts, gave a start and began looking around. A covered wagon stood a hundred yards west of the road, a saddled roan beside it, his reins trailing. Poe was putting up a tent beside the wagon.

"Damned if it ain't," Strang said. "I guess he didn't get the idea yesterday."

Swearing, Strang reined off the road toward the wagon. Poe stopped work and moved to the front wheel. There he waited.

"What are you doing here?" Strang bellowed.

Poe's pale eyes met Strang's. "Strang, what I'm doing here is more than just making a job for myself like you told the boys yesterday. I got my name Beans because there was a hell of a long time in my life when I didn't eat nothing but beans. I got my white hair when I was a kid. Want to know why?"

"No!" Strang shouted. "Just get off my land!"

"I aim to tell you about it," Poe went on coldly. "I saw my mother and father killed by a man like you who wanted more land than was good for him. I hid upstairs in our house for days and was afraid to come down because they were still outside. All the time the bodies of my father and mother were laying on the kitchen floor. From that time to this I've fought men like you. I'm settling here and I'll file on this quarter-section in Lakeview."

"You'll play hell filing on land that ain't open to entry. Now get off my range or I'll lay a quirt on you."

Again Poe's mouth held a faint smile as if he were enjoying a secret joke. "Strang, I'll kill you if you do."

Poe's guns were not on his hips. He stood straight and defiant, pale eyes challenging Strang. The big man swore, rage ruling him. He rode forward, swung his quirt down across Poe's right shoulder, lifted it, and swung it across the other shoulder. Poe did not flinch. He made no sound; his eyes still held the challenge.

"I'm coming by here tomorrow," Strang said. "If you ain't gone, I'll have you arrested for trespassing."

Strang reined his horse around and rode off, Dave beside him. Strang said, still wildly angry: "Who in hell does he think he is? If I let him stay there, I'd have every damned settler in Sage staking out claims all over the valley."

"That's what he figgers," Dave said.

"I'd better move him right now. No use waiting till tomorrow. May be too late."

Strang hipped around in his saddle. That was when it came, the report of the Winchester like a dry twig breaking clean. Dave reined up, looked back, and saw Poe standing beside his wagon, a rifle in his hands.

"Now what's he up to?" Dave asked.

He looked at Strang. Then he forgot to breathe, for Strang had pulled his black to a stop, a hand on his ribs, the other clutching his saddle horn. He whispered: "Help me down, Dave."

Dave swung to the ground, thinking it was the first time he had ever heard Matt Strang ask for help from anybody. He eased the big man out of the saddle. Strang fell back, his hat falling off as a gasp broke out of him. Only then did Dave realize how hard he was hit.

"I've got to get you back into the saddle, Matt," Dave said. "We've got to find the doc quick."

"Too late." Strang's fists clenched as pain racked him. "Look out for Mary, Dave. You'll be a big man here. I told Mary that from the first." He labored with his breathing, the agony of death upon him. "Let the law have Poe. Don't let Lundy or Kane start . . . any . . . shooting." His eyes closed and for a moment Dave thought he was gone. Then he whispered, "Tell . . . Mary . . . everything . . . that was good . . . in me . . . came . . . from . . . her."

That was all. His clenched hands fell off his chest to the ground, his body twitched, and Matt Strang was no longer a great block of granite. Just flesh and bones that would go back into the soil of this land that had been his.

Dave straightened, thinking of Poe. He heard the receding beat of hoofs. Then he saw Poe on the road, spurring his horse toward town. Dave's hand gripped his gun butt, lifted the gun, and dropped it back into his holster. Strang had said: *Let the law handle Poe.*

Dave lifted Strang's body into the saddle, tied him there, and rode back to Sage. He left the body with Doc Whitley who promised to bring it to the ranch the next day. Dave told him to fetch the preacher, remembering that Strang had said he wanted to be buried on the rim. Then he checked his gun and walked down the street, uncertain where he would find Poe. Hanna ran out of the jail to meet him, pale and trembling.

"What the hell happened, Dave?" Hanna asked. "Poe just came in and surrendered. Said he'd shot Strang."

"He did," Dave said. "Don't let him get away. We've got another hanging to attend to."

XIX

There are things a man thinks he cannot do, but when the time comes, he finds strength from some hidden source inside him to do the tasks that would have been impossible the day before. It was so with Dave. He told Mary, standing before her in front of the Red House with the reins in his hands, all the time feeling as if a knife blade was buried steel-deep in his middle.

Mary said, her face composed: "Do what has to be done, Dave. We'll bury him tomorrow." Turning, she looked past the house at the bleak, sharp-breaking rimrock. "Up there where he can spend eternity looking over his valley."

"I'll attend to things," Dave said, and stepped into the saddle.

It was as hard telling Clab Holland and Pablo Gonzales and the others as it had been telling Mary, for these men had started with Strang fifteen years ago when Strang, no older than Dave was now, had set out to build a fortune. These were men who had eaten and fought and drunk with Strang; they had breathed the dust of the drag with him, smelled the smoke of the branding fire; they had been soaked by the same rain and chilled by the same wind; they had sweated under the same sun. They had shared

287

each other's joys and disappointments, dreamed the same dream. Now the dream was becoming reality after fifteen years, but Strang would have no further share in it.

There was a long hushed moment. Then Holland asked: "Mary's burying him tomorrow?"

Dave said: "Yes."

Holland said: "We'd better ride. Might be some things that need doing."

Most of the townspeople came out the next day, the new people like Doc Whitley and Al Dillon who had stayed in the valley because of Matt Strang. Bob Joslyn was the only one of the old settlers who was there besides Hanna and Dave and the few who had come to work on S Star.

It was a simple service. There were tears, even Dave's and Clab Holland's and Pablo Gonzales's. The last scripture, the last song, the last prayer, and the grave was filled. Then the wagon tail-board was set in place and a few flowers that Mary had raised were laid on the mound.

There was the jangle of harness as teams were hitched up, the rattle of rigs being turned, and the final good byes, and they were gone, and Mary was standing on the porch of the Red House with the S Star men massed in front of her. It was only then that Dave noticed Mary had not been crying, but Nan had. Even now her eyes were red and she could not trust herself to speak, but Mary seemed as serene as she always did.

"I had to talk to you today," Mary said, "because I want to assure you that S Star will go on and you'll have your jobs. Nobody can take Matt's place, but we'll do our best to keep on building as he would have done and as he would want us to. As Matt said so many times, there's work for the next ten years." She nodded at Holland. "Clab will give the orders. I'm depending on you to work with him as you worked with Matt." She took a long breath, hands gripping the post beside her. "I have one more request. Before Matt died, he told Dave to let the law handle Poe. Al Dillon told me this morning that Poe will be indicted at once. I think all of you know that Matt believed in law so much that he would rather have his murderer go free than for any of you to take personal revenge."

Quickly she turned and walked inside, Nan with her. There was silence for a time and a shuffling among the men. Then Holland said: "You heard her. Hanna will hang Poe right and proper."

After the men had scattered, Dave pulled Holland aside. "Clab, I ain't sure they'll hang Poe."

"You're loco. If you tell your story like you told it to us, they can't help hanging him."

Dave shook his head. "The reservation's settled. There's a scattering of nesters around the valley. They're in the majority now, and they'll be in Sage for Poe's trial. Chances are they'll be on the jury."

Holland said: "If Poe walks out of that courtroom a free man . . ."

"That's what he'll do," Dave said in a tight bitter voice. "The settlers hated Matt just because they're settlers and he was a cowman, and they'll figger Poe's a hero. Poe savvied that, or he wouldn't have ridden in and given himself up like he did."

"I'll kill that damned Markham," Holland insisted.

"He's not to blame for Matt's death. He didn't want this to happen."

For a long time Holland stood staring at the house, a barren-faced bitter man. Then he said: "Most of my life I've done what Matt said. I suppose I'll go on doing it. I know what he'd say and we just heard what Mary wanted, but damn it to hell, they can't let Poe go."

Nan came out of the house, calling: "Dave! Mother wants you." When he walked up to her, she said: "She's in the sewing room." She put a hand on Dave's arm, her eyes searching his face. "I can't get used to him being gone. It's like a mountain you've looked at for months just disappearing."

"I know," Dave said, and walked into the house.

He paused for a moment in the cool gloom of the big front room, feeling the utter silence of the house. Then he went on to the tiny corner room that was Mary's. She was sitting in the rocking chair, some sewing on her lap, the last afternoon sunlight slanting through the window and touching her hair with its brightness.

Mary looked up when she heard him, smiled, and said: "Sit down, Dave."

He closed the door and dropped into the love seat, his Stetson clutched awkwardly in his hands, and it seemed to him she had never been more beautiful than she was now.

For a moment Mary did not say anything. There was just the faint squeak of her rocker. She sat with her head bowed over her sewing. A pile of shirts and socks lay on the walnut table, her scissors and spools of thread beside it. Suddenly she picked up the shirt that was on her lap and laid it on the table. She said: "I had him such a short time, Dave. Such a short time."

Dave opened his mouth and closed it, knowing he couldn't say what he had to say with the composure that was in Mary. He swallowed with an effort and cleared his throat. He said: "I didn't tell you before. I tried, but I couldn't. The last thing he said was to tell you that everything that was good in him came from you."

A sob broke out of her suddenly and violently, and then was gone. She sat with clenched fists, her handkerchief clutched in one hand. Then she said: "I'm sorry, Dave. For Matt's sake I can't let myself break up. We've got to keep this ranch going, you and me and Clab." She rose and stood at the window, her back to him, eyes on the rim. "Dave, you were more to Matt than you ever knew. He wanted a son. I would have liked to have given him one, but I couldn't. Then he said something I'll never forget. Just a few days ago. He said it didn't make any difference about not having children of his own. The ranch would go to you someday, you and Nan when she was older and not so foolish."

Turning, she stood motionlessly, looking at him, a strong rounded figure. "You saved his life, you know, the time he rode into Logan's Pocket and your mother tried to shoot him. He said that was why he offered you a job, but afterward he saw he'd done a bigger thing in hiring you than he'd known at first. You fought Clab and you rode the paint horse Clab was so sure would throw you, and you went after Walton and brought him out of the marsh. He said those were the things he would have wanted his son to be able to do." Mary went back to her rocker and sat down. "Dave, when he talked about having a lawn because grass was a good place for the kids to play in, he meant your kids, yours and Nan's."

"But she won't marry me," Dave burst out. "She wants to wait and save and start on our own in the Pocket."

"That's what I wanted to talk to you about. I understand Nan, Dave. You couldn't because you don't know what's behind us. There were some pretty rough years. You do know how she's been treated here. It's been a bitter land for us, but there has been some sweetness, too, and there will be more." Mary leaned forward. "Dave, try to understand this. Back of Nan's putting you off and her feeling toward Matt is something else that's hard to explain. My world was her world for so long that she has found it hard to adjust herself to a different life. When she was little, there were always men around me. Then Matt came. I suppose she learned to hate men and blame them for our trouble. She had always liked you, but you were a boy. Then, overnight it seemed, you were a man. She talked about marrying you, but she didn't know all that it meant. So be a little more patient with her, Dave. She does love you. I'm sure of that. When this is all over, ask her again. Tell her I need the two of you. I don't have anybody else to love. Now go away and let me cry."

He went out quickly and closed the door.

XX

Beans Poe was indicted for murder and the trial date was set for late summer. As Dave had foreseen, the settlers who had homesteads in the county accepted Poe as their champion and rallied to his defense.

A lawyer rode the stage in from The Dalles to defend him. The judge came from Lakeview. On the morning the trial opened, Sage was packed. Most of the transient settlers who had come to the valley seeking homes had gone on, a few were working for S Star, and only a handful had stayed, men without families who had been attracted to Poe and publicly swore that they'd never let him hang.

It was midmorning when Dave and Nan rode into town. Horses and rigs lined the street, the walks were crowded with settlers, and tents and covered wagons surrounded Sage.

"Looks like a circus has come to town," Dave said bitterly.

They reined up in front of the cabin where the McNairs had lived. The banker, Symonds, and his wife occupied it now, and Nan was to stay with them. She went in, and Dave took her horse to the livery stable. He left her gelding and his buckskin, and came along the runway and into the street again.

He went on to the courthouse and realized at once that he couldn't get in. The small room was jammed with settlers and there was a close-packed knot of twenty or more men around the door. Dave stood on his tiptoes, but there was little he could see, and the settlers refused to give way.

A man in the doorway said: "Dillon threw another one out. They'll be till doomsday getting a jury picked."

Turning, Dave walked back to Markham's place. Dixie Joslyn was standing on her porch, a hand shading her eyes. When she saw Dave, she called to him and, stepping down, crossed the yard to him. She waited in the corner of the picket fence, the usual good humor gone from her face.

"Are you going to make them hang him?" she demanded.

"They'd better hang him," Dave said grimly. "He shot Matt."

"They ought to give him a medal instead of a rope," she flung out in a shrewish voice.

Dave held his temper, giving her a long studying look, seeing little beauty in her face. There was anger and fear, and it puzzled him, for she had no stake in this thing as far as he knew. "I guess we've got nothing to talk about," Dave said, and started to turn away.

"Wait." She caught his arm and pulled him around to face her, suddenly frantic. "You don't know. Nobody knows but me and him. We've been meeting after dark. I'm going away with him as soon as he's free."

"No." Surprise pushed the word out of him. "Not you and Poe?"

"Don't tell anybody. I wouldn't have told you except that you're going to be one of the main witnesses." Her hand was still on his arm, gripping it convulsively. "Don't say anything that will make them hang him. If you ever loved me, Dave, save him."

"You don't know what you're saying. Poe's no good for you. He's no good to anybody."

"I don't care. He's the only way I've got to get out of here. You don't understand, Dave. I can't stay here. I've got to go where there's people. He'll take me. He's been everywhere." Her lips curled petulantly. "You're a fine one to talk about what's good for me. If you'd treated me right, I wouldn't have thought about him."

"Don't blame me because you're crazy about Beans Poe," Dave said indignantly. "If you go away with him, you *are* crazy."

"No I'm not. I'm just trying to get something I've got a right to have. People and nice houses and lights and a little fun. What is there here for us? Any of us? We'll just dry up from old age. Dave, can't you see how it's been, penned up in this damned valley a million miles from nowhere?"

"I like it," Dave said, and turned away, more troubled by what she had said than he liked to admit.

He went into Markham's cabin, nodding briefly in answer to Markham's greeting. He said: "Nan told me you think Poe should hang."

"It was murder, wasn't it?" Markham handed him a paper and pointed to a column. "Read that."

Dave glanced down the column Markham had pointed out, finding it hard to believe what he read, for Lacey Markham left no doubt of his position. *This is a test of justice in newly created Sage County. There can be no doubt of Beans Poe's guilt. Will the citizens of the jury see that justice is done? Or will they officially condone murder as a means of securing what they want? The* Sun *has consistently opposed monopoly. It will continue to do so. It fought Matt Strang when he was alive, and Strang fought back, but it was a fair fight with none of the ruthless brutality that marks so many range disputes. Since Strang's death his friends have exhibited admirable self-control in waiting for the law to take its course. Gentlemen of the jury, justice is in your hands.*

Dave tossed the paper back to Markham. "Lacey, which side are you on?"

Markham wiped a hand across his face, the gesture of a tired and disillusioned man. "My own, I guess. I've been wrong about a lot of things. About Dixie. About Nan, and I suppose I've been wrong about her mother. And I was tragically wrong about violence being the answer to violence. I saw that as soon as the settlers began coming in. I looked at their women and children, and I saw myself trying to make other men take human lives, something I lacked the courage to do. I would be to blame if they became widows and orphans. You were never more right than when you said I'd be sorry I ever thought gunsmoke would settle anything. So"—Markham made a sweeping gesture with his hands—"I've been in hell. It goes back to the day Strang broke McNair's arm and I sat there with a gun, hating him and doing nothing. I told you once I'd lick him. I didn't. He's dead, but he'll live forever. Maybe he was even right about this being a cattle country and nothing else. Time will answer that."

Dave thought of the hell Markham must have gone through before he could have brought himself to say these things. He said: "You put that paper out, Lacey, and I'll say you're as good an editor as you are a teacher."

Markham's face showed his pleasure. "I don't know about that, Dave, but I do know one thing. I've let my personal feelings warp my judgment. I thought, like Pilate, I was asking what is truth, but in reality I was closing my mind to it." He waved the thought aside. "Right now the question is what will happen if Poe is acquitted."

"I don't know," Dave said. "I wish I did."

"The cowmen could kill dozens of men who have done nothing worse than believe Beans Poe is a sort of Robin Hood. That's another mistake I made. I wrote to a man who had been marshal of Abilene, but he couldn't come. Poe heard about it through him and came without writing to me. Then I couldn't get rid of him." Markham gave Dave a searching look. "Now your people may wipe out the town to get square for Strang's death."

"I'll do what I can," Dave said. "I know what Matt would say and I know what Mary wants."

It took two days to pick the jury. Dave was in the courtroom on the afternoon of both days, and as he listened to the pulling and hauling between Al Dillon and Bert Chadwick, Poe's lawyer, it seemed to him he could judge the trend of events in the courtroom the same as he sensed the attitude of the settlers on the street. The way they saw it, Matt Strang's death was a victory for them; Poe's guns would open the valley for settlement. More settlement, or so their talk ran, would bring a railroad and a railroad meant prosperity for all of them.

The jury, as finally selected, consisted of two prospectors from the Blue Mountains, five men who worked at Cotter's mill, and five from the reservation, settlers who professed to have an open mind. It was not a good jury, but it was the best Dillon could get, and certainly better than if all twelve were settlers.

Holland and Pablo rode in the morning of the second day, Speck Hartzel and his crew that afternoon, and Lundy and Kane with their crews at dusk. Thus the scene was set for trouble. Within a matter of hours there were thirty cowmen in town instead of one. All were armed, and with characteristic confidence they considered themselves more than a match for the hundred odd settlers who were in Sage. The buckaroos loitered along the south side of the street or in the Gold Bar while the settlers held to the north side, staring belligerently across the silver strip that divided the town. Kane, Lundy, and Hartzel crowded into the courtroom and heard Dave tell the story of Strang's shooting in cold accusing words that could leave no doubt of Poe's guilt.

When Dillon finished with Dave, Chadwick jumped up and approached the witness chair. He was a big, ruddy-faced man with a great shock of black hair and a wide chin that gave him an impressiveness Dillon lacked. He stood before Dave, their eyes locking, and the courtroom quieted so that a fly droning against one of the front windows could be heard all over the room.

"Mister Logan," Chadwick said in his oratorical voice, "the defendant pleads not guilty by virtue of the fact that he shot in self-defense."

"That's a damned lie," Dave flung at him. "Matt had no idea of pulling a gun. Before we left the ranch, he told Missus Strang he wouldn't crack a cap. It was plain murder . . ."

"He can't say that," Chadwick raged at the judge. "It's not for him to decide what's murder and what isn't."

Dave swung to face the judge. "I was there. Who's in any better shape to decide?"

The judge pounded his gavel. "You're completely wrong, Logan. Answer the questions and keep your opinions to yourself." He nodded at the jury. "Forget what Logan said concerning whether the defendant's action was murder. That is *your* job."

Chadwick smiled triumphantly. "Now, Mister Logan, let us keep in mind that your testimony may be somewhat biased . . ."

Dave rose, temper a bright shine in his eyes. "If you're making out that I lied, I'll beat a few teeth down your throat."

The judge pounded the desk again. "Sit down, Logan," he said testily. He nodded at Chadwick. "I'll admit that our notion of court procedure is a little slack, but let me make myself clear on one point. When you ask a question, be sure it's a question."

Chadwick bowed. "Your honor, I hold that Dave Logan's position on Matt Strang's ranch will inevitably influence whatever he has to say.

He is in love with Nan Romney, the daughter of Matt Strang's widow. He had been closely associated with Strang from the day Strang drove his herd into this valley. Is it not natural, then, that everything he saw the day of Strang's death will be colored by his relationship with Matt Strang, Strang's widow, and Nan Romney?"

Dave rose again. He said: "Mister, what you've said is all true, but I still want to know if you're calling me a liar?"

Dave had mentally sworn before the trial to keep his temper. Now he saw Nan in the back of the room beside Clab Holland. Pablo, Kane, Hartzel, and Lundy were sitting on the same bench. They were leaning forward, tempers honed to a fine edge, and at once Dave knew that regardless of his own pride, he could not keep pushing at Chadwick.

There was this tight moment of silence. Then the judge was pounding his gavel again. "Sit down, Logan. The jury may consider what you have said, Chadwick. Continue with your questioning."

Dave dropped back into the witness chair. The lawyer faced him, asking in a carefully controlled voice: "All right, Mister Logan, I have four questions. Did the defendant have his belt guns on when you and Strang talked to him?"

"No."

"Did Strang quirt him?"

"Yes. I told you how it . . ."

"Did you see the actual shot?"

"No. I wasn't looking back . . ."

"All right. Now one more question. Did Matt Strang turn in his saddle?"

Dave held his answer for a moment, glancing at Dillon, but he found no assurance there, for Dillon was staring at the floor, his face thunder dark. Dave turned to the judge. "This Chadwick is going to make something out of what I'm saying that ain't true. Matt turned in his saddle all right, but he didn't make no move toward his gun."

"That will do, Mister Logan." Chadwick said crisply. "You have established that Strang did turn in his saddle."

Dave got up and walked to his seat on the aisle. He sat there, slumped forward, sickness crawling into him, the hum of the court coming to him over a great distance. He had told the truth, it should be enough to hang Beans Poe, but he was sure it wouldn't. Chadwick would point out that Strang had knocked Poe cold at the settler's meeting the day before, he would remind the jury that Strang had quirted Poe, and he would hammer on Dave's admission that Strang had hipped around in his saddle. Therefore Poe, thinking Strang was going to shoot him, had picked up his Winchester and fired.

The trial dragged on through a fourth day and

a fifth. Doc Whitley reluctantly testified that the bullet killing Strang had entered from his side, the final point that Chadwick needed to nail down Poe's plea of self-defense.

The jury went out at 5:00 the afternoon of the fifth day. Lacey Markham, standing beside Dave in the Gold Bar, said: "It is ironical that Strang should have turned in his saddle the very instant Poe pulled the trigger. They'll acquit him on that one fact."

Bill Hanna walked in then, white-faced and thoroughly scared. "There's a hundred and twenty men down there, and they're talking plumb wild. They say they'll wipe the cowmen out before sunup."

Holland came up with Kane. Dave jerked a hand at Lundy and Hartzel, and when they joined them, he said: "Tell 'em that, Bill."

Hanna said it over, but Kane dismissed it with: "I never seen a sodbuster that could hit the ground with his hat. If there's any wiping to be done, we'll do it."

"I figger the odds four to one," Dave said gravely, "and in a fight at close range, their scatter-guns will be mighty ornery."

"And even if they do the wiping," Markham added, "there'll be some widows and orphans who'll be hungry before spring."

"Then they better think of that," Kane said sullenly.

Lundy jabbed a finger at Markham. "It's damned funny, you being here. You wrote some rough stuff about Strang."

"I meant it," Markham said, "and I meant all I wrote about you. If Poe is acquitted and you hang him, I'll write some more. That's the question right now. As much as I hated the principle of monopoly that Strang stood for, I respect his stand on legal authority."

"Legal authority," Kane said contemptuously. "Just pretty words in a country that's got a majority of sodbusters. We know Poe killed Strang and we know he needs hanging. If that bunch of jackasses on the jury don't fix it so he will, we'll attend to it."

"What you're proposing is mob rule," Markham said coldly, "and mob rule does not know justice."

"Aw, hell," Hartzel grunted, "you auger better'n we do, Markham, but augering won't keep a rope off Poe's neck."

Dave's eyes were defiant. "I was with Matt when he died. He said to let the law handle Poe. We aim to see it does."

"It goes against my grain like hell," Holland said bitterly, "but that's the way it's gonna be."

Still Kane was not convinced. "If we let him go, he'll get some more of us. Then he'll run in, ask for a trial, and talk about self-defense. They'll acquit him again." He shook his head. "Maybe we didn't know Strang like you boys did, but we know what we've got to do."

"Then we know what we've got to do." Dave wheeled out of the saloon, Holland and Hanna with him.

It was dark now, and the heat of the day was rapidly fading. There was no wind, and dust smell was strong in the air, and there was the smell of people and sweat and horses. At that moment the town was without disturbance of any kind. It was the silence of angry men.

Hanna muttered: "I wonder why I ever thought I wanted to pack a star."

They were in front of the jail then. Across the street the settlers made a black line. Behind them in the rear of the courthouse a lamp in the jury room threw its finger of light into the darkness.

Dave said: "Only one way out of this. Get Poe's horse around to the back of the courthouse. Let him have his guns and tell him he's got five minutes if we're lucky. That'll be as long as we can keep the lid on."

Markham was running along the street, calling: "Dave!"

Dave said: "Wait, Bill."

Markham came up, panting. "After you left, Kane asked me something we'd better be thinking about. Suppose they find Poe guilty?"

"He'll get a legal hanging."

Markham motioned toward the silent men across the street. "They'll take him away from Hanna."

"There'll be hell to pay then," Dave said.

Markham ran a sleeve across his forehead. "I don't think I can stop them, but I'll try."

Dave watched him move across the street to the courthouse, Holland murmuring: "That boy's been eating raw beef, ain't he?"

Dave said: "Acts like it. Let's go back to the Gold Bar, Clab. Get hold of Pablo. I don't think that jury's gonna be out much longer."

Lundy, Kane, and Hartzel had called in their hands from the street. When Dave went back into the saloon, the place was packed. Smoke lay in writhing clouds below the hanging lamps, too thick to get a good breath, and liquor smell was heavy in the air.

Kane said challengingly: "You're a little out-numbered, Dave, if you're figgering on stopping us."

"I'll stop you," Dave said. "I'll stop you first, Ben."

"You're being the damnedest fool . . . ," Hartzel began.

"I guess not," Holland said, coming in with Pablo.

"Better figger a little more before you kick the lid off," Dave said. "We'll take you and Speck and Jim first."

Kane glowered at Hartzel. "Have they been eating locoweed?"

"I reckon," Hartzel said sourly.

Lundy scratched his nose, eyes thoughtful. "No. I've seen men like Strang. A few. They don't ever seem to die."

"That's right," Dave said. "Ben, there's no real trouble between us. We're trying to build something tonight. Don't tear it down."

Lundy nodded somber agreement. "It's a damned poor thing to fall out over."

"What the hell, Jim," Kane said incredulously. "Are you going to side these fools?"

"I'm a little older'n you and Speck," Lundy said. "Old enough to think of tomorrow. We've got settlers in the country. We'll have more. Hanging Poe won't do nothing but throw a fight into our laps."

Kane turned to the bar and poured himself a stiff drink. He said sourly: "If this ain't the damnedest thing."

They waited then, with nothing settled between them. Presently the banker, Symonds, came in. He said: "Markham tried to talk some sense into the settlers and got beat up. Doc's got him in his cabin now. Nan's with them."

Dave started toward the batwings. Symonds caught his arm. "Doc won't let anyone in there but Nan. He says Markham's got to be quiet."

Again they waited, the minutes piling up into

an hour. Others came in. Al Dillon. The barber. The stableman. The preacher, Naylor. All but Naylor were armed. Lundy had maneuvered so that his men were with him in the front of the saloon. Within the hour the situation had changed so that, if the showdown came, the odds would be nearly equal. Still Kane and Hartzel were not backing up.

Al Dillon left, saying nothing about where he was going. Another hour, and tempers, already drawn tight, were drawn tighter. Dave, looking at Kane's and Hartzel's barren faces, knew that this would go on until word came that the jury had acquitted Poe. Then it would end in a burst of violence. There would be no reasoning about it. Too much had happened, Strang's death and the passion aroused by the trial. It seemed to Dave that suddenly on this night everything Matt Strang had lived for was brought into sharp focus. Just as he had built his corrals and ditches and buildings to stand for generations, so he had made one belief a sound principle by which people could live together. Law had been a fetish with him. Now if Kane and Hartzel were allowed to have their way, this principle would be destroyed.

It broke then, but not in the way Dave had expected. Bob Joslyn pushed through the batwings, his white hair rumpled. He called hoarsely: "Dave!"

"You know anything?" Kane shouted. "The jury come in yet?"

Joslyn did not hear. He called again— "Dave!"—and stepped back into the street when Dave came to him.

"You've got to do it." He gripped Dave's arm, the words tumbling out of him. "You've got to. She wouldn't come back with anyone else. She's a thief and a common floozy, or she wouldn't have gone away with him. You're to blame, Dave. Damn it, I tried to raise her right. I lost her mother when she was a child. If you'd married her, it would have been different."

Dave shook Joslyn's shoulder. "What are you talking about?"

"Read that." Joslyn shoved a wad of paper at Dave. "I was asleep and Dixie was supposed to be keeping the store. I'd been up late ever since the trial started. When I woke up, she'd locked the store and was gone. I didn't know what had happened until I opened the safe and found this. She took a thousand dollars."

Dave flattened out the paper and held it up to the light from a saloon window. He recognized Dixie's fine straight-lettered writing.

Don't be angry with me, Dad. I told you I couldn't stay here any longer. I know they'll free Beans, and I'm going with him. I've made arrangements to meet him between here and Cañon City. I'm taking some money because I've earned it keeping house for you.

Dixie

"He's no good for her," Joslyn breathed. "Bring her back, Dave."

Dave stared at the letter, thinking of what Dixie had told him the day the trial had started. He felt none of the blame for her action that Joslyn tried to lay upon him. Still, he could not let her go with Poe.

He was standing there when Hanna crossed the street to him. Hanna said in great relief: "We pulled it off, Dave. Now I'm going in and get me a bottle of the best stuff Cowley's got and drink it dry."

"We pulled what off?"

"The fight. I mean we staved off a hell of a fight. The jury came in an hour ago. Not guilty, they said, so we put Poe on his horse and he vamoosed. Didn't auger none about staying, neither."

"An hour ago?"

"Yep," Hanna said happily. "I figgered, if this bunch didn't know it till he was gone, they couldn't do nothing. Got him out through a window. The settlers didn't know it till we told 'em just now."

Dave pushed into the saloon and stood there,

thinking of Dixie. It was her business. Maybe she had a right to the money. It was none of his affair if she wanted Poe.

Kane and Hartzel moved forward, waiting for him to speak. Joslyn was tugging at his coattail, pleading: "You're going after her, aren't you?"

Kane took another step forward, asking: "Well?"

Naylor moved between them, his face showing that he knew the danger he was putting himself into. "No trouble now, Kane."

Kane shoved him out of the way, saying again: "Well?"

But Dave was still thinking of Dixie and of Poe who was a killer. The $1,000 would be a lot to him, more than he could make by staying and fighting for the settlers. That was the way Dave came to his decision. He said: "You can go to bed, Kane. The jury acquitted him."

"Go to bed, hell!" Kane shouted. "We'll . . . !"

"Shut up," Dave said. "I'm going after him and I don't need any help." He stepped back, saying in a low tone to Joslyn: "Don't tell them about Dixie or which way Poe went."

Turning, Dave plunged through the batwings and raced on to the livery stable. He saddled, and left town in a wild run. Kane and Hartzel would suspect a trick, and would follow, so he went on past the junction of the Cañon City and the old Fort Pacific roads until he heard the drum of horses' hoofs behind him.

There was a clear sky and a full moon showing above the eastern rim. Dave let them see him, then pulled sharply to his right and waited in a dry wash until they roared by. He rode out of the wash and angled through the sage to the Cañon City road. Dixie would be waiting for Poe somewhere ahead in the timber.

XXI

It was still before midnight when Dave saw the fire through the pines. He had held one advantage over Poe. The road had been familiar to him as far as Cotter's mill, so he'd hoped to overtake the gunman, but he had not. Now he reined into the timber, made a careful check of his gun, and moved silently toward the fire, leaving his buckskin ground-anchored behind him.

He heard them talking before he could see them clearly, and although distance blurred the words, he knew from the tone of their voices that they were angry. Then he was at the edge of the clearing not more than fifty feet from them, and Dixie was saying: "I tell you I can't go on now. I'm tired. I'm not used to riding."

"I can't stop yet," Poe flung back, "and I sure as hell ain't leaving you here. Not the thousand dollars, anyhow."

"What have you got to worry about?" Dixie demanded. "The jury freed you, didn't it?"

"Some of those boys don't listen to a jury." Poe gripped her arm and jerked her toward her horse. "We're lighting a shuck out of here."

Dave had moved into the clearing. He said: "I reckon that thousand dollars makes her look mighty good, don't it, Poe?"

Poe whirled, releasing his grip on Dixie's arm. She fell away from him to the ground, clawed back up to her hands and knees, and crawled in her haste to get away from him.

Poe said coolly: "I thought you'd bring your bunch, Logan."

"This is my job. I'm taking Dixie back."

"I reckon not. I don't aim to let your outfit know which way I'm headed."

"You're a little late. Dixie left a note to her father."

Poe said: "The damned little fool." Dixie was on her feet now, breathing hard, and he turned to stare at her. "You damned little fool."

"She was fun for a while, wasn't she, Poe?" Dave asked. "As long as you had some use for her."

"She'll still be fun," Poe said. "For me."

"He promised me a lot of things," Dixie said. "I believed him."

"Did he promise you a wedding ring?" Dave asked.

314

"No," she said in a low tone. "He didn't promise me that."

Poe laughed. "What the hell, Logan? She wanted to get away from the valley. I said I'd take her. You're after me on account of Strang, ain't you?"

"No. Dixie's dad sent me to fetch her back."

Poe waved toward Dixie. "Take her along, Logan. Maybe you want her worse than I do."

Dixie ran toward her horse. "I'll go with you, Dave. I was out of my head, or I'd never have thought of this in the first place."

"Wait, Dixie," Dave said.

He stared at the gunman, the fire between them, the flames casting a red glow across Poe's lean face. Dave could not read his eyes; his mouth held the familiar smile as if he were enjoying his silent laugh. Carelessly Poe raised his right hand to scratch his nose. He said: "Get along with her, Logan."

Still Dave didn't move. Poe would not lose the money Dixie had brought, and he had no intention of leaving Dave alive. His actions were too casual for a man in his position. He carried two guns, and Dave was remembering Holland had told him a long time ago that there were a few men who could draw as fast with one hand as another. Dave thought: *He'll shoot me in the back if he has a chance.*

"Drift," Poe said. "I ain't holding her."

"You're moving first," Dave said.

"Sure, if that's the way you want it," Poe said, still smiling and still scratching his nose.

Poe half turned toward his horse, then wheeled, left hand whipping downward, but Dave had not been fooled. This was what he had practiced for; it was the sort of job Strang knew would someday come to him. That was why he had given Dave the gun. Holland had always said: *Most men that are fast ain't accurate. Their notion is to shake out a quick slug to scare the other man, but I'll put my money on the fellow who hits what he's shooting at.*

There was no feeling now in Dave, no revulsion against this thing he must do, and he did not doubt the outcome. He made his draw exactly as Holland had taught him—he heard the blast of Poe's gun, saw the red thread of flame. Poe was quicker, but he had missed. Then Dave had lined his gun on Poe. He fired three times, so fast that the shots boomed out together in one continuous roll of sound.

Once more Poe fired, a wild shot that racketed out into the fading echoes of the others. Dave stood motionlessly, watching, feeling no different than on countless occasions when he had sent a tin can kiting along the ground. Poe kept his feet for a moment, weaving like one of the tall pines behind him. The smile was gone from his lips now, for his ability to laugh was lost. For this short time he held to life, then the slack expression of death was in his face and he folded at knee and hip and fell face down into the pine needles. His hat came off his head and the firelight was bright on his white hair. There was no sound then but the creak of the pines in the wind and the sound of Dixie's crying.

Dave continued standing motionlessly, thinking of the time Strang had sent him to Cotter's mill, of his fear of the timber and the mountains; he thought of the mental storm that had struck him, the words that had burned themselves upon his mind: *The life Matt Strang had brought to the valley would end within this mass of timber.* It was only partly true. The best would live. Strang was dead and his killer was dead, but the law stood. Perhaps it had erred, but it stood.

Dixie came to him, still crying, and touched his arm. "Are you all right?"

He said: "I'm all right. Get on your horse and go down the road a piece."

She obeyed, and presently Dave joined her, leading Poe's horse, his body tied across the saddle. Dave mounted his buckskin and they rode downslope, past Cotter's mill and on out of the timber. Near dawn they came into Sage, the huddle of buildings black dots in the moonlight.

Dixie had not spoken since they had started. Now she said dully: "You don't understand, do you, Dave? It's always been Nan, hasn't it?"

317

He said: "Yes."

"I just wanted to get away. I just wanted him to help me get away."

A light was still burning in Joslyn's house, and he heard them as they reined up and came along the path. Dixie swung down and ran past him into the house, saying nothing to him.

"I'll take her horse," Joslyn said tonelessly.

"Go easy on her, Bob," Dave said.

Joslyn stared up at Dave, the moonlight touching his haggard face. "I can't understand what's happened. This isn't my country any more. Not since Strang came. I should have left when the McNairs and Tildie did. But you're different. You're the kind that'll stay." Then Joslyn took the reins and led Dixie's horse around the house.

Dave got Doc Whitley out of bed and left Poe's body in his back room. Whitley said: "The settlers pulled out right after you did. They didn't know you'd gone after Poe."

"The acquittal was what they wanted," Dave said.

"And a travesty of justice it was," the doctor said bitterly, "but there has been no flaunting of the law. Joslyn told me why you went after Poe."

Dave left the horses in the stables and went to bed with the pale light of day seeping out across the valley. It was noon when he woke. He shaved and put on a clean shirt, and ate a meal that was both breakfast and dinner.

Leaving the hotel, he stood for a moment on the boardwalk, feeling the peace and quiet of the town that had been so turbulent these last five days. Then he turned toward Markham's cabin. When he passed the store, Joslyn stepped into the sunlight, squinting at Dave. "Dixie took the Prineville stage out this morning. I thought you'd want to know. I'll be going as soon as I sell." He swallowed, and added: "I forgot to thank you last night."

"No need of thanks," Dave said. "I had it to do."

He went on to Markham's cabin. Markham was sitting up in bed, a bandage around his forehead. Nan stood beside him. She said: "Well, Mister Logan, I thought you were going to sleep all day." She wrinkled her nose at him. "And on your wedding day."

"Whazzat?"

Markham laughed. "Surrender, boy. Resistance is useless."

She moved to him, her face suddenly serious. "You said once I'd have to come to you. I'm coming now, Dave, on my knees if I have to."

"You don't need to get on your knees. I'm closing the deal before you change your mind." He put his left arm around her and swung her toward the bed, his right held out to Markham. "Lacey, I wouldn't shake hands with you once. I'd like to now."

Markham stretched out his long arm and gripped Dave's hand. "I suspect you still consider me an impractical idealist. Perhaps I am, but I've learned some things, Dave." He scowled at his press. "I guess you were right about me being a better teacher than an editor."

"We're being married here," Nan said. "Lacey can't get out of bed."

Dave nodded. "We can be married in the middle of the lake for all I care."

"I can't get out there. It will have to be here." Markham leaned back. "Dave, why did you want to shake hands with me?"

Dave thought about it a moment before he answered, wondering what strange alchemy had worked on Lacey Markham, changing him from the weakling who had watched Strang break McNair's arm into the sort of man who could live in Sage Valley. He said: "Let's say it was because you knew what the settlers would do to you when you talked to 'em last night, but you tried."

Markham lowered his gaze. He said in a low tone: "Better start looking for the preacher, Dave."

Ben Kane was waiting outside for Dave. He held out his hand. "I just had a look at what's left of Poe. I had you pegged wrong."

Dave took his hand reluctantly and dropped it. "No, you had me pegged right enough. I didn't kill Poe on account of Matt, and I never saw a man more wrong than you were last night. If things hadn't gone the way they did, you or me would be dead this morning."

"I reckon," Kane said, abashed.

"Let's get something straight," Dave went on. "No reason your outfit and S Star can't get along, but every time you figger it's your job to run things regardless, there'll be hell to pay."

Kane glanced at the gun on Dave's hip and brought his gaze back to Dave's face. "I'll remember," he said.

It was a quiet wedding. The only regret Dave had was the fact that Mary was not there, but as Nan said: "She doesn't feel like coming to town, and if we were married out there, she'd have to do a lot of work. After all, this is what she wants and she'll be happy."

Mrs. Symonds had supper for them with a tremendous wedding cake topped by white frosting; there were the usual rice and old shoes, one of them catching Dave on the back of the head. Then they were out of the Symonds house and running toward the hotel.

The morning sun was laying a scarlet pattern across the bed when Dave woke. He remained motionless for a moment, thinking he heard distant music that came from a thousand silver bells. He rubbed his eyes, realizing that the music was nine-tenths dream and one-tenth Nan's humming.

Nan, standing in front of the bureau brushing her hair, was wearing a wine-colored robe that Mrs. Symonds had loaned her. It was too small, but Nan had not had time to send to S Star for her things. Dave, looking at the shape of Nan's strong round thighs and her perfectly shaped breasts, at her hair that had grown darker this year, thought that it would not be long until she looked exactly like her mother.

Dave said: "You're the prettiest woman in the world."

She turned, startled. "I didn't know you were awake." She dropped the hairbrush and jumped on the bed. "I'll teach you to sneak a look at a lady when she doesn't expect it." She rumpled his already tousled hair and ended it by being drawn down to him and soundly kissed.

She lay beside him, her cheek against his. "Do you want to know why I married you yesterday?"

"I'm satisfied."

"I'll tell you anyway. Not all of it. I mean, there are a few things I don't really understand myself. I guess I just had to grow up, but there was one thing that made up my mind fast. Clab and Pablo told me how you stood up to Kane and Hartzel. They said, if there'd been a fight, you'd have been killed." She pressed harder against him, her arms around him. "I couldn't have stood losing you before I even had you, Dave. I just couldn't wait any longer. All of a sudden it seemed like there wasn't any reason to wait."

"Nan, Mary needs us on S Star. You want to live in the Logan Pocket, but . . ."

She placed her fingers on his lips. "Dave, I know now I love you so much I'll live with you anywhere you want to."

They were silent then, reluctant to let this moment go. Dave thought about the years that waited for them. He could not see what lay ahead, of the day when a railroad would come to Sage, when paved highways would cross the valley. When dozens of small ranchers would settle on land bought from S Star, when S Star would be talked about wherever men talked of good cattle and fine horses. When Mary Romney Strang would be the most loved woman in the valley, when there would be children and grandchildren playing in the grass under the tall poplars. When Dave would go to the legislature as Representative from Sage County, when he would be an honored pioneer who would he asked repeatedly to speak in Burns and Prineville and other eastern Oregon towns. And when he would help dedicate a monument to Matt Strang in front of the Sage courthouse.

No, Dave could not see these things, but they were ahead, their promise gleaming like a lit lamp down a long dark passage, for most of the bitterness was behind, most of the sweetness still to be had.

He pushed Nan away from him very gently and looked at her. He touched the tip of her nose that still held its freckles; he touched her mouth and she kissed his finger. He said: "Let's get dressed. We're going home."

ABOUT THE AUTHOR

Wayne D. Overholser won three Spur Awards from the Western Writers of America and has a long list of fine Western titles to his credit. He was born in Pomeroy, Washington, and attended the University of Montana, University of Oregon, and the University of Southern California before becoming a public schoolteacher and principal in various Oregon communities. He began writing for Western pulp magazines in 1936 and within a couple of years was a regular contributor to Street & Smith's *Western Story Magazine* and Fiction House's *Lariat Story Magazine*. *Buckaroo's Code* (1947) was his first Western novel and remains one of his best. In the 1950s and 1960s, having retired from academic work to concentrate on writing, he would publish as many as four books a year under his own name or a pseudonym, most prominently as Joseph Wayne. *The Violent Land* (1954), *The Lone Deputy* (1957), *The Bitter Night* (1961), and *Riders of the Sundowns* (1997) are among the finest of the Overholser titles. *Bunch Grass* (1955) and *Land of Promises* (1962) are among the best Joseph Wayne titles, and *Law Man* (1953) is a most rewarding novel under the Lee Leighton pseudonym. Overholser's Western novels, whatever the byline, are based on a solid knowledge of the history and customs of the 19th-Century West, particularly when set in his two favorite Western states, Oregon and Colorado. Many of his novels are first-person narratives, a technique that tends to bring an added dimension of vividness to the frontier experiences of his narrators and frequently, as in *Cast a Long Shadow* (1957) filmed as *Cast A Long Shadow* (United Artists, 1959), the female characters one encounters are among the most memorable. He wrote his numerous novels with a consistent skill and an uncommon sensitivity to the depths of human character. Almost invariably, his stories weave a spell of their own with their scenes and images of social and economic forces often in conflict and the diverse ways of life and personalities that made the American Western frontier so unique a time and place in human history.

| Books are produced in the United States using U.S.-based materials | Books are printed using a revolutionary new process called THINKtech™ that lowers energy usage by 70% and increases overall quality | Books are durable and flexible because of Smyth-sewing | Paper is sourced using environmentally responsible foresting methods and the paper is acid-free |

Center Point Large Print
600 Brooks Road / PO Box 1
Thorndike, ME 04986-0001 USA

(207) 568-3717

US & Canada:
1 800 929-9108
www.centerpointlargeprint.com